I0659400

Knights of The Golden Circle

A Rory Mack Steele Novel, Volume 9

Eugene Lloyd MacRae

Published by CreateSpace, 2013.

This is a work of fiction. Similarities to real people, places, or events are entirely coincidental.

KNIGHTS OF THE GOLDEN CIRCLE

First edition. December 18, 2013.

ISBN: 1927767105

Written by Eugene Lloyd MacRae.

Chapter 1

THE YOUNG BOY worked feverishly to rub the graphite pencil across the paper. The strange carving in the bark of the beech tree slowly took shape across the paper. His tongue worked itself back and forth to each corner of his mouth as he concentrated.

"I can't kill no kid," whispered the younger man.

"If you don't, he's gonna find the treasure," said the older man tersely.

"How do you know that? We don't even know where it is," the younger man said.

"We ain't the ones who are supposed to know where it is, you idiot. We're sentinels..."

"Oh yeah," the young man said in realization. Then he thought a bit as he watched the kid working his rubbing. "Does that make any sense? Shouldn't we know–?"

The older man slapped the younger man on the back of the head, "Never mind that. If you're going to take care of your castle, you need to take care of that kid. You wanted to get more involved, didn't you? Play a bigger part in everything?"

"Yeah. I'm proud to take my daddy's place...but–"

"Then do it!"

"Ain't this a job for a member of the military arm–?"

"This is *your* task right now."

"C'mon. Are you *sure* the kid can find it?"

"Are you willing to take the chance? You want to have to answer to Vernon P.?" the older man said sternly.

"No, that I don't want. But...it's a kid...maybe he'll only find a small cache...," the younger man reasoned.

"He had that slicker didn't he?" the older man said. "We both saw him with it yesterday."

The younger man nodded, rubbing the stubble on his day-old beard, "I wonder where he got it from? I've heard of them, but I ain't never actually seen one–"

"I ain't never heard of anyone else with one before either," interrupted the older man forcefully. "We'll go find it after. But right now, he's back here to get more signs and we need to do our part for the old south. Just like our daddys and our grand-daddys did. Ain't that what you said you wanted at your daddy's funeral?"

The younger man nodded, "You're right. You're always right. But I got a better idea. If I'm going to do my part, the kid just has to *disappear*. Just like the others, right? And I reckon that'll make Old Tuck happy."

The older man's face lit up, "Yeah, you're right. I never thought about that. And when we explain to Old Tuck that we saw this kid with a slicker...and if we *get* him that slicker...that's gonna work even better for us. Two birds with one stone and all that."

"Old Tuck always wants information like that," agreed the younger man.

The older man slapped him on the back, "And he never forgets who gave him the information."

The younger man nodded. Taking a deep breath, he slipped expertly through the trees towards the freckled faced youngster.

Chapter 2

GOLDEN, SOUTH CAROLINA

RORY MACK STEELE sat sipping his early morning coffee in Martha's Diner. The place was full and noisy, the smell of bacon and eggs, waffles, toast, and coffee was full and rich and he loved the old-time feeling of this place. It fit perfectly with the small town he had glimpsed through the tall, stately trees before he had pulled into the parking lot. Rory was a private investigator in the family business, Highlander Investigative Services, with offices in both New York and Toronto, Canada. Having Canadian-American Dual Citizenship allowed Rory to work both sides of the border. He had recently finished a job in Atlanta, Georgia and was now on his way to his next assignment. But with Greenville, South Carolina only a fifty mile drive up I-85, and since he didn't have to meet the client until tomorrow morning, he decided to linger a little longer and enjoy the atmosphere. He looked around for his waitress to get a refill but he didn't see her. He could wait. Looking back out the window, he watched an elderly couple getting into a large motor home. He smiled at the antics of their golden retriever, wagging his tail hard and pushing between the two, apparently eager to get back on the road.

"Want a little more coffee, hon?"

Rory looked up to see a tall, white-haired waitress with crazy red glasses pouring him a refill. She had been working the other side of the restaurant when he had first come in.

"Yeah, thanks," Rory said as he reached for the sugar.

"You'll have to forgive Donna-Lou, she hasn't been the same since she lost her son," red glasses said.

Rory poured some sugar onto a spoon and dropped it into his coffee. He assumed Donna-Lou had been the waitress who had served him. He poured a second spoonful and stirred, "What happened?"

"Young Corry just up and disappeared about two months ago. Was on CNN for two full days. All kinds of news vans here and lots o' police. Then some big political scandal knocked it off the news before he could be found. He was all she had, poor thing."

Rory tipped more cream into his coffee and stirred, "How old was he?"

"Ten. And he was so sweet. Not one of those back-talking kids you see so often now. Never gave Donna-Lou an ounce of trouble or concern. That kid was off in the woods treasure hunting every single day, rain or shine. And once school was out for summer, that's all he did from sunup to sundown. Then one day he's gone. He just disappears." Red glasses shook her head sadly before turning and walking away to offer a refill to another customer.

Rory sipped his coffee. A few minutes later he saw his waitress come back in from a door in the back. She was dabbing at her eyes with a Kleenex. Donna-Lou was a black haired beauty with a trim figure. He imagined she must have had her son at a young age. He didn't think she was more than 26 or 27 years old. No wedding ring. He was all she had red glasses had said. His heart went out to her.

RORY WALKED ACROSS the parking lot to his Jaguar XK-S. It was a nice, warm southern day that reminded you of those proverbial iced teas and mint juleps. Pulling out of the parking lot, he turned left onto the access road, skirted the edge of Golden and pulled back onto I-85. Rory turned the satellite radio on and set it for the local station to check for traffic. The local news finished off with weather and the traffic as Rory drove at the speed limit. Usually, he had a lead foot, but he wasn't in any hurry to barrel through a pleasant day.

"Okay, this is Chet Calhoun. And we're back on with author and newspaper columnist Nora Jackson. Nora, you were talking about the statistics on missing persons...."

"Right, Chet. Every day in the United States 2,300 people go missing. Every single day."

"Every day! That's astounding," Chet said.

"Yes, it is. It's hard to believe but true. Now we have to understand that most of those missing persons are adults. And they do include people who may have just run away from their old life for some reason or another without telling anyone. And there are also those who are involved in drugs, elderly people who wander away because of memory problems..."

"So they're not all what we consider as stereotypical abduction cases of young'uns," Chet said.

"Exactly," Jackson confirmed. "And most of the missing reports for youngsters are apparent abductions over custody battles, that kind of thing."

Chet prodded his guest, "So what has your bee in a bonnet right now? I think that's how the FBI and our own Sheriff Luther Ponder and Circuit Court Judge Vernon P. Teague described your concerns...."

Jackson was sarcastic in her correction of the title, "You mean the *Honorable* Vernon P. Teague,"

Of course, I stand corrected," Calhoun chuckled. He was loving this.

Jackson was bitter, "Both Sheriff Luther Ponder and the *Honorable* Vernon P. Teague are a disgrace to local law enforcement, that's all I can say. There's *nothing* honorable in either man."

Rory reached over to switch to another station.

"Consider *this*," Jackson said forcefully. "Only 100 missing child cases reported every year in the *entire* United States are true stereotypical abductions by strangers. Yet we have nearly that number here in the southern states *alone* this year!"

Rory's hand froze in mid-air.

"And we're only halfway through the year," Jackson continued. "Two-thirds of those reported missing are usually between the ages of 12 to 17. But Chet, *we* have 78 youngsters missing, boys and girls who are ages 10, 11 and 12 years of age."

"I would say all those missing young'uns sounds like a cause for worry," Chet reasoned.

"The local law doesn't seem to think so," Jackson said. "And again, this is not throughout the entire US that I'm talking about. These 78 children have disappeared mysteriously in the last six month in Tennessee, Mississippi, Virginia, the Carolinas –"

Rory pulled over to the edge of the road.

Chet's voice rose an octave, "And what *has* law-enforcement said about this? I know you've been talking to them Donna-Lou. What have they been saying about all this?"

The disgust was evident in his guest's voice, "It's an anomaly is what they called it. A statistical anomaly."

"Unbelievable," Chet said. Then Chet switched gears to that of an announcer, "Okay, folks. We have to go to break. We'll be right back after this message. Don't go away, you hear?"

Rory's senses, honed from years of helping people in hundreds of situations as a private investigator, told him something was wrong. Rory thought about the waitress back at the diner. She had been heartbroken at losing her young son. He was one of the statistical anomalies the police were talking about. He considered going back and talking with her...but that didn't make any sense. What would he say? He leaned over and pressed a tab on his GPS screen, looking for the local radio station. He decided talking to this Nora-Jane Jackson would make more sense. She seemed to have a handle on what was going on. With the coordinates for the radio station entered, he let the woman with the mechanical voice lead him down the road.

"MS. JACKSON?"

The short, attractive brunette in the blue pantsuit stopped her sprint for the front doors of the radio station and looked back at the receptionist, "Yes?"

The receptionist smiled broadly and pointed at Rory who was sitting in a chair on the far side of the room, "This gentleman was waiting to talk to you."

Rory rose and approached Nora Jackson, extending his hand, "Hi, my name is Rory Mack Steele."

"So?" She let his hand hang out there in the air.

Rory felt like a scam artist under the scrutiny of someone who was extra cautious when meeting people. He lowered his hand, "I was hoping I could talk with you for a moment."

"So talk," Jackson said curtly. "I'm heading for my car. I don't have time." She turned, took two steps and pushed open the front glass door, stepping outside without a look back to see if he was following behind her.

Rory turned to the young receptionist, "You'd think we were married."

The young receptionist smiled, "Well, you better hurry after her or you ain't getting any...."

Rory raised an eyebrow.

"...talk that is." The receptionist winked.

Rory winked back and then hurried out the front door of the radio station, leaving the giggling receptionist behind. He jogged down the walkway, "Ms. Jackson, I was hoping to get some more information on those missing children I heard you talking about earlier."

"Why? What's it to you?" Jackson said over her shoulder as she began walking across the parking lot. "Are your FBI bosses pissed at me again because I won't play nice and pretend they care about all those missing children?" Jackson extended her hand and pressed the key fob, unlocking a dark-blue Lincoln MKS luxury sedan just ahead.

"I'm not with the FBI," Rory said as he finally got up with her.

Jackson opened her car door and looked around at Rory, "You're not? You look the type. What's your interest in this?"

"I look the type?" Rory said in amusement.

"Yeah, tall and good-looking," she said sarcastically. "Look. I don't have time Mr....?"

"Steele. I'm a private investigator with Highlander Investigative Services and –"

Jackson threw her purse forcefully into the car and turned on Rory, her hands on her hips and anger on her lips, "Now look here Buster. These people don't need any more shysters promising things and taking their money. I've had enough of your kind trolling for information–"

"I'm not after money –"

"Right. But you *do* have expenses and you *do* have leads that will require cash incentives...blah, blah, blah. We've heard it all before, so beat it, pal!"

Rory stood there in stunned silence as Jackson jumped into her car.

In a moment, the tires on Nora Jackson's dark-blue Lincoln squealed, leaving a black trail of rubber behind as she left the parking lot in anger.

Chapter 3

"NORA-JANE IS RIGHT, YOU KNOW."

Rory turned around to see a stocky man, carrying an old battered briefcase, walking across the parking lot behind him. "Pardon?"

"I say, Nora-Jane is right," repeated the man. "She's from here, you know. That's her full name, Nora-Jane Jackson. She dropped the hyphenation thing when she went up to the big city in Atlanta, then New York itself some years ago and became a big-time journalist as plain Nora Jackson. But she's from here. She knows these people as well as anybody and she's right. Folks here are tired of opportunists showing up and trying to take advantage of a sad situation."

Rory nodded his head. He could understand the situation. In his experience, there were always cons ready to pounce on every single opportunity to make a fast buck. And people in grief and desperate were always easy targets.

The man kept walking as he eyed Rory. He approached a battered old Chevrolet Impala, placed the old briefcase on the hood and then hitched his pants back up under his old checkered sports jacket. "Can I ask, what *is* your interest, friend?

Rory just took a deep breath and let it out. Truth was he wasn't sure himself.

"Just a hunch, huh?" the man said.

Rory looked at the man and cocked his head.

The man shook his head and smiled as he walked over to Rory, hitching his low pants up again. He stuck out his hand, "Chet Calhoun. I'm the local announcer, newsman, weatherman and jack of all trades for the radio station here. Even got it on the Internet thing now."

Rory shook his hand, "Rory Mack Steele."

"I've been interviewing people for a long, long time and I can tell when someone has something in his britches bothering him. Something more than a rash," Calhoun added with a chuckle.

Rory smiled, "I'm not sure if it isn't just a rash this time. It's just...I was over at the diner and one of the waitresses was looking down in the dumps. One of the other ladies said she had lost her son—"

"That would be Donna-Lou Haney and her son Corry," Chet said grimly. That's the kind of news report I hate to make."

Rory nodded at the mention of the names. "Maybe just seeing the waitress, and the sadness in her face made it a little more personal. And then, when I was driving, I heard your interview with Ms. Jackson...."

Chet nodded, "And something just didn't sound right. We all feel the same way. But the state troopers and the FBI don't seem to see it the same way. Neither does the local sheriff. But then, he doesn't do a single thing without the state troopers anyway. Sheriff in name only."

Rory shook his head. "You would think with all those youngsters going missing..."

"Tell me about it. I've been talking it up every chance I get. Done a number of shows on it. Interviewed people. But no one in authority has paid any mind past a quick look it seems," Chet said ruefully.

Rory shook his head in disbelief.

"Which is why I called Nora-Jane," Calhoun explained. "And when she told me she had already been looking into it for a possible newspaper article, I invited her down for the interview. Thought it would get things going again. She dug up all those stats...aw heck...who am I kidding? They ain't going to look into it much more." He started walking back to his Chevrolet Impala.

Rory took a couple of big steps to catch up, heading for his own parked car, "But you're still trying."

Chet nodded, looking sad. "Kinda got a little personal for me too, I guess. I had to do an interview with an old girlfriend, Josie McDaniel. She married one of the other guys from school and moved over to the next county," Chet said. "Real looker, you know. I was a little backwards with the ladies and missed the signals...hells bells missed the entire boat...never had a chance with anyone else after that. Anyway, broke my heart when I had to talk to her about her youngest girl. Little tom-boy who disappeared while she was out treasure hunting."

Chet continued walking but Rory stopped in his tracks.

Chet took a couple more steps and stopped, looking back at Rory, "Something wrong?"

"You said she was out treasure hunting? They said the same thing about the boy...."

Chet put his hands in his pockets and shrugged, "That's just what a lot of the young'uns do around here. Doesn't really mean much. Heck, we did it when I was a kid. Me and Bobby Fin used to treasure hunt these woods around here for years."

"What for?"

"The treasure," Chet said as if he had expected Rory to know all about it.

"The treasure? What treasure?"

"The one buried by the Knights of the Golden Circle."

Chapter 4

GOLDEN PUBLIC LIBRARY

RORY STEPPED INSIDE the old building and was immediately surprised. The large open space was filled with ornate wooden carvings, gleaming old tables, polished oak chairs and even smelled like an old library. The smell of old books and yellowing newspapers was powerful. But he also saw bright lighting and dozens of computers with patrons tapping away and printing out reams of paper. At the far end of the room, he could see dozens of youngsters gathered around a number of tables, talking softly and laughing and keeping an eye on the older ladies who were obviously the staff or 'library police' who kept them in line. Rory looked over at the staff and saw the small, short woman he wanted. She was sitting behind an old, wooden desk that had the sign 'Information' on it. Her name tag read: Sara Madison.

Rory stepped to the desk, "Ms. Madison? Chet Calhoun said you could help me find information on The Knights of the Golden Circle."

The small woman looked at him over her glasses, "Oh, he did, did he? Do I look like a personal information kiosk for Calhoun's friends?"

Rory felt uncomfortable under the woman's steady gaze. "Well...I'm not really a friend. I just–"

"Smartest thing you've said so far," Sara Madison said. Suddenly she broke into a cheeky grin. She pulled off her glasses as she got up, letting them hang from a chain around her neck. "I suppose I can help you. What is it you need to know?"

Rory felt an embarrassed grin linger on his lips. He wasn't sure if he was the butt of a joke or she was really happy to know he wasn't Chet's friend. "Well, maybe you can tell me who these Knights of the Golden Circle were. And about this treasure–"

"Ah, the treasure," Madison said as she tapped the side of her nose. "Is that what this is all about. Want to find, it do you?"

Before Rory could answer, the woman moved away, waving for him to follow her.

The small, short woman talked back over her shoulder as she walked across the library floor, "Back at the end of the Civil War, nine trains were sent to get Confederate President Jefferson Davis and the other politicians up in Richmond, Virginia. That was the Confederate Capital at the time. Union troops were moving in and they had to evacuate Richmond to avoid capture But the trains weren't just there to carry people," Ms. Madison stopped and turned, lowering her voice to a conspiratorial hush. "It was also a treasure train. Loaded on board was the Confederate treasury, the assets of six Virginia banks and a whole lot more. A *lot* more. It was loaded onto the trains and driven into Georgia, where it disappeared. Poof," she said with her hand simulating an explosion.

"Poof?" repeated Rory. "No one knows anything about what happened after–"

"Oh, of course they do. Stop trying to ruin the story," Ms. Madison complained as she shook her head, "some people just don't have a sense of mystery, I guess."

Rory opened his mouth and then closed it, a smile lingering on his lips.

The small, short woman turned and continued her walk across the library, explaining more of the story as Rory followed, "It was buried somewhere, is what happened. Legend says it was turned over to the Knights of the Golden Circle, who buried it."

Rory wondered why he had never heard about this, "The Knights of the Golden...?"

"Circle. The Knights of the Golden were a secret society in the 1800s. Legend says it was started in Lexington, Kentucky, on the fourth day of July in 1854. The circle refers to the geographic circle of countries they were going to take over as part of an economy built on slavery. Their plan was to create a virtual monopoly on the world's supply of tobacco, sugar, and cotton. The circle was centered on Havana, Cuba–"

"I would have thought it would be centered on the southern rebel states. Why Cuba?" Rory asked.

Ms. Madison stopped in front of a filing cabinet. "I'm not really sure, to tell you the truth," she admitted with a frown. "All I know is it was to be centered on Havana and included our Southern states, as well the West Indies, parts of South America and Mexico. Maybe they figured a lot of those places would be easy to invade and take over."

"If the train went down into Georgia, why would people be looking for the treasure up here in South Carolina?" Rory asked.

"Well, for one thing, the legend says caches of money were buried all over the place by the KGC in anticipation of the South rising again. You'll find KGC signs supposedly leading to caches all over the Southern States and even as far west as South Dakota. But you also have to understand it in the context of local history. The Knights of the Golden Circle had their start in the formation of what were called Southern Rights Clubs in a number of southern cities in the mid-1830s. These clubs were inspired by the influences of John C. Calhoun. He was a Senator from South Carolina and a vice president under John Quincy Adams and ole Andrew Jackson himself."

"Calhoun? Any relation to Chet Calhoun?" Rory asked.

Ms. Madison tapped the side of her nose with a finger, "No lint collecting on you. His great–great–great grand-daddy. Family legend says Ole John C. his-self had a son name of Daniel Jackson Calhoun. And Daniel Jackson was the one who reorganized the Southern Rights Clubs into the KGC on that day over in Lexington, Kentucky. At the very least, he was a *very* influential member. It was under *his* instructions, that the treasure train was unloaded in Atlanta and supposedly a large wagon train brought it up into South Carolina. It only traveled at night, but a lot of people reported its passing. Wagon after wagon after wagon were said to squeak under the heavy load of the treasure. After the Civil War, the KGC went underground and became even more secretive, if that was possible."

"Why didn't Chet say anything about that?"

Ms. Madison looked left and right, then, lowered her voice again, "Well now. According to ole John C's political theory of republicanism, it included the automatic approval of slavery. And remember what I said about what the Knights of the Golden Circle wanted to create...?"

Rory nodded, "An economy built on slavery."

Ms. Madison tapped the side of her nose and nodded, "Like Chet, most of us here have to live with the stupidity of our ancestors and it's not something we like to talk about openly."

"I can understand," Rory said in sympathy.

Ms. Madison turned her attention to the filing cabinet, pulling open the top drawer, "Anyway, these are our files on the Knights of the Golden Circle and the events regarding that part of our history."

Rory looked dismayed at all the files stacked in the cabinet drawer.

"Yeah, tell me about it," complained Ms. Madison. She bent over and tapped three other drawers underneath the one she had pulled open, "All of these are filled with more information. Despite the state grants to get all those computers and Internet connections, we still don't have any of those fancy machines to scan and store everything digitally so...."

Rory nodded his understanding, "Thank you."

Ms. Madison started walking away, leaving Rory to his chore of research.

As Rory put his hand on the open drawer, Ms. Madison turned and said, "Oh, and there's more information in the books on top of the filing cabinets. And those long shelves of books beside you have more information, including local history."

Rory took a deep breath as he looked around, wondering if he really wanted to go through all of this information. Then he pulled out several folders and set them on an old wooden table. Sitting down, he started looking through the files.

"WHATCHA DOIN'?"

Rory looked up.

It was a young girl, about nine years old, dressed in blue jeans and a t-shirt that had the name and picture of some pop singer across the front. The young girl's red hair and freckles reminded him of his sister Skye Steele when she was about the same age. The young girl was leaning on the other side of the table, elbows on the table and both hands propping up her chin.

"Just looking at some things," he said as he looked back at the file in front of him.

"You going to look for the treasure?" the young girl asked.

Rory looked at the young girl and shook his head no, "Just looking."

The young girl was quiet for a minute and then sat down in a chair, "I used to look for the treasure all the time. But now momma says I can't go out in the woods no more."

Rory looked across at the young girl again. Her hands were crossed on the table now and she looked sad. "Why not?" he asked.

"Cause momma says she doesn't want me to be kidnapped like Corry. That's where he was when he was kidnapped, in the woods looking for the treasure," she said.

"That would be Corry Haney? I heard about him," Rory said.

The little girl nodded her head, "Me and Corry used to go out into the woods all the time looking for the treasure."

"I see."

The little girl put her hands on the side of her mouth and spoke to Rory confidentially across the table, "Corry was my boyfriend."

Rory suppressed a smile but nodded. "Did Corry know he was your boyfriend?"

The little girl covered her mouth and giggled, shaking her head no. "But I was working on him," she added. "Just like momma said she did with daddy. She had to work on him a loooong time." The girl looked down at the table, "He died in Iraq."

Rory's heart went out to her, "I'm sorry to hear that."

The little girl nodded, "I don't really remember him. But momma says he was nice. Corry's daddy died in Iraq too. They was best of friends."

Rory didn't have to say much in return. The story of two best friends from a small town, fighting for their country and each leaving behind their young family was difficult enough for older folks to handle, let alone a young girl.

The little girl got up and walked around to Rory's side of the table, "Would you like me to help you figure anything out? Corry was really smart when it came to this stuff. And he taught me a lot about it."

"He did?"

The girl nodded emphatically, "Showed me how to read the signs. And how to find more—"

"Signs?"

"The treasure signs," she said as if he should know.

"What are the treasure signs?"

She looked at Rory like he had two heads. "If you're gonna look for the treasure, you *have* to know about the signs. C'mon," the young girl said. She reached out and took Rory's hand, pulling to get him to stand up.

Rory got up and allowed the young girl to lead him towards the back of the library.

She walked right to an exit door and pushed it open, leading him outside. They moved across an open expanse of grass at the back of the library, then over a sidewalk and onto the street.

Rory felt a little awkward, being led by a young girl and he didn't even know her name. "Where are we going?"

"Not far," she said simply.

Reaching the sidewalk on the other side, the little girl pulled Rory to the left and past a number of old single-dwelling houses with louvered shutters, metal roofs, and white, weather-beaten boards that needed paint. A few minutes later, they were walking past larger, two-story homes with big wrap-around porches and double-hung windows.

Rory noticed a police car sitting further down the street. He hoped the officer behind the wheel would ask questions first and not shoot the stranger in town, walking with one of their young children.

"This way," the young girl said as she pulled Rory to the right, across a lawn and between two of the large, two-story houses. They entered a large, sparse backyard and headed for an old, gnarly tree at the back. She stopped at the tree and pointed, "That right there on the tree is one of the signs from the Knights of the Golden Circle. It leads to treasure."

Rory cocked his head and looked at the tree. He saw the amazing outline of an old, old stick figure carved into the thick bark. It looked like a star above a man riding on a horse. Or was it?

Rory moved in for a closer look, feeling the contours of the figure in the bark with his fingers, "How do you know what it means?"

The young girl stepped closer and pointed, "See how the head on the horse is looking forward?"

"Okay...."

"But the head of the rider under the star is looking back? Corry said that means—"

"Emma?"

Rory turned and saw a woman standing back by the house

"Hi, Mrs. Haney," Emma said as she waved. "I'm just helping this man figure out the treasure stuff."

Rory realized the woman was Donna-Lou Haney, the waitress back at the diner and the woman whose son had been kidnapped.

The black haired beauty with the trim figure looked with concern at Rory. She waved Emma towards her, "I think your momma is calling for you."

Emma cocked her head and she listened intently, "I can't hear her...."

"Emma-Mae Houston, you just go on now, you're momma is calling," Donna-Lou insisted.

The young girl glanced at Rory and waved, "Okay. Bye." She then skipped past Donna-Lou Haney and towards the front of the house.

Donna-Lou Haney crossed her arms as the girl disappeared around to the front of the house, "Who are you? And why are you in my yard?"

"I apologize for that," Rory said with a nod of his head. "Emma is not easy to ignore. I was talking earlier with Chet Calhoun —"

"You know Chet?" Donna-Lou asked. She tilted her head in a questioning look.

Rory shook his head no, "I just met him. I was over at the radio station and we got talking. He suggested I look up some information at the local library. Which is where I met Emma and she dragged me over here—"

"If you don't mind, I gotta get back to work," Donna-Lou said as she turned and headed for the front of her house. She took a few steps and then turned, giving Rory a look that said he should be leaving too.

Rory followed several feet behind her and back towards the front of the house.

Donna-Lou Haney stepped around towards the front porch.

Rory kept walking towards the sidewalk.

A car pulled to a stop in front of the house. Two honks on the horn sounded, "Hey Donna-Lou, how are you?" Chet Calhoun was leaning out the driver side window, grinning and waving.

Donna-Lou Haney smiled and waved back.

"Hey there, Mr. Steele. You need a lift?" Calhoun asked as Rory stepped onto the sidewalk.

"I left my car over at the library," Rory said. It's just a short walk —"

"Hop in, no need to wear out shoe leather when you don't have to," Calhoun said amiably.

Rory nodded and walked around to the other side of the car. He looked over the roof of the car at Donna-Lou Haney.

She was now staring at him with her arms crossed.

Rory opened the car door and got in.

Calhoun honked twice and yelled goodbye to Donna-Lou Haney. As he pulled away from the curb Chet looked at Rory, "Find anything out at the library?"

Rory shook his head no.

Calhoun drove, not a peep from him for a moment. And then he glanced sideways at Rory, "Find out anything from Donna-Lou? About her son, I mean?"

Rory glanced at Calhoun and then shook his head no, "We didn't have much of a conversation, I'm afraid."

Calhoun nodded, "She ain't been the same since Corry was took. Too bad. Beautiful woman like that. Smart as a whip too. Everybody figured she was headed to a big-time university. But she got pregnant with Corry. Husband was Merle Haney, star quarterback for the local high school football team. He got a scholarship from Alabama but decided to fight for his country like his daddy and his granddaddy and his great granddaddy did. Family tradition, I guess. Got killed over in Iraq a week before Corry was even born. Real shame. Nice guy."

Rory simply nodded at the info dump.

Calhoun pulled to a stop beside Rory's Jaguar, "What you gonna do now?"

Rory gave that some thought for a moment. Then he said, "I guess I'll just head for Greenville. I have someone to meet." He reached over and extended his hand, "But it's been nice meeting you, Chet. Maybe I'll be back this way some day and I'll look you up for a coffee or something. Learn a little more about that treasure."

Chet Calhoun shook Rory's hand vigorously, "That would be nice. It's been a real pleasure meeting you, Rory Mack Steele. Almost a good ole southern name that."

Rory nodded and got out. A few minutes later, Rory gave Chet two honks, received two honks in return, and headed for Greenville, South Carolina.

Chapter 5

GREENVILLE, SOUTH CAROLINA

THE SUN WAS HIGH AND WARM, the sweet fragrance of the nearby tulip trees carried across the air on a light breeze as the three large men stood side by side across the wide laneway, fully intent on intimidating ninety-year-old Grace Patterson.

"I already told you," the elderly lady said, "I don't want to sell the business. I'm keeping it for my grandson. Once he finishes college –"

The large man on the right, sporting long dreadlocks, took a step forward, bits of gravel on the asphalt crunching under his heavy, steel-toed boot, "You wouldn't want something serious to happen to your Todd, now would you?"

The man's two companions each took a step forward as well, glaring menacingly to emphasize the pain they would inflict on Grace Patterson's grandson.

Grace Patterson thrust her chin out, "I've already signed the papers to transfer the business. You're too late–"

The big man on her left, sporting a red Mohawk, growled in a low voice, "No you haven't. You were gonna do it tomorrow. If you do that old lady, little Toddy is going to be in a world of hurt."

He raised his right hand and slowly formed a fist, "That is *if* he survives the hurt."

Grace Patterson's old gray eyes narrowed at the man, "Now, how in the world would you know I was going to the bank *tomorrow* to sign the papers? Who have you been talking to young man?"

"We have ears everywhere, grandma," said dreadlocks "you can't escape this–"

Grace Patterson wagged a finger at the big man, "When that young Detective Berenson catches up with you, with all three of you, he's going to give you the whipping of your life."

The three men laughed. "He's probably going to give us a high-five," dreadlocks said to red Mohawk. Then he looked back directly at Grace Patterson, "Time to stop playing games, old lady." He made a motion with his head to red Mohawk, "Pit Bull, knock a few teeth out. If the old crow has any left."

Pit Bull flashed a gap-toothed smile, "My pleasure, Digger." Pit Bull took a step toward the old lady, pulling his fist back to throw a hard right. But before he threw the punch, his eyes widened in shock, he howled, clutched his right side in the back and dropped to his knees.

Rory Mack Steele had been waiting behind the old garage where Grace Patterson kept her car at the back of her two-story house. Three long strides and one punch to Pit Bull's kidney from behind had done the job.

Digger was taken by surprise and slow to respond as he watched Pit Bull drop over onto his face. By the time he was turning towards Rory, it was too late.

Rory landed a punch to Digger's jaw and watched the big man drop to his back on the asphalt. Looking to the third man, a big, 6-foot barrel of a man, with a shaved head and a goatee, Rory saw him go into a defensive crouch. Rory had learned his street name was Fat Boy, but there was a lot of hidden muscle under the three hundred pound frame.

Fat Boy swung his arm and made a whipping action with his wrist.

Rory hadn't expected that. Fat Boy had a collapsible fighting baton in his right hand. Only now it wasn't collapsed. It was rigid and ready to strike. He had expected a man with his girth would use that size and bulk. *I guess not.*

Bringing the weapon up to his left shoulder in a well-practiced move, Fat Boy whipped the baton down in one quick motion to strike Rory's right thigh.

Rory stepped back but was not quick enough. The end of the baton caught his thigh muscle. Pain shot through his body and his right leg collapsed under him. His right knee screamed in pain as his kneecap slammed into the asphalt.

Raising the baton over his head, Fat Boy moved ahead in attack mode. He brought the baton down with two hands and a loud shout.

Rory raised his left arm, fist over his head, elbow down at the shoulder and deflected the baton with this forearm. He emitted a cry of pain from the deflected blow, but he kept his head. He brought his right fist up between the man's legs.

Fat Boy saw the blow coming and twisted to the left. It struck him on the inner right thigh and he yelped in pain, staggering back a couple of steps.

Rolling over backward, Rory came up on his feet. The pain in his right thigh was still immense and he nearly lost his footing.

Seeing the stumble, Fat Boy moved his bulk forward again quickly, bringing the baton up over his head, aiming a vicious two-handed blow at Rory's head.

Rory brought his left arm up again at an angle. Thrusting his arm forward in one smooth motion, Rory deflected the blow with his elbow and then thrust a flat left-hand blow towards the man's face.

Fat Boy reacted by pulling his head back.

Rory used the reaction to go on the offensive and disarm the big man. Dropping his hand down between Fat Boy's arms, Rory then circled his hand up and back, twisting the big man's arms. He reached for the baton with his right...but it wasn't there!

Fat Boy was grinning. He had anticipated Rory's move and had simply dropped the baton. Now he threw a hard left cross and connected.

Rory staggered from the hard blow to his jaw.

Now shifting his weight, Fat Boy threw a right uppercut between Rory's arms.

But Rory countered by moving his upper body back and the punch missed by barely a quarter of an inch. Bringing his upper body forward and angled to the side, Rory threw a body punch with his right to the man's now exposed left side.

Fat Boy's face was a mass of agony as he dropped to his knees and collapsed onto his face from the vicious body punch.

Before he could deliver another blow, Rory felt pain exploding across his upper back and he collapsed to his own knees.

Digger now stood over Rory, holding the baton Fat Boy had dropped. He grinned maliciously, blood from Rory's first punch coating his teeth and his lips. He raised the baton and brought it down on Rory's back again.

Rory collapsed face down in pain. He ignored the hurt and got to his knees but a steel-toed boot caught him in the stomach, knocking him over onto his back.

Pit Bull had recovered from the kidney blow and he was now striding towards Rory, teeth clenched in anger as gravel crunched under his own steel-toed boots, "Let's finish this little bastard."

Fat Boy had recovered as well and was only a few feet away, his voice a growl, "Yeah, you're going to die, buddy."

Digger spit out blood, "Naw, I wanna play a little more." He raised his arms and brought the baton down from way over his head.

Rory rolled to his left. He heard the baton strike the asphalt hard just behind him and roll brought him over on his hands and knees. He was wondering how he could fight all three without the element of surprise when he spotted a page from a discarded newspaper. It was lying against the back of the garage, lightly flapping in the breeze that had carried it there. The headline caught his eye and everything changed in a heartbeat. Adrenaline raced through Rory's body.

Pit Bull attacked, aiming another vicious blow at Rory's midsection with a steel-toed boot.

Rory rolled over, letting the boot pass and then rolled back towards Pit Bull. His maneuver had worked. The man with the red Mohawk was now like a defenseless punter, his right leg lifted high in the air. Rory spun around on his back like a break dancer and threw a leg kick at Pit Bull's left knee.

The sound of bone snapping was loud. Pit Bull screamed in agony and he fell hard in a heap.

Rory kept moving on attack. He spun back, rolled over and threw a left punch directly between Fat Boy's legs.

Fat Boy wasn't expecting the blow and he clutched his groin, rolled over and vomited in agony.

Digger's face was a mask of rage as took two strides and attacked with the baton, bringing it down hard from over his head.

Rory rolled right and came up to his feet as the baton struck the asphalt again.

Digger shifted his stance and attacked with a left-handed baseball swing, aiming to catch his opponent in the side.

But Rory countered by stepping forward to the inside of the swing and securing a hold on Diggers' right arm with both of his. Rory locked Digger's elbow, then twisted and pulled on the locked arm at the same time.

Digger was spun around by the force of Rory's move. He dropped the baton and fell hard to his back.

Rory stepped forward and stomped between Digger's open legs, connecting solidly with the tender bits of the big man.

Digger howled in pain and curled up in a fetal ball, clutching at his genitals.

Rory heard a noise on the gravel behind him and he turned.

Fat Boy was standing there, holding the baton, looking at Rory menacingly. Smelly vomit ran down his jaw and his shirt and the three hundred pounder snarled, "I'm gonna crack your skull _"

Grace Patterson held her arm out, pressed down with her thumb and launched a pepper spray attack.

Fat Boy dropped the baton and his hands shot to his burning eyes as he screamed in agony.

"How's that you son-of-a-bitch," hissed Grace Patterson as she moved to the side as the police had taught her and continued the attack.

Rory took advantage of the situation, stepped forward and kicked Fat Boy squarely between his legs.

Grace Patterson continued her spraying as the man collapsed to the ground in agony, "That'll teach you to attack us."

Fat Boy rolled up in a ball, trying to protect his face with one hand as the other hand instinctively clutched between his legs.

Grace Patterson stopped spraying and looked over at Rory, "That was a job well done, Mr. Steele. I especially like the way you used their family jewels in a non-traditional way."

Rory nodded as he pulled several sets of plastic handcuffs from a pocket.

"Mrs. Patterson, are you okay?" a middle-aged man yelled as he ran up to the fight scene. It was Howard Chub, Grace Patterson's lawyer.

"Of course, Howard," Grace Patterson said with a look of why-wouldn't-I-be. A big grin swept across her face, "Mr. Steele and I took care of matters. Didn't we, Mr. Steele?"

"Yes we did," Rory said as he finished applying the last of the plastic handcuffs. All three men were now cuffed with her hands behind their backs, still in obvious agony.

"I'm sorry, Mr. Steele," Chub said, "I know I was supposed to be here as a witness but my car broke down...."

Rory stepped over to a garage and retrieved a small video camera. He stopped it from running and handed it to Chub, "No problem. I made sure we had video evidence of the whole incident. I figured they would use this isolated spot as their point of attack. Mrs. Patterson says she comes out this way every day to walk through the park."

Chub nodded eagerly, "Good. Good. With the videotape we did of Detective Berenson last night, when Mrs. Patterson told him she was going to sign the papers transferring the business, we will have more than enough to put them all away for good. I already have a police Captain who is a friend primed with the whole sordid tale of extortion."

"Thank you so much, Mr. Steele," Grace Patterson gushed. "Todd will be set once he graduates and I can...."

But Rory wasn't listening. He had stepped back over to the page of the newspaper he had spotted while rolling around on the ground from the attack. He bent over and picked it up. It was yesterday's front page of the Greenville Gazette. Rory smoothed out the wrinkles and stared at the picture. It was the young girl from the library. There was no mistaking her sweet, innocent face. And the name clinched it. The headline read; Another Missing Child. And under the picture was the name: Emma-Mae Lynn Houston.

Chapter 6

GOLDEN, SOUTH CAROLINA

RORY SAW FLASHING LIGHTS in his rearview mirror. A state trooper was pulling him over. Rory had been using the cruise control on his Jaguar so he knew he hadn't been speeding. And he had stayed in his lane all the way from Greenville without passing. He couldn't think of any other traffic violations he had committed. Nevertheless, pulled over to the shoulder and rolled his window down.

A heavy-set State Trooper, wearing the prototypical sunglasses, stepped from his vehicle.

Rory heard the man's boots crunching across the gravel as he approached the side of Rory's vehicle.

As the state trooper reached the rear bumper he called out, "Wanna get out of the car, sir."

Rory thought it was strange. In the side mirror, he could see the trooper standing with his thumbs hooked in his gun belt at his waist. Rory checked for traffic and stepped out, closing the door, "What's wrong officer –?"

The state trooper spoke in a no-nonsense tone, "I'll ask the questions. Step back here please,"

Rory walked towards the back of the Jaguar.

The state trooper backed up a couple of steps and pointed to the trunk area, "Hands on the car."

"I don't understand —"

The state trooper raised his voice, "Turn and place your hands on the car." He pointed to the trunk area again, "Do it. I won't ask you again." His hand went to the butt of his weapon.

Rory couldn't see the state trooper's eyes but the hard set of his jaw told him all he needed to know. Rory kept his face passive as he complied. He stepped carefully around to the back of the Jaguar. Bending over slightly, he placed his hands on the trunk.

The trooper stepped forward and kicked at Rory's feet, "Spread 'em."

Rory complied, spreading his feet apart.

The trooper began to pat Rory's body. "Any weapons on you?" he barked.

"No sir," Rory said in a compliant voice. He had his Baby Eagle 9915 RL Polymer 9mm handgun in a lock box in the trunk. He expected to be asked about weapons in the vehicle next, but that question never came.

The state trooper drew his weapon and placed it against Rory's right temple.

Rory's blood ran cold.

The big trooper's left hand grasped Rory's shirt in the back and he twisted the material to hold him in place. He leaned over, his voice a hiss in Rory's ear, "I saw you talking to that little girl, Emma-Mae Houston."

Rory could feel the trooper's hot breath on the side of his face. He smelled the stale coffee and cigarettes. This must have been the trooper who was parked down the street when Emma led him into Donna-Lou Haney's backyard. Rory could understand the state trooper's harsh demeanor. He had watched a stranger talking to a young local girl. A young girl who was now reported as missing –

"What were you two talking about?"

That question threw Rory a curve ball.

"The trooper pushed on Rory's back, "Answer me."

"I met her at the library. She took me down to Mrs. Haney's house to show me something."

"And what was that?"

"A sign...on a tree in the backyard–"

The state trooper pressed the gun barrel hard into Rory's temple, "That's it?"

Rory winced in pain, "Yes sir–"

"I ran your plates," growled the state trooper. "Your name is Rory Mack Steele...dual U.S.-Canadian citizenship...a big shot investigator from a company in New York City called Highlander Investigative Services. Now, what would a big-time, private investigator from New York want with a little girl and treasure signs down here in the south?"

"I was just passing through and–"

The state trooper pulled the gun barrel away from Rory's temple, then thrust it back harder.

Rory winced and grunted from the pain in his temple.

The trooper's voice was loud and angry, "You think I'm a fool? Huh, sport? You think I'm a stupid country clown? You think I just fell off the turnip truck?"

Things didn't look good right now.

His voice dropped to a hiss again, "Now, Mr. Private Eye, *what* exactly are you doing here?"

Roy opened his mouth, but he didn't know what else he could say.

The trooper's hot breath came closer. The smell of stale coffee and cigarettes was stronger.

Rory waited for the gunshot. Would he hear it?

The sound of a car approaching them from somewhere behind broke the tense silence.

The state trooper held the gun in place for a moment as the sound of the car drew closer. A moment later, the trooper pulled the weapon away from Rory's head and holstered it. Then the trooper stepped back as the car slowed to a stop on the road beside them.

Rory looked to the left, wondering what was going to happen next. He watched as the passenger window on the stopped car slowly lowered.

The driver leaned over and Rory recognized the face of Chet Calhoun, peering across the seat.

"Hey Buck, how you doing?" Chet said to the state trooper. "Looks like you got yourself a real criminal there." He looked over at Rory and grinned, "Hey Mr. Steele. What are you doing back here?"

Rory didn't say a thing. He was actually afraid for Chet, not sure where this whole thing was going.

"You know this guy, Chet?" growled the state trooper.

"Well, I met him at the radio station the day I was interviewing Nora-Jane Jackson," Chet explained. He opened his car door and stepped out.

The state trooper grabbed the back of Rory's shirt and hauled him upright to his feet. "That one's just another busybody, interfering in police business."

"Now you know Nora-Jane, Buck," Chet said as he leaned on the roof of his car. "She's good people and means well –"

The state trooper leaned into Rory and spoke in a low menacing voice, "Don't stay in town too long or we'll be meeting again. Do you understand me?" His eyes were hard as he looked at Rory. Then he straightened up and tipped his hat to Chet Calhoun. Turning, the big trooper walked back to his vehicle.

Rory turned slowly and watched as the state trooper got into his vehicle, floored the gas and did a U-turn, disappearing down the road.

Calhoun watched the police pursuit vehicle disappear as well and then looked at Rory, mirth in his voice "Just keep your speed down and mind your P's and Q's and you'll be okay with Buck."

Shaking his head softly, Rory looked at Chet like he had two heads, "You're kidding. Right? He pulls me over for no reason and pulls his weapon?"

Chet waved his concerns away, "Aww, he's just blowing off a little steam. Don't mean nothing by it. I think his nose is just out of joint with the FBI coming in again and taking over his turf for a couple of days."

Rory didn't buy Chet's soft-pedaling of the trooper's attitude but it was his other comment that caught his attention, "What do you mean the FBI was just here a couple of days? I just read about the disappearance of Emma-Mae Lynn Houston. After the disappearance of the other kids, I would think they'd be here for weeks."

Check shook his head sadly, "No. As I said, nobody really takes this thing too seriously. The FBI said they couldn't find any indication of foul play. I pressed the state troopers to keep looking on their own but they wouldn't. I even went to the Circuit

Court Judge, Vernon Teague to get them back, but he thinks Emma-Mae just ran away. Which is ridiculous, little girl like that...." His voice trailed off in frustration.

Rory couldn't believe what he was hearing. Something was definitely wrong. And it wasn't just the disappearance of a little girl. Or even a little boy like Corry. It was the attitude around the disappearances. He stared down the road where the state trooper had disappeared. The way he was stopped and the attitude of the trooper was troubling as well. He chewed on his lip for a moment and then asked Chet, "What's Buck's full name?"

"Buck Walker Harrison. Why?" asked Calhoun.

Rory decided to deflect the question for now. He simply shrugged his shoulders, "Just want to make sure to call him *Mr.* Harrison if we meet up again."

Chet laughed as he stopped leaning on the roof of his car up, "That would probably puff him up bigger than he already is. You just passing through again?"

Rory shook his head slowly no as he continued staring down the road, "Probably stay for a day or so."

Chet tapped the roof of his car twice, "Tell you what. Why don't you come by the radio station just after five? I'll buy you a beer and something to eat and we can talk more."

Rory looked to Chet and nodded, "That sounds like an offer I can't pass up."

Chet nodded and gave him a quick wave, "See you then." Chet got in, closed his door, put the car in gear and drove off.

Rory watched Chet Calhoun drive away. Then he looked back in the direction where the state trooper had driven off. Rory's radar was up. Buck Walker Harrison had seen Rory with a little girl. A little girl Rory didn't know. A little girl who had just disappeared. Yet the state trooper *never* asked Rory where the little girl was. He *never* asked Rory if he took her. He was more interested in *what* they had been talking about. And the state trooper's comment was a concern; 'what would a big-time private investigator from New York want with a little girl and treasure signs.' Rory stroked the side of his chin. Why would a state trooper seem to be more concerned about treasure signs than the little girl herself who was missing? Who exactly are you Buck Walker Harrison? And what is your endgame?

Chapter 7

RORY SAT ACROSS from Chet Calhoun in Martha's Diner. The marvelous smells from the cooking were mouth watering and the meal they had just shared had proven how good it really was. And just like the first time Rory had been here, the diner was full and noisy. From the number of out-of-state license plates in the parking lot, there were a lot of tourists here. But the majority of folks at the tables seemed to know each other. They greeted each other cordially, even talking across from table to table. This was obviously the local watering hole.

Chet sat back and patted his stomach, "Didn't I tell you the shepherd's pie they make here is the best in the South."

Rory nodded as he picked up his coffee, "I don't usually have seconds so I have to agree with you."

"I've been trying to figure out the secret for years." Chet tapped the side of his head with a finger, "I figure they use a bay leaf or two along with Heinz ketchup."

Rory smiled, "All I know is it tastes great."

Chet picked up his coffee and saluted Rory, "That it does, Rory-Mack. That it does."

The tall, white-haired waitress with the crazy red glasses appeared with her coffee pot, "Is Chet here still trying to discover our secret ingredients in the shepherd's pie?"

"I'm not saying a thing," Rory said as he held his coffee mug out for a refill.

"Come on now Jesse, it's just normal for a man to be inquisitive," Chet said as he watched the waitress fill Rory's coffee mug. He lowered his voice as he held out his own coffee mug, "I won't tell a soul."

Jesse refilled his cup and gave him a skeptical eye, "Yeah. And come tomorrow morning, you'll be flapping those gums on your radio show, telling everybody in the county." She looked at Rory and shook her head, "Man can't keep a secret know-how."

Chet scowled good-naturedly as the waitress wandered away to her other customers.

The two men sat there, drinking their coffee and looking out the window at the passing cars and the customers who were either coming or going. It was a beautiful summer evening and Rory thought about the strangeness of the whole thing. Life in the community carried on while two local children were being held somewhere. Or maybe buried somewhere nearby.

"Penny for your thoughts."

Rory looked across at Chet. He shrugged and set his coffee down.

"Little Emma's disappearance is really bothering you, ain't it?" Chet said quietly.

"I guess meeting Emma, even briefly, makes it a little more personal," Rory admitted. "But...the whole thing is bothering me, Chet. Not just the disappearance, but the attitude of law enforcement." He shook his head, "I don't know, everything just seems...off."

"Not much we can do about, I guess," Chet said. "The FBI and State Troopers *did* have people out searching for a couple of days." He shook his own head in frustration, "Couldn't find a blasted thing. I talked it up on the radio. Asked people to phone in, with even the slightest thing that might pertain to Emma's disappearance, and nothing came of it. It's just like she...like the two of them young'uns...dropped off the face of the earth. You know what I mean?"

Rory nodded. He took a sip of his coffee, thinking. Rubbing his hands around the mug, feeling the warmth, Rory said, "Abductions by a stranger are rare. That's what your Nora-Jane Jackson said in that interview. Right?"

Chet thought about it for a moment and then gave Rory a nod, "That's true. She did say that." He shifted uncomfortably in his seat, "But...and no offense to you...but we do have a lot of people passing through this small community. Lots of people traveling between Atlanta, Georgia and Greenville, South Carolina. I mean, a *lot* of tourists come and go through here."

Rory just continued feeling the warmth of the mug, thinking, without looking up at Chet.

Chet sat there, looking at Rory for a moment. Then he narrowed his eyes and shifted forward in his seat, lowering his voice, "You're not suggesting somebody local did this? Are you?"

Rory's looked Chet directly in the eyes, "I'm not suggesting anything, Chet. But you have to take everything into consideration, don't you? Or does that make you feel uncomfortable?"

Chet sat back, chewing on his lower lip, drumming his fingers lightly on the table, considering what Rory had said. "Truthfully," he finally said, "I'm more uncomfortable with the fact we got two missing young'uns." Chet gave it some more thought as he looked at Rory. Then he straightened up and leaned forward, "You got something on your mind, don't you? I can tell there's something there...."

Rory looked out the window, watching a young couple play with a pair of greyhounds. They looked happy and carefree. The direct opposite of how those young children must've felt the day they were taken. It made him angry inside. He looked back at the man across from him, "Chet, I've been doing investigations into all sorts of situations for quite a while now. And you end up with a nose for things...."

"And...?"

"And my nose tells me the disappearances have something to do with this local treasure," Rory finally said. "Call me crazy, but...."

Chet had a concerned look on his face as he scratched his chin, "I'm sure by now you know about my family connections to the treasure...?"

Rory nodded, "That Sara Madison at the Golden Library said your three-times great grand-daddy was involved at the start."

"So...you're not suggesting...?"

Rory shook his head, "No, Chet. I don't think *you* had anything to do with it."

Chet let his breath out and sat back, looking relieved.

"But you do know a lot about the subject. Right?"

Chet nodded his head, "Spent my whole childhood looking for it."

Rory tapped the table with a finger in emphasis, "Just like those missing children." He paused and then asked, "Did the FBI or your Sheriff follow up on the treasure angle?"

Chet did some thinking, then shook his head no, "They said...if it was kidnappings...it looked to be what they called 'crimes of opportunity'. Young'uns being out alone in the woods and the kidnapper comes across them. That would make it nearly impossible to crack the case they said. Course, when they couldn't come up with anything, they just decided the young'uns ran away from home. Jackasses. Just covering their behinds cause they couldn't figure it out."

Rory nodded, "Now, I may be wrong, but I'd like us to work together, to see what we can find out following the treasure lead. You game?"

"Sure," Chet said. "But how exactly do we do that?"

"Well...you said you searched for it as a kid. Where would these kids go to hunt for the treasure around here?"

"Oh wow, there are dozens of spots. There are signs on rocks and trees and the like all over," Chet said.

Rory shook his head a little in frustration, "I was hoping there would be one particular spot. But I guess not. Emma showed me one of the signs in back of Donna-Lou Haney's house."

Chet nodded, "Yeah, I know about that one. But I'm not sure if that sign would do anybody any good anyway."

Rory looked at Chet in surprise, "Why not? Isn't that one of the signs from The Knights of the Golden Circle?"

"Oh yeah," Chet replied, "But where those houses are built, I was told by my granddaddy that it used to be one of the old apple orchards. The old farm, the orchard and some of the hillside and trees were removed when those houses were built over the years. There was even a filling station near there at one time that's now long gone. Anyways, sounded to me like a lot of the signs were destroyed. You see each sign that was there was part of a larger network of signs that crisscross and point to other signs or some other type of clue."

Rory nodded in understanding, "I guess members of the Knights of the Golden Circle weren't expecting progress to wipe out their signs."

"No, I suppose they expected the Old South to rise long before then," Chet said.

"Anything helpful passed down through your family tree?"

Chet shook his head sadly no, "I had the vague recollection that my daddy and grand-daddy *were* a part of the KGC, from the stories that I remember hearing. And they did teach me a few things. But when I was six years or so, my daddy and my grand-daddy were killed in an accident–" Chet sat up straight in his seat again.

"What's wrong?"

Chet's eyes moved back and forth, like he was looking into the past, "It's just...I remember momma getting frustrated with me, even mad at times, when she found out I was out looking for the treasure. I remember my aunt Nell saying to momma when she would visit, 'that boy is gonna get his-self killed too.'" He looked at Rory, "That's exactly what she said...'too'. Momma would agree and forbid me to go out treasure hunting again." Chet shook his head softly, "I hadn't thought about that since I was a boy. But now...."

Rory cocked his head, "You think your father and grandfather were killed because they were looking for the treasure way back then? By who?"

Chet looked across at Rory as if it should be apparent, "By the KGC."

That didn't make any sense to Rory, "But why would they kill them if they were part of it?"

Chet took a breath and let it out slowly, "Keep in mind the Knights of the Golden Circle were a secret society, Rory. Members were *forbidden* to reveal anything about the society, on the penalty of death. The organization even had their own army, going way back to 1860. Once they began burying money in anticipation of the South rising again, they appointed members of the army to be Sentinels. Those sentinels were expected to keep watch, guard the caches and *kill* anyone who got too close...or kill any *member* who talked...."

"But that was the 19th century! We're in the 21st century and–"

Chet shook his head somberly, "The task of being a KGC Sentinel is said to be passed down from generation to generation, Rory. It's an honor and it's taken seriously. Every person looking for the treasure has heard of recent accounts of armed Sentinels who responded to incursions by outsiders into treasure areas. Tourists who were treasure hunting around here have claimed they was run off by men on horseback, if you can believe it."

Rory leaned forward, "So you believe the Knights of the Golden Circle still exist? That there are *still* armed Sentinels guarding the treasure?"

Chet gave Rory a shrug but his face was dead serious.

Rory rubbed his chin as he contemplated what Chet was saying, "I was thinking more along the lines of someone wanting the *information* these kids might have figured out. Figuring it was their ticket to a personal lottery. But I never thought about someone *protecting* the treasure in this day and age. A secret society...."

"And I have a hard time believing someone around here would be that evil. Scaring people off is one thing. But killing young'uns?" Chet said. He looked at the people around them, eating, drinking, laughing and talking.

"I'm sure you've watched enough television to know how people with a cause have used children and didn't care if their ambitions resulted in their deaths."

"In other countries maybe, But this is the United States of America," Chet countered, still having a hard time believing it.

"Maybe...."

Chet nodded solemnly as he gave it some thought. Then he got up and stood by the table. He hitched his pants up and said firmly to Rory, "If there are KGC Sentinels around here like that - then me and you can give them more than a couple of young'uns to worry about."

Chapter 8

CHET'S OLD CHEVROLET IMPALA slid to a stop in front of Donna-Lou Haney's two-story dilapidated house. The paint on the clapboard siding was faded and peeling in spots. The rain gutters were rusty and the curtains were faded from the sun as well. Coupled with the bare spots on the lawn, the overall appearance gave the impression the residents of the house were struggling financially.

Rory peered out the passenger side window at the place, knowing full well where he was, "What are we doing here?"

Chet turned the vehicle off, "I told you, we're going to give those bozos something more to worry about than a couple of young'uns." He opened his door and got out.

Rory got out and stood on the sidewalk, shaking his head softly, "I don't know about this Chet. The last time I was here, the lady of the house wasn't too happy to see me."

Chet hitching his pants up as he joined Rory on the sidewalk, "As Nora-Jane Jackson said, a lot of outsiders came and tried to take advantage of the situation. And you *are* an outsider, so you can understand her skepticism, finding you in her back yard and all."

Rory nodded. As Chet headed for the front door of the house, Rory glanced down the street. A police car was sitting further down the street. Just like that day with Emma. Rory chewed his lip, pondering the threats the state trooper had made.

"Coming?"

Rory looked over to see Chet looking at him, waiting on the wrap-around porch at the front door.

Rory nodded. He walked up the three steps and stood on the porch, waiting apprehensively while Chet knocked.

Donna-Lou Haney opened the door. She was wearing a white blouse, blue jeans and stood there in her bare feet. She looked surprised to see Chet Calhoun standing on her porch, "Chet?"

But Rory could also see a hint of delight in her eyes.

"Hey there, Donna-Lou, glad we could find you at home," Chet said. He took one step to the side and gestured towards Rory, "This here is Mr. Rory Mack Steele."

Donna Lou squinted her eyes at Rory, then crossed her arms, "You're that man who was in my backyard with Emma-Mae Houston!"

"Yes, ma'am," Rory acknowledged with a slight nod of his head.

Donna-Lou looked sharply at Chet Calhoun, "What's going on here? We reported him to the FBI as the stranger we saw last with Emma-Mae before she went missing! They were gonna check him out–"

Rory's eyebrows rose as he looked at Chet.

Chet gave Rory a half-apologetic smile, "Everybody was just concerned with Emma going missing. Don't take no offense to it."

"None taken," Rory replied, "it's understandable."

Chet addressed Donna-Lou, "The FBI *did* check him out. I talked to the FBI guys myself and they said there was nothing there. I still wasn't satisfied, cause the FBI dropped the ball before. So I went up and pushed Circuit Court Judge Vernon P. Teague to pursue it further. But he made a few calls and told me his-self that Mr. Steele was in Greenville, helping another family with an extortion case. That's what he and his family do. Investigate and help people. That's why I asked him to come here with me today, to help. Not only with Emma-Mae but with Corry too."

Donna-Lou Haney looked startled and her eyes misted over at the mention of her son.

"We both know the authorities ain't doing a damn thing," Chet said harshly. "But we're not giving up," he said, gesturing at Rory. "We're not giving up one bit, Donna-Lou," he added firmly as he hitched up his pants.

Donna-Lou nodded her head, "I know you've never given up, Chet. I've heard you on your radio programs. And you've been a good friend over the years."

Chet nodded, his own eyes misting up. He took a deep breath and gestured at Rory again, "Mr. Steele here has an idea he'd like to follow up on –"

Rory interrupted, "As I understand it, Mrs. Haney, no one really knew where your son was when he...."

"Disappeared," Donna-Lou added.

Rory nodded.

Chet's face brightened just a bit. He understood Rory didn't want to reveal exactly what they were fearing. He looked at Donna-Lou, "That's right. I mentioned to Mr. Steele how Corry was always off hunting for the treasure. I know Corry was always making graphite etchings of the signs on paper...."

Donna-Lou smiled and nodded as she rubbed the back of her neck, "He was always coming home, so excited to add another rubbing to his collection."

Rory jumped into the conversation again, "It's a long shot, but I was hoping that...if we could look over his collection...maybe we could figure out where he was when he...disappeared."

"That's right, maybe gives us a lead," Chet added.

"Chet here tells me he searched for the treasure when he was a kid," Rory said. "Maybe he can figure out where your son was and that would give us a starting point to look for him."

Donna-Lou looked at him for another moment and then took a step back from the door, "Sure. C'mon in and I'll take it up to his room. Please take your shoes off, if you don't mind."

Chet stepped into the house.

Rory stepped in behind him, "Thank you, Mrs. Haney." Rather than the musty smell he had expected from the run-down appearance of the house, Rory's senses detected the pleasant fragrance of a flower and herb potpourri. Chet slipped his shoes off and Rory followed his lead, setting his to the side as he glanced around. They were in a wide hallway with tall ceilings. There was a curved archway to the left and the right and dead ahead of them was a stairway to the second-floor.

Donna-Lou looked at Rory for a moment, then said, "And you call me Donna-Lou."

Rory nodded.

Donna-Lou turned, walked down the hallway and started up the stairs.

Chet, looking concerned, whispered quickly to Rory, "Sorry about the FBI thing...."

"Like I already said, it's fine. And understandable," Rory whispered in return. He motioned for Chet to follow Donna-Lou.

Chet looked relieved. He hitched up his pants, walked down the hallway and started climbing the stairs behind her.

Rory stepped forward and took a moment to glance off to the right. He saw a neat and tidy living room, filled with faded, beat-up furniture. The walls were decorated with faded print wallpaper and the old ceilings were quite high, with the surface up there looking faded as well. On his left, he saw a neat and tidy kitchen area with beat-up linoleum floors and appliances that had seen better days 30 years ago. Despite struggling financially, the woman was working hard to maintain a good home for her son. Not wanting to appear too nosy, Rory then took quick steps and followed Chet and Donna-Lou to the second floor.

Every stair squeaked with age as each person moved from one to the next. At the top of the stairs, Donna-Lou led them down a long, high hallway, sections of the old floorboards squeaking softly as each person passed.

Rory passed a bedroom on the left, filled with more beat-up furniture.

Donna-Lou gestured as she passed another open door on the left, "That's Corry's bedroom. I haven't changed a thing since the left that day...." Her voice trailed off.

Rory thought Donna-Lou would lead them into the bedroom but she didn't. She kept on walking down the hallway.

Chet obviously wondered the same thing because he turned and shrugged his shoulders and raised his eyebrows.

Donna-Lou walked to a door at the far end of the hallway, pushed it open and stepped inside. "This is Corry's treasure room," she said as she stepped to the left side of the door.

Chet stepped into the room and stopped walking, just standing there, staring.

Rory stopped directly behind Chet and just outside the doorway, wondering what the problem was.

After a moment, Chet took a few steps to stand beside Donna-Lou, turned and looked at Rory.

Rory could see Chet had a look of surprise on his face. He wondered why. Rory walked in, looking across the room...and stopped dead in his tracks.

Chapter 9

THE ROOM WAS HUGE, covering the entire back side of the house. There were two tall, narrow windows at the back with a wide, beat up old oak desk standing directly between the two. A computer, a computer monitor, and a laser printer sat on top of the desk. Every other single space along the walls was covered with maps, pictures of trees and rocks with symbols on them, pencil sketches and graphite rubbings of signs and symbols and photocopies of news articles.

Chet Calhoun stepped across the floor and ran his hand over some of the papers, "This is amazing. Some of these treasure signs I've seen. But some of these others...I've never seen them before. Where did he get these?"

Donna-Lou smiled, "Corry was always out looking for new signs to copy. Or he was on that computer, on the Internet, visiting different forums for treasure hunters. Anything he could find, he would print out and put up on the wall. At first, I didn't like him making holes in the walls with his stick pins, but it gave him so much pleasure. When you think about all the things a young boy can get caught up in today, it was such a relief to see him doing something harmless like this."

Rory walked over to the right to a large whiteboard that was on a stand. It had more pencil sketches and etchings of treasure signs taped to it. "Any idea why these aren't on the wall?"

Donna-Lou shook her head, "No. I had no idea what that boy was thinking when it came to treasure signs." She emitted a soft laugh, "That big whiteboard? I was told he charmed a teacher out of it. Apparently, they weren't using it the school anymore. I don't know how they got it here but apparently Emma-Mae helped him."

Chet walked over to stand beside Rory, "I've seen these signs in various parts of the woods around here. Not sure why he would have them all together on this board though."

"How do the signs work, Chet?" Rory asked.

Chet hitched his pants up, "The signs can work alone or in a group or a cluster. When you find a sign on a tree or rock, it usually points you in a direction. When you go in that direction you usually find another sign or a clue. The thing you have to understand though is that you may have to go for a long ways before you find the other sign. You could travel for miles before you find it. And they're not always easy to spot. So that's where other signs in the area come into play. When you plot each one of them on a map, they usually converge on the area that you need to search. That's where you find another sign that may lead you to the next group of signs." Chet's eyes lit up, "Or...it might be a sign that says there's a cave or a mine or something buried nearby like a treasure cache–"

"Just another big kid," Donna-Lou said. Her arms were crossed over her chest but she had a smile on her face.

Chet looked over at her, a sheepish grin on his face. He hitched his pants up, "I guess we all stay little boys, especially when it comes to treasure. Remember Bobby Fin?"

Donna-Lou nodded, "I sure do."

"Me and Bobby Fin used to sneak out at night, after everyone went to bed, to check out treasure signs we found during the day," Chet said with a shake of his head. "We figured we were gonna find the big cache –"

"Corry used to do the same thing, sneak out at night," Donna-Lou said. "I always knew when he did it. We may be poor but I always kept this house spotlessly clean. He would sneak in and leave a little dirt here and there on his way up to his room. He could never figure out how I knew. He'd sneak in a through a different door or a different window and I always knew...."

Chet shook his head and laughed, "I'm glad my momma never figured that one out."

"That's why I knew one of Corry's friends snuck in here last night," Donna-Lou said. "Little bugger left a little trail from the back window up into this room and back out."

Rory's blood ran cold.

Chet looked over at Rory, the smile gone from his face.

Rory gave him a subtle shake his head.

Fortunately, Donna-Lou changed the subject, not seeing the looks of concern between the two men, "Would you two like a coffee? Also got some cake you can have while you look through here."

"Just coffee would be great," Rory said.

Chet nodded, "Yeah, that would be great, Donna-Lou. Thank you." He waited until Donna-Lou left the room, then turned to Rory, "You thinking what I'm thinking?"

Rory looked around the room and then at the whiteboard, "I'm sure this kid was on to something. And this little break-in episode just convinces me all the more. But it also makes me worried about Donna-Lou. If there is something in here...."

"Think we should say something to her?" Chet asked. He had a worried look on his face, "Maybe we call the police...?"

Rory looked at Chet for a moment, then broached the subject, "Did you notice that police car down the road when we came in?"

Chet's brow furrowed and he shook his head, "No, can't say I did. Why?"

"I think it was the same police car that was parked on the road that day Emma took me here to show me the sign in the backyard," Rory revealed.

Chet hitched his pants up and shrugged, "One police car looks like the other. Maybe Donna-Lou already told them about the break-in and they're just keeping an eye out?"

"Maybe. You can ask her when she comes back up with the coffee. But she's already chalked it up to one of Corry's friends coming in. Right?"

Considering it for a moment, Chet gave a brief nod, "Right."

"So, if she didn't tell the police about it...?"

Chet shook his head slightly, "I have a hard time believing the local sheriff or any of the state troopers that run the roads outside our little burg would have anything to do with this. They're all local boys. Went to school here. I've known Luther Ponder, the Sheriff, all my life...Buck Harrison too."

Rory decided to move away from the subject for the time being. No sense getting Chet worked up. Rory gestured back to the whiteboard, "Anything catch your eye on this board?"

Check hitched his pants up as he looked over the white-board. "Well... as I said...if I recall correctly...not all these signs are from the same area around here." He rapped a knuckle on one sketch, "This one here is to the north of us. While this one here is right out here in the backyard. That's the one Emma-Mae showed you–"

"No, I don't think it is," Rory countered as he looked closer.

"Sure it is," Chet said firmly, convinced he was right, "I've seen that one plenty of times as a kid. The rider on the horse. Every schoolboy knew about this one out back of this house."

Rory pointed, "Take a look at the circle that represents the head of the rider. The one on the tree in the backyard has the rider's head looking *backwards*. With this one, the circle indicates the rider is looking *ahead*."

Chet looked closer and then a look of astonishment came over his face, "You're right. I never even noticed that. You're pretty observant...."

Rory shook his head no, "I wouldn't have known if Emma hadn't pointed it out to me that day. And guess who told her?"

Chet nodded his head, "Corry Haney." He looked over the other pieces of paper taped to the whiteboard, "Still...it doesn't make sense why he would have all these particular signs on this whiteboard. As if they were all in one area, but they ain't. That's not how I would do it, if you want to find the treasure." He took one of the papers off the whiteboard and showed to Rory, "And this bird one. I've *never* seen it around here. I've seen something similar but not this one. These downward marks or feathers mean you go a certain distance in the direction indicated by the beak or the tail. But this isn't even a sketch or a graphite rubbing, like we used to do when I was a kid."

Rory took the paper from Chet's hand and looked at it. He rubbed the paper with his fingers, "This feels like a photocopy...maybe a photocopy from a page in a book?"

Chet nodded. He looked over the whiteboard again and pulled another paper off, handing it to Rory, "Same with this one. Photocopy from a book. And nothing I've ever seen around here."

Rory took it and looked at both papers, "Looks like they're from two different books as well. But no indication what books."

Chet looked over the whiteboard for a few more moments and then reached out to the two photocopies, "If you don't mind, I have an idea. My cell phone is in the car and I'd like to call someone about these."

Rory nodded, handing the photocopies over to Chet.

Donna-Lou was just coming back into the room, holding two steaming mugs of coffee.

"I'm just going down to my car and I'll be right back up," said Chet as he hurried past her and disappeared down the hallway.

"But you are coming back, right?" Donna-Lou called after him.

Rory noticed a hint of disappointment in her eyes.

"Yes," Chet yelled back to her.

Donna Lou's eyes brightened. "I swear that man was always rushing around when it came to the treasure when he was a kid." She shook her head as she turned and walked across the room.

"You went to school with Chet?" Rory asked.

"He's about five years older than me, but I remember him." She handed Rory one of the mugs, "I'll just put his over on the desk for when Chet comes back."

Rory took a sip of his hot coffee and cast his eyes over the whiteboard again. Something caught his eye up in the top left-hand corner. He moved closer for a look. There was a narrow wooden border around the outside of the whiteboard and a stick pin was stuck through a small torn remnant of a yellow-tinted, semi-transparent material.

Donna-Lou walked back over to Rory, "Looks like something has got your attention. Boys and their treasure maps and stuff," she said with a smile and a shake of her head.

"Yeah, not sure what it is though," Rory said. He handed the coffee mug to Donna-Lou, "Could you hold this for a minute?"

Donna-Lou took the mug and watched as Rory held the fragment with one hand and pulled out the stick pin with the other.

Rory put the stick pin back into the tiny hole on the whiteboard and examined the scrap of material in his fingers, "It feels like a skin of some type." He held it up to the light, "It's semi-transparent. Any idea what it is?"

Donna-Lou took the fragment from Rory and handed him back the coffee mug. She felt the scrap of material with her fingers and held it up to the light as well, "It's an oilskin of some type. It's how they used to make raincoats. My grandmother taught me about it. They would use a fine-woven cotton canvas or flannel and treat it with linseed oil in a process to make it water repellent." She put her head down, thinking as her fingers rubbed over the material.

"Penny for your thoughts," Rory said after a few moments of silence.

Donna-Lou broke out of her thoughts and gave Rory a sheepish smile, "Sorry. It just brought back memories of when I was a kid." She looked back at the material, "I remember my grandfather having something like this. His was cotton I think, coated with linseed oil, just like this. I hadn't thought about it for years...."

Rory took a look at the other three corners of the whiteboard. Two of them had bent stick pins. The third corner had an elongated hole. He looked down on the floor to see another bent stick pin. He bent over and picked it up, inserting it back into the elongated hole, "It looks to me like your son had something like a large oilskin pinned to each corner over top of these papers. Do you know where he got it from? What it was for?"

Donna-Lou handed the fragment back to Rory, crossed her arms and looked at the whiteboard, puzzled. She shook her head no after a few moments, "I have no idea. And I don't remember ever seeing anything draped across this board."

Rory looked at the material in his hand and wondered.

Chapter 10

RORY TOOK A LOOK AROUND the room as his fingers caressed the material. There was a lot of information in here. The problem was, nothing made much sense to him or stood out. He was definitely going to have to rely on Chet to help him figure this out.

"Penny for *your* thoughts now," Donna-Lou said in amusement.

It was Rory's turn to feel sheepish. He just shook his head as he looked at the papers clustered around the walls of the room, "I'm just not sure where to start. Or how to use this information. Maybe I'm even on a wild goose chase...."

"Well, at least it's a chase. Which is more than anyone else has been doing," Donna-Lou said. "So thank you for that."

Rory nodded, appreciative of the support, but not sure whether he merited it. Rory wandered around the room, trying to make sense of the signs. He glanced through newspaper articles young Corry had photocopied or printed out and pinned onto the wall, trying to get an overall sense of the young boy's search for the treasure.

Donna-Lou stood by the whiteboard, looking at it thought-fully, as Rory wandered around. She was silent for the longest time and then she said, "Rory, would you do something for me?"

Rory turned and nodded, "Sure. What is it?"

Donna-Lou gestured for Rory to follow her out the open doorway, into the hallway. She walked back to a spot between the two bedrooms, the boards squeaking softly under her footsteps. Stopping, she pointed up at the ceiling, "There are old pull-down stairs up there for the attic. Can you grab that short cord and pull it down?"

Rory looked up to see a rectangular section in the ceiling. A short discolored cord hung from one end. He had missed that when they first came through. He positioned himself right un-derneath and reached up.

"Careful. It's old and it's been a long time since anyone used it," Donna-Lou cautioned as she took a step back.

Rory nodded and did a little jump, grabbing hold of and tug-ging on the cord in one motion. He stepped back as the stairway began to drop.

"Ooo," Donna-Lou said with a giggle as Rory bumped into her.

"Sorry," Rory said as he watched the bottom of the stairway bump into the old floorboards.

Donna-Lou looked confused as she stepped around Rory, looking up into the opening. "That's strange. I thought there'd be a lot more dust coming down."

Rory hadn't thought about that aspect, but she was right. He wondered if someone had been up there not long ago. Maybe the same person who had broken into her house?

Donna-Lou shook the stairway vigorously to make sure it was safe. Satisfied it was fine, she began climbing.

As Rory watched her climb, his eyes settled on her shapely bottom in the blue jeans.

Placing one foot on the attic floor, Donna-Lou stepped up into the attic, turned and looked down at him.

Rory wondered if she had caught him looking at her bottom. They had only just met and–

"Are you coming up or not? Or you afraid of the dark?" She smiled.

Rory cleared his throat, shook his head and started climbing.

Donna-Lou disappeared from view.

As Rory's shoulders emerged through the opening in the ceiling, Donna-Lou turned on a large, bare light bulb attached to one of the rafters and he got his first look at what was up here. Piled across the attic floor, in no particular order, were old wooden chairs, small tables, bits of furniture, pictures and pictures frames wrapped in cloth, assorted lamps, and boxes. Dozens and dozens of boxes of various sizes, some cardboard and some wooden, were placed around the attic. Most of the boxes had labels scrawled across the side; books, dishes, cutlery, knick-backs. A number of labels were faded and unreadable in the dim light off to the edges of the attic. Rory stepped foot on the old attic boards and saw more items off in the dark corners of the attic.

Donna-Lou was working her way through items and boxes, heading to the far end of the attic, toward the back of the old house.

"What exactly are we doing up here?" Rory asked as he took a few tentative steps on the old boards, heading in her general direction.

Donna-Lou talked over her shoulder as she continued walking along the old boards, looking for something, "My grandfather had an old trunk that fascinated me when I was just a kid. I don't remember ever seeing inside it. But I do remember that was where he kept that oilskin I mentioned. My grandmother had some of the men put the trunk into the attic after his wake here in the house. I can remember them struggling to get it upstairs on and then into the attic."

"They held a wake here in the house! Really?"

Donna-Lou nodded as she moved a couple of boxes, "That's what they did in those days. I don't remember much about it, except for the crying and wailing. Stayed with me for a long time as a kid. Can you move those boxes over there, out of the way?"

Rory stepped forward and slid four boxes over to the right and away from where Donna-Lou was working, "Why are you looking for the trunk?"

"I just thought it might be helpful to see what an old oilskin looks like. Move this over there too, please," Donna-Lou said as she slid a larger box towards Rory.

Rory slid that box over with the others.

"Maybe it helps, maybe it doesn't," Donna-Lou said. She slid another large cardboard box to the side with a grunt, "And here it is."

Rory slid the larger box further to the side and out of the way.

Donna-Lou was now bent over, hands on her knees, in front of another large box.

Rory couldn't see exactly what it was but he caught a glimpse of a large, fancy-looking steamer trunk with a heavy, brown patina.

"Can you pull this out for me?" Donna-Lou asked, "I'd like to get it more into the light."

"Sure." Rory stepped forward. As Donna-Lou moved to the side, he now had a better look at the trunk. It was four foot long, two feet across and nearly two feet high. The color was a deep, rich caramel with a gilded, gold framework, crisscrossed by half-inch, gold metal straps, gold latches, and gold carry handles on each end. Rory ran his hand over the surface between the metal bands, "Amazing. The material is actually leather. This thing looks really old."

"It is," Donna-Lou confirmed.

Rory grabbed one of the gold handles on the end. He grunted as he barely slid it a foot, "Wow. Is it ever heavy." He tapped the top, "There is thick wood underneath the leather. Someone really wanted to protect the contents."

"As I said, those men struggled and cursed all the way up. My grandmother had us kids leave so we wouldn't learn bad language. Little did she know we already knew the choice swear words," Donna-Lou said with a laugh. She took a step forward and grabbed the other gold handle, "I'll do my best...."

Rory grabbed the handle again and waited for Donna-Lou to get herself set. She gave him a nod and working together, they slowly slid each side back and forth until the old steamer trunk was free of the surrounding items.

Donna-Lou knelt in front of the trunk, breathing heavy from the exertion. She pulled down on the lock, "Crap, locked. And I don't remember where the key is." She waved at the items around them, "Find me something to hit it with."

"Are you sure?" Rory asked. "That trunk is probably worth a fortune as an antique."

Shrugging, Donna-Lou said, "Like I said, I don't know where the key is

Rory bent over, looked at the keyhole in the lock, estimating the size with a fingertip. He remembered seeing something he could possibly use. He turned on his heels and went over to an area of the attic floor where he saw some kitchen items and one other thing he felt he could use. A minute later he found the boxes marked 'kitchen' and a heavy cast piece for hanging pots on top of one. And wrapped around one of the prongs he found the small roll of black, stovepipe wire. Grabbing it, he uncoiled one end as he went back to the steamer trunk, "This should work."

Donna-Lou slid over on her knees and watched Rory kneel and insert one end of the wire in the keyhole.

Rory worked the wire inside the keyhole, feeling for the locking mechanism and was rewarded with a dull click. Pulling the wire out he slid over to allow Donna-Lou to move back. "You can do the honors," Rory said. He reached over and put the coil of wire on one of the cardboard boxes.

Donna-Lou slid over on her knees and undid the two gold latches first. Then she put her hand on the lock and looked at Rory, a twinkle in her eye, "Do you think we'll find KGC treasure?"

Rory pretended to grumble, "We'll never know if you don't open it."

Donna-Lou smirked, then turned her attention back to the trunk. She slowly opened the lid, leaned over a bit...and Donna-Lou Haney gasped.

Chapter 11

RORY COULD FEEL HIS OWN AMAZEMENT as he looked at the contents inside the old steamer trunk. Right on top of everything was a gray-colored, Confederate cavalry stetson, also known as a stag hat, with a gold acorn cord. The gold insignia on the hat consisted of the figure '8th' surrounded by a gold laurel.

Donna-Lou reached in and gently picked it up, turning it in her hands.

"Did that belong to someone in your family?" Rory asked.

"I have no idea," Donna-Lou answered in a voice filled with wonder.

Rory glanced inside the trunk at the gray material that had been underneath the stag hat, "Is that a jacket?"

Donna-Lou's brow furrowed as she looked at the material, "I don't know...."

Rory reached in and pulled the material out. Holding it up, he let the gray material unfold.

"It is a jacket," Donna-Lou exclaimed. "That's a Cavalry Officer's shell jacket! I never knew that was in there all this time."

Rory turned the coat this way and that, examining it in detail, "It's still in great shape." There were four rows of 1/8 inch gold, flat braid on the sleeve with gold edges on the cuffs, gold piping on the collar and two rows of gold buttons running down the front of the jacket. The letters CR were embroidered in gold stitching on the shoulders.

"That insignia on the collar says that jacket is part of a Major-General's uniform," Donna-Lou explained. "I know because the boys used to do a lot of their talks in school on the Confederacy."

"Do you think these are original?" asked Rory.

Donna-Lou shrugged, "Maybe. But I'm not sure why we would have that."

"Maybe your family bought it an auction," Rory suggested. "You'll have to get a museum expert to take a look at it for you. It could be worth a lot of money."

Donna-Lou nodded as she looked back into the trunk, "Oh my." She set the cavalry stag hat on her lap and reached inside. She carefully pulled out a folded Confederate flag. Unfolding it, she ran her hands over the old cloth, "It looks like it's been repaired at some point. There's a seam running diagonally across the entire flag. And one of the stars has some extra stitching around it."

"The flag looks old. Maybe there was a hole in the star and they just added another one in," Rory said

"No, I don't think so," Donna-Lou said. She set the Confederate flag down her lap and reached into the trunk again. She pulled out a long cylinder, about 4 feet long and 2 inches around. "It looks like it's made from rabbit fur and coated with a wax-like substance." She pulled a waxy plug out of one end and held the tube up to her eye, "It's empty."

"Anything else in the trunk?" Rory asked.

"Yeah, two mahogany boxes," Donna-Lou said. She set the cylinder behind her. Then she reached inside the trunk, putting her hands around one of the boxes.

"Wonder what's in them?" Rory reached into the trunk when he saw Donna-Lou struggling and helped her lift a mahogany box out. They set it on the floor.

Donna-Lou leaned over and undid the catch, opening the mahogany box. She peered inside, "What...?"

Rory leaned over and helped her pull out a brass object with a wonderful mellow patina. The brass object consisted of a triangular attachment on top, an eleven-inch scope below that and a six-inch circular gauge with a needle under the glass. "It's a surveyor's transit," he said in surprise. He felt the heft, "It weighs about twenty pounds."

"It looks really old," Donna-Lou said. "I don't remember anyone in my family doing any surveying." She reached in and pulled out the other mahogany box, opening it, "Oh my...."

Rory set the surveyor's transit carefully down on the floor and looked into the box. It held a two-tone gold handgun that had an intricate series of Confederate symbols etched across it. He reached into the box, slipping his fingers carefully around the weapon and lifting it out. His eyes sparkled as he held it up, "*This* is a LeMat revolver. I've only seen pictures of them. It was invented by Jean Alexandre LeMat of New Orleans. It was used by the Confederate army during the civil war, including some members of the Confederate Cavalry." Rory ran his fingers over the weapon, "See those Confederate symbols?"

Donna-Lou leaned a bit, looking at the old weapon in Rory's hands, "Yeah." She turned her head this way and that, "It looks like the gun has two barrels."

"It does," Rory confirmed as he looked weapon over. "The top one is a .42 caliber, cap & ball black powder barrel. The secondary one is a smooth-bore barrel, capable of firing 16 gauge buckshot." He looked into the box, "You've got everything here. The powder horn, balls...."

Donna-Lou whispered as she shook her head, "I didn't know it was up here. I never wanted guns around once Corry was born."

Rory set the gun carefully back in the case and closed it, setting it on the floor, "Anything else in the trunk?"

Donna-Lou looked into the trunk, then sat back on her heels, shaking her head, the disappointment evident in her voice, "No. There's no oilskin in here at all. That's what I really expected to see. I'm positive my grandfather kept it in there."

"No problem." Rory reached behind her and picked up the long cylinder, looking inside it again, "It might have been rolled inside this thing at one time. And someone's taken it."

Donna-Lou nodded, thinking, "It must've been taken a long time ago. I haven't been up here for years–"

"Hello?"

It was Chet, yelling from below.

Donna-Lou turned, a smile lighting up her face. She put her hands to her mouth and yelled, "Yeah, we're up here, Chet. C'mon up."

Rory noticed her smile as he heard Chet climbing the ladder. He looked back and a moment later, Chet's head and shoulders popped through the opening from below, "What are you doing up here?"

"Just looking through some old stuff," Rory explained. "Did you get a hold of that person you were calling about those photocopies? You were gone quite a while."

"Yeah. Actually, I was calling Nora-Jane Jackson." Chet climbed into the attic, hitched up his pants and walked across the old boards, "She has contacts in the historical archives down in Atlanta. A lot of our old local history books were moved down there some years ago and they might know where those photocopies were taken from. As luck would have it, she was actually back in town because of Emma. She was just over by the library and she drove over and I gave her the copies–"

"Are you sure that was a good idea?" Rory asked gently.

"Oh, sure. They'll be safe. She's headed over to her momma's old place and then down to Atlanta."

"No, I mean–"

"Oh, wow," Chet exclaimed when his eyes saw the old Civil War items. He hustled across the old boards, hitching his pants up again, "I never knew you had this stuff, Donna-Lou."

"Really didn't know I had it either Chet," Donna-Lou admitted. "This was an old trunk of my grandfather that was placed up here when I was a kid. Never looked at it before today."

Chet stopped beside Rory and he swallowed, "That's...that's a Cavalry officer's stag hat...."

Donna-Lou passed to Rory, who handed it up to Chet, "Donna-Lou is not sure who it originally belonged to."

Chet looked at the hat with big eyes. His hands passed over the gold insignia almost in awe.

"What is it, Chet?" Donna-Lou asked. "Do you recognize it?"

Chet didn't answer. He handed the stag hat back to Rory and took a step.

Rory and Donna-Lou each shifted to allow Chet some room.

Kneeling by the gun case, Chet opened it slowly, placing his hand on the LeMat revolver inside. His fingers traced the gold etchings, his eyes lit up with wonder and delight. Then he quickly held his hand out for the shell jacket.

Rory passed him the gray jacket.

Chet took the shell jacket by the shoulders, stood up and held it out in front of himself. He had a goofy grin on his face and shook his head.

Rory exchanged a glance with Donna-Lou and looked up, "You do recognize these things, don't you Chet?"

Chet just nodded.

"Boys and their toys...or uniforms," Donna-Lou said with mirth in her voice.

"No, it's more than that," Chet said, almost reverentially. "The gold insignia on the stag hat identifies this as the uniform belonging to the 8th Cavalry of South Carolina. The same thing is etched into the revolver. And see that CR designation on the shoulders of this shell jacket? That stands for Calhoun's Raiders."

Donna-Lou shook her head, "Calhoun's Raiders? I don't remember *ever* hearing that name. And you would think we would have heard of it around here, considering your family and all."

Chet nodded as he kept staring at the uniform, "It wasn't supposed to exist. At least, that's what all the history experts say. My family and a lot of old timers around here say it did. But there were never any records found in the archives that proved them right. But this does. It's exactly as they described it."

"Any idea why *my* family would have it?" Donna-Lou asked.

Chet shook his head no. Then he closed his eyes as he was thinking back, "If I remember from what I was told as a kid...the leader was a Major-General Jeb Pinter–"

"Pinter?" Donna-Lou exclaimed. "Are you sure?"

Chet opened his eyes and nodded. Both he and Rory looked in surprise at Donna-Lou's outburst.

"Pinter was my grandmother's maiden name," she said in astonishment.

Chet shook his head in amazement, "My grand-daddy and my uncles said Calhoun's Raiders were the main military arm of the Knights of the Golden Circle."

"You're kidding me?" Donna-Lou said. "My family was a part of the KGC?"

"Apparently," Chet said. "And what's more...they were responsible for taking the treasure from Atlanta up into South Carolina."

Donna-Lou looked down at the trunk and shook her head, "I never knew...."

"What made you look through this stuff?" Chet asked after a moment of silence.

"I was looking for an old oilskin my grandfather had. It should have been in here too," Donna-Lou said.

Chet's back straightened, "What oilskin?" He looked from Donna-Lou to Rory and back.

Rory took the material from his pocket and handed it up to Chet.

Chet gave Rory the shell jacket and took the fragment of material from him.

Glancing at Donna-Lou, Rory raised his eyebrows in question

Donna-Lou gave him a shrug in return.

Chet's voice was a whisper as he glanced to the trunk, "You found this in there?"

"No," Rory said. "I found it under a stick-pin on the white-board. It looks like Corry had an oilskin draped across those pictures. Someone ripped it off, leaving behind that small fragment in the upper corner of the whiteboard."

"We think it was in this tube," Donna-Lou said. "Why? What does it mean?"

Chet took a deep breath and let it out, licking his lips before he spoke in a low voice, "Slickers or old raincoats worn by folks back in the old days...including the ones worn by the Knights of the Golden Circle...were made from this material."

Donna-Lou nodded, "That's what I told Rory."

"Why are their raincoats so important?" Rory asked.

Chet looked at the remnant again and took another breath before he answered, "When KGC operatives buried their money caches, they would inscribe signs on rocks and trees as directions back to where they left those caches. To start with, the signs were made from a template. They had a basic set of signs but each time they hid something, the signs they put on the trees or rocks or whatever would have subtle differences. In the sign in the back yard, the rider's head was looking back, so you go in the direction it's looking to find another sign. A similar sign might point in a different direction. As I said before, where two signs intersected you would find another sign or maybe a clue of some type. The larger caches would have an extensive set of signs that could lead you over miles and miles and miles of terrain. To find the hiding spot again, you would go to each sign in the area and draw them on another slicker, one by one in the pattern according to where you find each one. The pattern on the semi-transparent slicker would then be an overall template to find the treasure spot."

"So you think that's what my grandfather had in here? That kind of slicker with a pattern of signs?" Donna-Lou asked.

"Maybe. Or a map and the original set of signs and how they were laid out," Chet said. "That would be neat."

Donna-Lou pointed to the surveyor's transit, "Maybe they used that thing to set everything up."

Chet looked down at it and shrugged, "Could be. I'm not really sure how they set it up. But that would make sense."

"So whoever has that oilskin can find the treasure?" Rory asked.

Chet shook his head no, "You don't really need the oilskin. You could just re-create the original map by sketching the signs on paper, just like Corry did. Like we all did as young'uns."

"But if it was that easy, why has it been so hard to find these treasure caches?" Rory asked.

"Ah, the secret," Chet said. "You needed the template *and* the knowledge of two things, the keystone and the guide."

"Template, keystone and guide?" Rory repeated.

Chet nodded, "To relocate the cache, the signs were copied onto a slicker in the exact pattern in which they're found in an area. The slicker would then be placed over top of a topographical map, scaled to fit the area where the signs were found. This produced a very specific and accurate map. Now...one of the signs in the area was the keystone. You had to align some feature of the template over the keystone and something on the template would indicate a direction. But still not the exact direction. Or the distance. The cache could still be miles away from the area where the signs are found. And that brings up something my grand-daddy told me about, something most people don't know. One of the signs was the guide. You had to align the template over the keystone *and* the guide to tell you the specific direction. *And* one of the signs would then tell you how far in that direction you needed to go–"

"What would the template look like?" Rory asked.

Chet shrugged, "I'm not really sure. I've heard some of the smaller templates consisted of a Confederate soldier's uniform with one of the seams pointing in the direction–"

Donna-Lou's eyebrows shot up, "A seam?" She looked down at the Confederate flag. She held it up to Chet, "Like the seam in this flag?"

Chet gave the piece of slicker material back to Rory and took the Confederate flag. He ran his hand along the seam, "Oh wow!"

Donna-Lou and Rory stood up.

"One of the stars has stitching around it as well," Rory said as he pointed to the flag.

Chet took a closer look. He then looked at Donna-Lou. "Remember that sign in your backyard? It has a five-point star over the head of the rider?"

Donna-Lou nodded.

Chet looked at Rory, "And the one on the whiteboard?"

Rory nodded, "It has a star as well. But the head is looking a different way."

"If this is a template...and you align this star with either star...and you follow the seam..."

"That's the keystone," Rory said in realization.

Chet nodded.

"What about the guide?" Donna-Lou asked.

Chet looked at the Confederate flag for a moment and then shrugged, "I'm not sure what it would be. We would have to have all the signs in the area to figure that out."

Donna-Lou crossed her arms, looking at the items from the trunk, "Maybe that's why there wasn't any dust when we pulled the attic stairs down. There should have been. Maybe Corry came snooping up here and found my grandfather's oilskin in this old trunk. And all of this other stuff...."

"And he went looking for the treasure," Rory added.

"And got closer than somebody liked," Donna-Lou concluded sadly.

"Can we use any of this to figure out *where* he went looking, Chet?" Rory asked.

Chet shook his head, "Not that I can see. We have one big problem."

"What's that?" Rory asked.

"As I already said, at least a couple of those signs on the whiteboard are *not* from around here. That I'm positive about."

Rory looked at Donna-Lou, "Was your son ever away from home overnight or...?"

Donna-Lou shook her head no emphatically, "Never. Home every night. Never really strayed far from home. No field trips for the school. Nothing that I can think of. Sorry."

"So...does any of this really help us...or not?" Rory asked finally.

No one had any answers.

Chapter 12

NORA-JANE JACKSON pressed down on the gas, hitting 90 mph. It was a little risky on these older back roads, but she was determined and excited. She glanced over the two photocopies on the passenger seat. She had no idea if this far-fetched lead from Chet Calhoun would pan out. But at least *something* was being done for all those missing children. Months and months of pressing the authorities had done little good. Experience told her to keep pressing until something gave.

A low mechanical growl took her out of her thoughts. Nora-Jane looked in her rearview mirror. She could see a vehicle far behind her, too far to tell who it was. Then again, she had been living elsewhere for years and couldn't identify the locals by their vehicles like she could before she went away.

Her thoughts went back to the photocopies on the passenger seat. Everybody here knew about the treasure legends, but she wondered if people would be so low as to harm children over protecting caches. Then again, in the years since she'd been away, she covered a lot of people who were willing to do a lot of cruel things for money or power. But that was the big city, not small-town Golden. She slowed down, anticipating the three twisting turns coming up. She remembered nearly losing it through this stretch when she was first learning to drive. Taking the twists on her bicycle had been a lot easier, she remembered with amusement. She dropped her speed a little more just to make sure, took the turns with caution and then entered the straightaway. This was always a pretty part of the drive. Large mature trees lined the two-lane road with a wall of lush green. She pressed down on the gas again.

A few minutes later Nora-Jane heard the mechanical growl behind her again. Only it sounded louder. She glanced in the rearview mirror and saw the vehicle coming around the last corner. The idiot behind her must have kept his speed up and had been lucky not to lose it around those sharp bends. Nora-Jane could now see it was a red, heavy-duty pickup truck with an extended cab and an extended rear cargo area. She learned those terms from her cousin Granville, who had a similar blue truck with four-wheel drive. And like him, this one had those big tires –

The red, heavy-duty pickup truck growled louder once it hit the straightaway.

Nora-Jane could see it was coming fast. Idiot!

The pickup closed the distance to Nora-Jane's Lincoln rapidly.

The newswoman felt herself tighten her butt cheeks as the pickup came up so fast she thought he was going to ram her.

The growl was loud as the pickup stayed mere inches away from the Lincoln's bumper.

Nora-Jane couldn't see the driver through the tinted windows. Who was this idiot? She contemplated slowing down and letting the driver pass. But he was so close! She wondered if he wouldn't react in time. She pressed down on the accelerator.

The big pickup began to fall back, the sound of the engine dropping away.

Nora-Jane felt some relief. She consciously tried to relax her body.

Suddenly, the 310 hp engine of the red pickup truck growled harshly again.

Looking in the rearview mirror, Nora-Jane's body tightened up as the heavy-duty pickup truck shot forward like a cannonball to within inches of her bumper again. She swore and yelled, "Why don't you just pass, you idiot!"

But the pickup truck just stayed glued to the Lincoln's bumper.

Nora-Jane squinted, trying to figure out who the driver was. And what his game was. She couldn't see anything through those stupid tinted windows. Nora-Jane pressed down more on the accelerator, opening a gap again.

The red pickup reacted by accelerating and closing the gap again.

Nora-Jane gave her car more gas.

The pickup accelerated just enough to stay on the Lincoln's tail.

"What are you doing, you idiot," she yelled again. She gripped the steering wheel tighter and gave it more gas.

The heavy-duty pickup upped its speed to close in again. Then it began to weave back and forth in the lane, mere inches from the Lincoln's bumper.

That angered Nora-Jane. Playing a stupid game like this at high speeds was reckless and dangerous. She didn't know what to do. She was afraid to slow down. If he wasn't expecting it...bang.

If he accelerated while she slowed...bang. A collision at this speed wouldn't be pretty.

A moment later, the pursuing vehicle swung left into the opposite lane and the engine growled as it accelerated. The nose of the bonnet moved up to the back door of the Lincoln.

Nora-Jane shot a look down into the side mirror.

Was he finally passing?

She still couldn't see the driver through the tinted windshield. And the passenger side window was tinted as well. As the truck drew parallel, she couldn't tell if someone was sitting there looking across at her. Why was he...she...they...doing this?

The pickup stayed in the opposite lane, matching the big Lincoln's speed.

The scared woman glanced ahead, afraid even a glance might set off some burst of anger. Usually there weren't many vehicles on this road, but if one came along now–

Suddenly slowing, the pickup dropped back and then moved back in behind the Lincoln.

What in the world? What was he doing? Nora-Jane wondered.

The heavy-duty pickup began to weave back and forth again, inches from the Lincoln's bumper.

Nora-Jane Jackson pounded the steering wheel in frustration. "What are you doing!" she yelled. She wished she could just pull over and give the jackass a talking-to. This must be what road rage feels like, she thought.

The red pickup stopped weaving. It slowed and moved back from the Lincoln's bumper.

Nora-Jane felt relief.

But she also felt sick at her stomach.

Stupid games!

The truck's engine growled and the vehicle accelerated again, coming back hard at the Lincoln's bumper.

Nora-Jane gripped the steering wheel in anticipation of getting rammed!

The huge pickup loomed large in her rearview mirror

Nora-Jane screamed. He was going to hit her this time, she was sure of it.

The pickup slowed down and backed away.

Nora-Jane Jackson almost threw up.

Vomit burned her throat.

The pickup accelerated again.

Nora-Jane tensed, anticipating the collision again, but it never came.

The pickup slowed down again and backed away. He did it several more times, coming up close at high speed and then backing away quickly.

Nora-Jane yelled as she hammered at the steering wheel again, "Son of a bitch. Why are you doing this?" She floored the gas. The big Lincoln accelerated away from the heavy-duty pickup. She glanced in the rearview mirror. She was getting away. Nora-Jane kept the gas pedal to the floor. She tried to remember how far to the next curve. She heard a roar and glanced into the rearview mirror.

The huge pickup accelerated and chased the Lincoln.

Nora-Jane pushed her foot down on the gas pedal, trying to get more speed. She felt like the gazelle trying to escape the lion in those nature shows her mother used to watch.

The red pickup roared, coming closer...closer....

Nora-Jane glanced back and forth from the road ahead to the rearview mirror.

The pickup closed the distance and hung on to the Lincoln's bumper again.

Nora-Jane willed her car to go faster, bile rising in her throat.

The pickup swung left into the opposite lane again, the engine growling as it continued accelerating.

Looking across, Nora-Jane could see the pickup truck was right there now, right beside her. It was taller than the Lincoln, she could only see the lower half of the passenger side window. But she still couldn't see anything through the tinted glass.

The pickup truck moved a foot away and she could see more of the passenger side window. It was like a big black evil eye staring at her. Then it suddenly swung sharply left, away from the Lincoln and almost off the road.

Nora-Jane looked ahead quickly, thinking a vehicle was approaching ahead of them. But the road ahead was empty. She looked back at the pickup truck, wondering....

The big red pickup growled and swung back towards her.

Nora-Jane Jackson let out a surprised scream as her Lincoln was bashed from the side. Her right wheel hit the gravel shoulder on the right and she nearly lost control. Holding the steering wheel tight with a death-grip, she fought to get the big luxury car back onto the pavement.

The pickup truck swung to the left in its lane again, then aggressively moved back to pound the side of the big Lincoln again.

Nora-Jane felt the jolt and the big Lincoln luxury sedan swayed and she fought to maintain control as her right wheels fought with the gravel shoulder.

The pickup truck moved left again.

Nora-Jane got the wheels back on the pavement.

The pickup truck came back at the Lincoln even harder this time.

Nora-Jane actually felt her driver-side door buckle inward from the blow.

The red pickup move left and came back again, crunching in the Lincoln's left front fender.

The 4,200 lbs of the Lincoln was a poor match for the 6,000 lbs of the heavy-duty pickup truck. Nora-Jane's right wheels left the pavement again, hitting the gravel. She fought to maintain control as the Lincoln shuddered half on the pavement and half on the shoulder. The trees on the right were just a blur.

The pickup moved to the right, not hitting her again but keeping pace.

"You're not running me off the road," she yelled.

The trees were right there, certain death at this speed.

The red, heavy-duty pickup truck stayed put, never wavering in its path.

Nora-Jane struggled to maintain control as the right wheels continued to fight with the soft gravel of the shoulder.

The pickup truck kept pace, a huge menacing hunk of red metal.

Nora-Jane Jackson felt hot tears stream down her cheeks as she realized what was about to happen. He wasn't trying to run her off the road. Her brain sent the signal but her foot only made it halfway from the gas to the brake. The Lincoln MKS stopped dead as it hit the steel framework of the Knox River bridge.

Chapter 13

IT WAS EARLY MORNING, an hour after sunup, and Rory sat in a window seat in Martha's diner, eating a breakfast of bacon, eggs, toast and great coffee. Donna-Lou Haney had insisted he and Chet meet her for breakfast. He hadn't expected her to be serving and paying. But she was extremely grateful at having someone looking for her son beyond the cursory search she felt the FBI had done. Chet hadn't shown up yet, which Donna-Lou thought was unusual. Chet was a regular and loved this place.

Jesse had said she was surprised he hadn't shown up either. She kept one eye on Rory, making sure his coffee was topped up, and one eye on the door.

The diner had been filled to the brim with locals and tourists when Rory first came in. But right now it was thinning out as people headed off to work or wherever they were going for the day.

As he watched people leaving through the large window overlooking the parking lot, Rory finally saw Chet Calhoun's battered old Chevrolet Impala pull off the road. The Chevy took a spot a few cars down from the diner.

Chet got out and headed for the door of the diner.

Rory noted the walking with his head down like he was thinking heavily about something. And he looked somber.

Chet gave a subdued greeting to a couple of locals who passed him on their way out.

Rory watched him weave his way through the tables, head still down as he headed towards Rory. Something wasn't right; he could see it in Chet's walk. And he never once hitched up his pants.

Chet sat down heavily across from Rory without saying a word. His head was still down.

Jesse hustled over with her pot of coffee, "Well, ain't you just an old sleepyhead."

Donna-Lou Haney moved in beside Jesse, "We was getting worried about you, Chet. It isn't like you –"

Chet Calhoun slowly raised his head. His eyes were brimming with tears.

Jesse put her hand on his arm, "What's wrong, Chet? What is it?"

"Nora-Jane Jackson–" the words caught in his throat.

"What about her?" Donna-Lou asked.

Chet cleared his throat, trying to say something.

"You're worrying me, Chet," said Jesse with concern. "What's happened?"

"She died last night," said Chet simply. He let out a sob.

Rory sat up straighter, "What? What happened?"

Chet cleared his throat again, "Her...her car hit the Knox River bridge."

Jesse took a step back like she had been hit with a brick, "What!" "How can that be? She's drove that road for years, knew it like the back of her hand. That's impossible."

Chet nodded his head as tears spilled out, "I know...I know. I heard it on the police scanner this morning, just after I got up. I went out there to see it for myself. They've taken her body up to the morgue in Greenville. Teddy Atkinson brought her car in on the flatbed and put it in the scrap yard behind his auto body shop. She went off the road and hit dead center into the steel-work...."

Jesse broke down in tears.

Donna-Lou Haney broke down in tears as well, putting her arms around Jesse.

The locals still sitting in the diner heard the news and came over, talking and consoling one another.

Rory stayed quiet as he set his fork down and sat back, watching the grief etched on the faces of everyone around him.

Chet Calhoun stayed sitting on the other side of the table, his body sagging under the weight of his own grief. His voice was hoarse and low as he looked out the window, "I never thought I'd be making a radio announcement like this for Nora-Jane Jackson. First those kids, now this...."

Rory sat there. Not much he could say at a time like this. But as he watched the grief-stricken people around him, his radar was working overtime.

Chet Calhoun looked up at Rory, wiped a tear from his eye and made a gesture with his head toward the front door of the restaurant.

Rory watched Chet slide across on his seat on the other side of the table and stand up.

Jesse embraced Chet and they said a few words to each other.

Rory slid out and got up. He rested a hand on Donna-Lou's shoulder for a moment. He received a slight nod from her as she embraced one of her friends. Rory looked at Chet and Jesse, then headed for the front door. He stepped outside into the sunlight, leaving the darkness of death temporarily behind him. He put his hands into his pockets and waited, thinking about the woman he had only just met. The woman headed for a cold slab in the Greenville morgue.

Chet Calhoun stepped out of the restaurant, wiping tears from his red eyes, "Sorry...but I just didn't want to stay in there a moment longer. I never was much good with all that grief stuff since my daddy and my granddaddy's wake." He looked back into the restaurant and didn't say anything for a moment. Then he slid his hands into his pants pockets and looked straight at Rory, "Did I just get her killed?"

Rory didn't know what to say.

"Did I?" Chet asked in a broken voice. Tears rolled from his eyes again and he wiped them away with his right hand.

Rory reached out and placed a comforting hand on Chet's shoulder.

Chet took a deep breath and cleared his throat. He looked back into the restaurant for a brief moment and then shook his head softly, "I can't believe this."

Squeezing the man's shoulder, Rory, "If you're up for it, I think we should go over to see the car...."

Rubbing the stubble on his chin, Chet gave a slight nod of his head, "Yeah. Yeah, we should do that."

TWENTY MINUTES LATER, Chet pulled his old Chevrolet Impala into the driveway of Atkinson Auto Body Shop & Repair.

A large number of cars were lined up along the side and at the back of the building. A few looked new, some were old and damaged and others looked like they were being cannibalized for parts.

In the passenger seat, Rory watched as a tall, skinny man in his 60s came out of an old building, the screen door snapping shut behind him.

Chet rolled down his window, "Hey Teddy."

"Chet," acknowledged Teddy Atkinson.

The scent of motor oil and gasoline from Atkinson's beat up ball cap, shirt and coveralls reached Rory as the man leaned over and placed his elbows on Chet's driver side window frame.

"What can I do for ya?" Atkinson asked Chet.

"I've got to make a news report on Nora-Jane," Chet explained. "Thought I would get the make and model of the vehicle. Just need to fill in the details, that kind of thing."

Teddy pushed the ball cap back on his head, revealing salt-and-pepper hair, "You sure? I can just give it to you. Make it easier...."

"Thanks, but I'd like to do it right. Just like Nora-Jane would do," Chet answered.

Teddy looked across at Rory for a moment. Then he nodded his head, "Yeah, that's how she would do it too. Go ahead, take your time. It's way in the back, over on the left. If I can do anything, you can find me in the shop." He patted Chet several times on the shoulder, then headed back for the screen door.

Chet took a deep breath and put the Chevrolet in gear. Driving around into the back and around several piles of junk, they reached Nora-Jane Jackson's dark blue, Lincoln MKS luxury sedan. The front end was demolished. Chet stopped the Chevy ten feet from the wreck and stared.

Rory waited for a moment, then got out and walked to the luxury sedan.

Chet got out, hesitated for a moment and then walked over to Rory on the driver's side of the Lincoln. "They used the jaws of life to get the door open. She was already gone, though."

Rory nodded. The driver side door was a crunched pile of junk, hanging from one hinge.

"She hit the right side of the bridge dead on," Chet said. He put his hands in his pockets.

Rory bent down and looked into the vehicle, "Did you see those photocopies? The ones from the books that you gave her?"

Shaking his head, Chet said, "No. I never really had a chance to look. The shock of it and everything...."

Rory stepped back and looked at the side of the Lincoln. He walked towards the back, fingers lightly touching the surface of the back door.

Starting for the passenger side, Chet said, "I saw her put them on the passenger seat before she drove off. Maybe they're still there."

Rory walked around the back of the Lincoln and then up to where Chet was looking into the passenger side of the car.

Chet stuck his head partly through the opening where the window glass should be, "But I don't see anything in there. Not on the floor either." He straightened up and looked at Rory, "What do you think...?"

Taking a step back, Rory looked at the vehicle for a few minutes. "Notice how the passenger side window is gone?"

Chet took a step back as well and nodded, "Yeah. Probably from the accident. Maybe the photocopies got tossed out–?"

Rory shook his head, "No, I don't think so." He pointed at the front windshield, "Notice how the front windshield is totally shattered but still intact?"

Taking a step to the side, Chet looked at it and nodded, "Yeah?"

"That's because it's made from laminated glass. It's created to shatter into a million pieces rather than a few sharp pieces to protect the passengers. But it's actually two layers of glass with a plastic sheet in the middle, so the actual glass fragments stay together as a whole piece. You can kick your way out but it takes a little time."

Chet nodded his head as he looked at the windshield. He hitched up his pants and looked at Rory, "Okay...?"

"On the other hand, the side glass is made to shatter into tiny pieces much easier, so you can kick your way out if necessary," Rory explained.

"Right, such as when a car accidentally goes into a lake or river and such," Chet said.

"Exactly." Rory reached out and tried to open the door. It wouldn't open. He stepped back, "Notice how the passenger side door is buckled out just a little as well?"

"That's from the accident," Chet said. "It's wedged shut."

Rory nodded in agreement, "Right. Now think about this. If the window had shattered in the accident, you would expect the glass to come out this way from the force as well, wouldn't you?"

Chet looked at the hole where the glass had been, then looked into the car, "The glass is shattered inward. Some of it is still on the seat." Chet looked at Rory, realizing where he was going with his train of thought, "Someone couldn't open the door so they smashed the glass in...*after* the accident."

Rory nodded again, "It might have been someone like a paramedic or trooper, getting to Nora-Jane but...."

Blinking his eyes, considering what Rory was saying, Chet licked his lips, "Rory...Nora-Jane put the photocopies right on this seat...."

"And someone reached in and took them," Rory concluded.

Chet cursed. "Do you really think...?"

Rory motioned for Chet to follow him back around to the driver's side. He ran his hand along the surface of the back door and then along the driver's side door, "See anything?"

Stepping back a foot, Chet narrowed his eyes. Moments later, he opened them wide, "Red paint traces?"

"Yeah. It looks to me like someone collided with the side of her car. And there are paint traces where the front fender is buckled in."

Chet looked closer at the driver's side door, "It looks to me like there was some gray paint under the red."

Rory looked at where he was pointing, "You're right. Someone repainted a gray vehicle."

"I should check with the Sheriff about this," Chet said. "See if he saw this. Could be important."

Rory thought about it for a moment, "Why don't we go over to the crash site first? Can we do that?"

Chet shrugged, "Sure. But don't you think –?"

"Just humor me. Please?"

THIRTY MINUTES LATER, Chet stopped his old Chevrolet Impala as Rory asked, on the gravel shoulder of the roadway, twenty feet away from the Knox River bridge. The accident scene was on the other side of the bridge. Chet got out and stood beside Rory at the front of the vehicle, "What are we looking for?"

"Not sure. Let's just take a walk and go take a look," Rory said as he gestured to the other side of the bridge.

"I just couldn't believe it when I first saw her car crunched into the steel girders," Chet said as they walked across the bridge. "Like Jesse said, Nora-Jane knew these roads like the back of her hand." He wiped a tear from his eye.

Rory looked over the edge of the bridge at the fast flowing water below. Nothing stood out or caught his attention. A few moments later they were on the side where the accident had occurred. Rory took a cursory glance at the steel girders, where the car had come to its final resting spot, and then he continued walking.

Chet kept stride with him, not saying a word.

Rory didn't say anything either. He just kept walking along the pavement, looking for anything that might give them a clue as to what had happened.

Chet walked along beside Rory for one hundred yards, wiping a tear or two from his eyes as he thought about his friend and her last trip along this road.

Stopping, Rory turned around and began the walk back towards the bridge. But he went slower this time. He kept looking from one shoulder to the next.

Chet walked along beside him, silent.

Rory stopped when they reached the bridge again. He turned around and looked back up the road.

"You see anything?" Chet asked.

"Not really," Rory answered.

"I guess we'll never really know –"

No, Chet. Think about it," Rory prodded. He gestured back down the road, "Why *don't* we see anything?"

Chet looked at Rory with confusion on his face, "What you mean?" He looked back down the road, then at the bridge, "If there's nothing to see, there's nothing to see, right?"

Rory pointed down at the gravel shoulder near the point of impact, "What do you see in the gravel on the shoulder where her car was sitting?"

Chet looked down and thought about it. Then he shrugged, "Just the drag marks from when Teddy Atkinson pulled her car onto the road to get it onto his flat bed truck."

"Why nothing else?"

Chet's face screwed up in confusion again. He scratched the back of his head as he looked at the drag marks, then further up the gravel shoulder. "Sorry...I don't...."

"Did the sheriff or the state troopers do any measuring or accident scene reconstruction when you were here?"

Chet shook his head no, "Probably done it before I got here –"

Rory's saw realization come across Chet's face.

Chet looked down at the gravel shoulder. His gaze followed the gravel shoulder all the way back to the hundred yard mark, where they had been standing only a few moments before, "There are no skid marks or any kind of tires marks along on the shoulder. Someone has smoothed out the gravel shoulder all the way back and beyond."

Rory nodded, "The only marks left were when they pulled the car out to put it on the flatbed. And you were here. So...?"

"So they left those. They had to," Chet said with a nod. He did some thinking. "I heard the report that they had found her car and I came right out here. There were only a couple of state troopers and the sheriff. They would have headed out here at the same time as me. And when I got here, they were *not* doing any measuring or accident reconstruction. We all just stood there and watched as Nora-Jane's car was pulled out from against the steel girders."

"And they can't do any measuring now because all the evidence has been wiped out," Rory added.

"You think someone tampered with the scene, right after they took the photocopies?" Chet asked.

"Maybe. Or maybe somebody else did."

"Like the police? I have a hard time believing that. I've known most of those guys all my life here," Chet reasoned.

"Both you and Nora-Jane Jackson were frustrated that the authorities, including the local police, didn't take the reports of all those missing children more seriously."

Chet nodded then whispered, "You're right. Nora-Jane pushed me in that direction as well. I just didn't want to believe it, I guess. And I guess I just got her killed...."

"No, someone else did that," Rory said firmly. "We just need to find out who...and why?"

Chapter 14

RORY SAT QUIETLY as Chet drove them back into town. There was no doubt some kind of conspiracy was going on here. But even Rory found it difficult to believe that a group of grown men would be willing to kill children who were coming close to their beloved treasure. Children were victims of war and there were child soldiers created in Africa, but this was America he kept telling himself.

A cell phone rang. It was Chet's and he reached over and picked it up from the cup holder he had it sitting in. Driving with one hand, he pressed a button and set it back down, "Chet Calhoun," he answered. "You're on speaker phone."

"Mr. Calhoun, this is Desmond Beck from the Historical Archives in Atlanta. Do you have a moment?"

Chet looked over at Rory, puzzled. "Yes sir, what can I do for you?"

"I just heard about Nora-Jane Jackson on the news down here," Beck said. *"I'm very sorry for your loss."*

"Thank you," Chet said.

"When are they going to have the funeral? Has it been set yet?"

"Not sure," Chet answered.

"Still too soon, I imagine."

Rory mouthed, 'Who?'

Chet just shrugged.

"I'll send you a text message with my cell phone number if you don't mind," Beck said. "I'd like to know when the funeral is so I could attend, if possible."

"Of course," Chet said. "I'll send you the information as soon as I get it."

"Thank you. Now to the matter at hand. I trust you still want the information on those photocopies you gave to Nora-Jane?"

Chet nearly drove off the road. He looked at Rory, surprise written across his face. "You have the photocopies, Mr. Beck? How? Nora-Jane hadn't left yet –"

"She took images with her cell phone and sent them to me," Beck answered. "She was very anxious to find information on them as quickly as possible, so she sent them on ahead of her arrival. She was the same right to the end, wasn't she? Diligent, always working away–"

Chet pulled over to the shoulder and stopped, "Yes, she was. Did you find anything out? Were you able to figure out where those pages came from?"

"Oh yes. Not all that difficult a task really. Just took a bit of patience, which we have lots of here. Have to, you know? Anyways, the original images appeared to be from a tintype, which became very popular during the American Civil War," Beck explained. "So we started our search from the start of the Civil War in April of 1861 and worked forward. Very simple really."

"And...?" Chet prompted.

Rory could see Chet's knee bouncing up and down.

"And we found where they were copied from. Back about seventy-five years ago, there was a project to gather copies of historical

books from around the southern states. A number were sent to us from the Golden area. Those images were in a book sent here for that project and the book pinpointed them to being taken back in 1887."

"Do you know where?" Chet asked. His knee was bouncing harder.

"Oh yes. Let's see...they were taken up near a geographic point designated as Cherokee Ridge."

Chet's knee stopped bouncing, "Are you sure? I've been up in that area. All of us young'uns around here hiked up into that area. I'm positive we would've seen those signs if they were there–"

"Oh no, sir. You wouldn't. They aren't there today," Beck assured him. "In fact, they haven't been there for a long, long time. They would have disappeared somewhere around 1888."

"How do know that?" Rory asked.

Beck hesitated, only now aware that someone else besides Chet Calhoun was listening. "Well...that was when the Cherokee Dam was put in. There are other pictures taken up there around that time, probably to preserve the–"

Chet spoke slowly, "Cherokee Dam...Cherokee Dam...I vaguely remember hearing something about that when I was a boy."

"It was only used for a few years. There was an attempt to get a sawmill working up there, using power from the dam," Beck explained. "They put up bunkhouses and a cook shack, but there was a lot of opposition from locals for some reason. There were a few deaths and the company that put in the dam and sawmill had to hire guards at great expense. The project eventually proved to be economically unviable when the opposition continued, as well as dangerous–"

"Hold on. You said a few deaths? Any idea how they died? And who died?" Chet asked. He looked over at Rory, wondering...

No. But I could look back into old county records, newspaper reports for the time, that sort of thing," Beck offered. *"Why? Is that important, Mr. Calhoun?"*

Rory looked at Chet and shook his head no.

"No, that'll be fine. If we need more information on that we'll get right back at you," Chet said.

"Alright, then," Beck said. *"Oh! And Nora-Jane also asked me to find out if anyone else had asked about this information. Let's see...I found an interlibrary request from your local library for one of their patrons...a Corry Mark Haney."*

Chet looked at Rory.

"I hope that helps," Beck said.

"It does. Very much so. Thank you," Chet said. "And one last thing, Mr. Beck. When you send me your text message could you also send me the images of the photocopies sent to you by Nora-Jane? I haven't been able to retrieve the ones from her car...."

"Of course, I understand," Beck said. *"If I can be of any further help, please don't hesitate to call me. Goodbye."*

The phone clicked off. "Goodbye," Chet said quietly. He sat there motionless, looking out the windshield.

"Is this Cherokee Ridge very far from here?" Rory asked after a moment.

"Not really," Chet said as he stared through the windshield. "We used to hike up there in the morning as young'uns, hunting for treasure signs all the way...and be back home just before sundown. We would pack a lunch...we had a great time...."

"So Corry could've easily gone up there and be back, without his mother knowing it," Rory said.

Chet nodded his head, "Sure could. *Our* families never knew when we went up there. As far as they all knew, we was just gone all day long, playing in the woods."

Rory sat quietly himself, thinking.

"I wonder how Corry knew to look for those old history books?" Chet asked after another moment.

"Donna-Lou said he was always looking for more information on the treasure. He would frequent forums on the Internet, talk to anybody he could about it," Rory reasoned. "Someone may have tipped him off about the old historical books from the area being sent to the Historical Archives in Atlanta. Or he may have come across references to them when he was going through all the local historical books and records still in your library here. Either way, he sent for the books and came across the signs."

Chet shook his head slowly, "Kid was sure a lot smarter than we were."

Rory looked at Chet, "Are you up for a hike to Cherokee Ridge?"

Chet nodded slowly, "Probably attract a little attention as we go up there."

"That's what I'm counting on," Rory said.

Chapter 15

CHEROKEE RIDGE

CHET CALHOUN HAD TO STOP for a moment, muttering to himself, "This was easier as a kid. I've got to start exercising." He wiped sweat from his brow, hitched up his pants and then shifted the small backpack up a little higher, tightening the straps. It was only an hour into the hike up here from his house, but the slight uphill climb was already beginning to take its toll. The heat wasn't helping either. As he took the brief rest, he looked around. Chet had to admit, the one thing he had never taken notice of when he was a kid, was the beauty and serenity of this area north of the little town he had grown up in. He breathed in the smells of fern, honeysuckle and wild rose, also something he enjoyed as a kid. Unfortunately, other thoughts intruded on the enjoyment. He fully expected to be shot at any time. His thoughts went to Corry Haney, Emma Houston and Nora-Jane Jackson. He was doing this for them. And for all those other missing children. Somebody was responsible and maybe he could help uncover who it was. He took a deep breath and let it out slowly, trying to calm his nerves. Time to move on. He hitched up his pants again and started walking again.

An hour later, Chet crossed a large clearing and stopped just before he entered the tree line again. He grabbed the canteen on his belt and took a drink. The water was cool and refreshing as it went down his throat. Funny how the little things in life can become so pleasurable. Putting the canteen back, he made a show of pulling out the rolled-up piece of paper sticking out of the top of his backpack. He unrolled it, looked at it and then looked around at the trees and the rocks around the clearing. He walked a few feet, then stopped and looked at the paper again. He wondered: *Will I hear the gunshot that kills me? Is that what happens to people who die? Do they see it coming? Do they hear it?*

Bird songs and the chattering of squirrels were the only sounds in the forest. A woodpecker hammered away in the distance over to the left.

Chet rolled up the paper and put it back over his shoulder into the backpack. Time to move on.

"Don't move."

Chet froze. He could feel something pressed against the back of his head.

"Take off the backpack," instructed a low voice behind him. "And do it real slow."

Chet unhooked the backpack and felt it pulled away from his body. Whatever was against the back of his head was taken away.

"Whacha you got here, Chet?"

Chet turned slowly to look behind him.

Someone was sliding the rolled up paper from the backpack that was now sitting on the ground.

The figure straightened up and Chet saw a familiar face, "Buster?"

Buster Connor, 5'10 inches and 150 pounds and dressed in green camouflage clothing, stood twenty yards away, holding a .308 Winchester rifle with one hand as he unrolled the paper.

Chet turned right around, "What in the world are you doing, Buster?"

Buster Connor glanced up at Chet, a half smile on his face as he continued unrolling the paper.

Chet stepped forward and reached for the paper, "Stop fooling around –"

Bringing the Winchester up, Buster pointed it menacingly, "Stay right there or I put a bullet in you."

Chet stopped dead in his tracks. Confusion etched across his face.

Buster stared as he chewed on a large wad of tobacco in his cheek. Then he took a step back, keeping a wary eye on Chet while he went back to unrolling the paper. "What the–?" The paper had sketches of various KGC signs right across the paper, in no particular order. Buster looked up the Chet, "Where's the map?"

"I don't have a map, Buster," Chet said. "Look. You don't understand what's going on here–"

Buster let the piece of paper fall to the ground as he brought the .308 Winchester rifle up to his shoulder, aiming it directly at Chet's head, "We know you've been snooping, hanging around over at Haney's house. That kid put a lot of things together. What did you find? Where's the map?"

Chet Calhoun's blood ran cold. "You're...you're part of the KGC?"

"I'm part of the military arm," he said as he spat tobacco juice on the ground. "My daddy was, my grand-daddy, all the way back..."

"I...I never knew. We went to school together –"

"You'd be part of it too," Connor snapped as he lowered the rifle. "Except your family was a bunch of traitors. Weren't willing to stick to the cause."

Chet shook his head and held his hands out, "W-what are you talking about?"

Connor snickered, "Yeah, figures. Nobody in the family ever told you."

"Told me what?"

Connor spit tobacco juice on the ground and then sneered at Chet, "Your family said there was too much killing. They was in charge of caring for the treasure and working with the sentinels. But they was going to turn it over to the government." Connor spit harder, the tobacco juice hitting the grass with a splat, "Same government that killed our ancestors, the ones who destroyed our way of life. The very same government that *still* wants to take away our freedoms and our guns. It ain't gonna happen."

The faces of Corry and Emma flashed in Chet's mind. "And you kill children to protect a damn treasure!" he snapped.

Connor spit a blob of tobacco juice at Chet's left foot.

Chet jumped back.

Connor shouldered the .308 Winchester rifle again, closed one eye and aimed at Chet's head, "Tell me what you're lookin' for up here. Spill it all...before I put a bullet between your eyes."

Chet blinked his eyes, "W-why should I? Y-you're probably going to kill me anyway...."

"Probably."

"Why kill those kids though, Buster?" Chet asked in a shaky voice. "Who put you up to it?"

Connor stared. And he never denied the accusation.

Chet could hear the birds twittering. The sun caressed his face, probably for the last time he thought. Something hit a tree off to his left with a sharp clunk.

Buster swung the Winchester right and fired, placing a bullet into the bark of a tree thirty feet away.

A green and brown blur shot from the trees and hit Connor at waist height with a vicious tackle. Conner was carried backwards ten yards and slammed to the ground, the .308 Winchester rifle flipping another twenty yards away.

Rory Mack Steele got off Buster Connor and hauled him to his feet. He turned the dazed man roughly, walked him back ten yards and slammed his back against a large tree. "Sorry I didn't act sooner, Chet. But I was hoping he would give us something."

Chet was white and shaking as he walked over to Rory, "No, I understand. Although I have to say, I thought I was a goner –"

Crack!

It was a rifle shot!

Rory ducked and whirled around.

Chet half ducked, frozen in place.

"This way," Rory said urgently. He grabbed Chet's arm and pulled him towards the trees and away from the clearing.

Chet stumbled and nearly fell.

Crack!

Chet flattened to the ground, trying to burrow into the pungent earth.

Rory stopped, wheeled around and went back to Chet, "You're still in the open, Chet. C'mon, you have to get –"

Crack!

Chet had started to move and the bullet gouged a hole in the ground barely an inch or two from his eyes. Swearing, Chet realized it was meant for his head and just missed by that much. He rose to his feet and ran hard beside Rory, trying to match stride for stride–

Crack!

Bark exploded from a tree just beside Rory and he dove head first for cover.

Chet stumbled, caught his balance and then dove to the ground behind a pine tree. Scrambling around on the ground, Chet sat his back up against the tree.

Rory already had his back to the tree to Chet's right. He looked over at him, "You hit?"

Chet shook his head vigorously no. Then his face took on a look of alarm, "Buster!" He rolled over onto his knees and looked around the pine tree and back towards the clearing.

Buster Connor lay on his side, on the edge of the clearing, facing towards Rory and Chet. There was very clearly a bullet hole between his eyes. A blood stain was also spreading on his chest.

Rory pointed across the clearing and towards a higher ridge of trees, "I think the shots came from up there. Do you see anything?"

Chet shook his head, "No–"

Crack!

A narrow branch just above Chet's head was cleaved from the tree and fell to the ground.

Chet rolled back behind the tree.

Rory did the same.

Licking his lips and shaking his head, Chet said, "I expected to draw some attention coming up here. I just didn't expect it to be so scary...."

Rory rolled around to his knees and slowly peered out from behind the tree.

Crack!

Sharp bark fragments flew off the tree just above Rory's head. He ducked back behind the tree.

"Why didn't they shoot us when we were out there in the open?" Chet asked in a strained voice.

"Those first two shots were meant for your friend. Probably wanted to make sure he was dead first. And then we were on the move...."

"He *was* a friend...not so much after today," Chet said. He licked his lips, looking at the dense trees around them, "What if they sneak up behind us?"

Rory sat with his back to the tree, "Probably will." He pulled his Baby Eagle 9915 RL Polymer 9mm handgun from the holster under his camouflage jacket, "But they'll do it slowly since they don't know if we're armed or not."

"Well, you're armed, I'm not. My old handgun was in that backpack. Stupid Buster." He shifted a little to peek around the tree, "Unless I could go and find that rifle–"

Crack!

Bark shot in the air as the bullet clipped the tree.

Chet pulled his head back in, pressing his back against the tree again, "Not gonna happen."

"Just keep an eye for any movement," Rory told him.

Cursing, Chet said, "Movement? There's probably going to be a bowel movement in my pants!"

"You'll be fine," Rory said.

"Yeah, right." After a few moments of scanning the trees behind them, Chet's back straightened as a thought struck him. He got around onto his knees, "Rory. We should get back into town. I was just thinking about what he said about us being over at Donna-Lou's place. If we don't make it out of here...and they go over there...I'd never forgive myself...."

Rory nodded his head after a moment, "You're right. Okay, I'm going to fire a shot. That should make them pull their heads in for a moment. You run through the trees over there towards the left."

"Why not straight back where there's more cover?"

"Just trust me."

Chet took a deep breath and let it our hard, scared. But he nodded and squatted in a running position.

Rory got around on his knees behind the tree and then shifted the Baby Eagle handgun to his left hand, "On three?"

Chet nodded once and then watched Rory's fingers count down.

3-2-1.

Chet was off in a low run.

Rory leaned out and quickly fired a shot across the clearing and high towards the ridge. Then he turned and sprinted off after Chet.

Crack!

A bullet clipped the branch just to the left of Rory's shoulder.

He wheeled left, fired two shots from his Baby Eagle and continued running.

Crack!

A bullet exploded through a small sapling a foot behind Rory.

Up ahead of him, Chet was breathing hard, fear driving his legs. He clambered over a fallen log, scrambled down a small gully and used his hands to make it up the other side before driving through the trees, swatting branches aside.

Rory was now right behind Chet, running low.

The only sound was their raspy breathing and the sounds of leaves crunching underfoot. Needles scratched their skin as they ran through a dense stand of Loblolly pines. A hundred yards through the trees, they burst into another clearing.

Chet stopped dead in his tracks.

On the other side of the clearing was a two-man, green and brown all-terrain vehicle sitting in the foot high grass.

"It's okay," Rory said. "It's the one we brought."

Chet's face showed instant relief, "Oh right. I forgot." He joined Rory at a run across the clearing. They jumped into the all-terrain vehicle, Rory on the driver side, Chet on the passenger side. They were both breathing heavy.

Rory put his weapon on the dash in front of him and started the vehicle, "I was pretty sure they would use one of those clearings to stop you."

"Pretty sure? As in not positive?"

Rory put the vehicle in gear, "I caught sight of that Buster guy in my binoculars after you moved through that last clearing. Have to admit I missed the other guy. Or however many there are out there." He accelerated, left the clearing and began to weave through the trees.

Chapter 16

RORY DIDN'T DRIVE STRAIGHT for the road; he took an arc through the woods, hoping to avoid any other gun-wielding attackers. It didn't take long before they were approaching the spot on the Clarkson Sideroad where he and Chet had left their vehicle. He slowed to a stop, still inside the tree line, and turned the all-terrain vehicle off.

Chet sat up a straighter in his seat, "Do you see something?"

"No. Just sit quiet for a second. Do you hear anything?"

Chet leaned forward, his hands on the dash, listening intently. "What are we listening for?" he whispered after a few moments.

"For anything," Rory said. "I just wanted to make sure anyone back there didn't have an all-terrain vehicle and they're moving in to cut us off at the road."

"Oh, okay." Chet swallowed and turned his head, listening.

They sat there for a few minutes and then Rory reached down and started the vehicle, "I think we should be okay." He slowly accelerated the ATV and within moments they were beside the Ford pickup truck they had borrowed from one of Chet's friends. Rory had backed it thirty feet off the roadway and into the trees to hide it.

Chet jumped off as Rory maneuvered the all-terrain vehicle to the bottom of the portable ramps still sitting against the lowered tailgate of the pickup. As soon as Rory had the all-terrain vehicle parked up on the bed of the rear cargo area, Chet was tossing the ramps up beside it.

Rory placed his weapon back inside the holster under his camouflage jacket and then worked to secure the ATV to the truck's bed with the rubber tie downs.

Chet closed the tailgated and locked it. He ran for the passenger side door as Rory jumped down and got in the driver's side. Both of them rolled their windows down, listening and watching carefully as Rory slowly drove the truck forward towards the roadway. A growl off to the left made him stop just to the side of a large tree.

A red, heavy-duty pickup truck flashed by on the road just ahead.

Chet turned quickly to Rory, "Did you see that?"

Rory nodded, "There was damage and paint scratches on this side."

"And that looked like a couple of streaks of dark blue paint on the front fender," Chet said. "And Nora-Jane's Lincoln was–"

"Dark blue," Rory said as he pressed his foot hard down on the gas pedal. The Ford's tires spun through grass and dirt and then across the gravel shoulder. The back end of the truck fishtailed as they hit the pavement. Rory straightened the vehicle out and accelerated. The tires squealed, leaving wide, black marks on the gray pavement as they began their pursuit of the heavy-duty pickup that was already out of sight.

"He's headed into town," Chet yelled. "You have to go. Don't lose him."

Rory nodded and he was pushing 80 mph when they finally spotted the back end of the heavy-duty pickup truck. They were entering the start of a double S bend and he took his foot off the gas.

"Don't slow down, we'll lose him," Chet yelled again.

"I know, I know," Rory yelled. "But he knows these roads better than I do. Won't do us much good if we go off the road."

Chet banged his hand on the dashboard in frustration.

Rory had to slow to 60 miles per hour through the back-and-forth turns and it was still dicey. When they reached the last turn, Rory accelerated.

Slamming his fist down on the dashboard, Chet cursed. There was no sight of the heavy-duty pickup ahead.

Rory slowly pressed his foot down on the accelerator. He had no idea how fast he could go without losing it on the narrow back road. A few more minutes and they would be into town.

Trying to sit up higher, Chet staring down the road through the front windshield. Finally, he yelled and pointed, "There. Just ahead. See it?"

Stretching his neck, Rory's saw the heavy-duty pickup truck was turning left just up ahead at the first stop sign in town, "Yeah, I see him." Rory kept his speed up, waited to brake at the very last minute and slid to a stop.

Chet was leaning forward, hands on the dashboard as he tried to spot the truck down the road to their left, "Those dang bushes are in the way. I can't see the pickup." He yelled and banged the dashboard again, "Hurry, hurry, hurry! We can't lose sight of it."

Rory made the left turn quickly and accelerated.

Chet leaned forward and pointed down the road ahead, "There it is. It's moving really fast for being in town. We gotta go."

Nodding, Rory accelerated. But there were old houses on either side and he kept his eyes darting left and right as he drove.

"You're gonna lose him again," Chet yelled.

"And if a dog or a child runs out, we'll kill them," Rory said forcefully. "That driver may not care, but I do."

Frustration crossed Chet's face but he nodded in understanding.

"Just keep an eye on the pickup. Watch for any turns," Rory said as he continually monitored the houses on either side.

Chet nodded, staring ahead intently. After a moment, Chet sounded panicky, "I don't see him. I don't see him, Rory."

Rory cursed. The seconds passed like hours. They reached the end of the line of houses. Trees now lined both sides of the road.

Chet pounded his fist into the dashboard again, cursing hard.

Taking his foot from the accelerator, Rory peered down the road ahead of them. Nothing. Maybe if they turned around and went back and checked to see if –

"Stop! Stop, stop, stop," Chet yelled.

Rory screeched to a halt, fishtailing back and forth on the road.

"Back up, back up back up," Chet said urgently. He turned around in his seat, looking back to the right.

Rory put the pickup in reverse and accelerated.

"Stop, stop, stop," Chet said in an urgent whisper. He was looking out at something.

Rory hit the brakes and the Ford slid to a backward stop. He turned in his seat, looking at where Chet was looking and realized he had missed the gap in the line of trees where a large, rickety barn sat back off the roadway. To the right, behind the line of trees, he could see a number of other outbuildings and an old two-story house. Somebody was pulling the barn doors shut, but Rory caught sight of the front end of the red, heavy-duty pickup truck inside.

Chet's voice was an amazed whisper as he stared, "That's Luther's place. That can't be."

"Who's that?"

Chet turned his head and looked at Rory. After a few seconds, he said, "Sheriff Luther Ponder."

Rory was surprised. But at the same time, he wasn't.

Shaking his head, Chet stared at the dashboard, "I can't believe he would have...."

Rory put the truck in gear and drove forward quickly before pulling to the shoulder of the road where he parked, hidden from the barn by the trees. He pulled out his Baby Eagle 9915 RL Polymer 9mm handgun, "Only one way to find out."

"But...we can't...he's the sheriff...."

Rory looked across at Chet, "And why would the sheriff be putting possible evidence of a murder in that old barn? Because that's what that truck is. Is that barn your local evidence locker? Is it?"

Chet licked his lips. Then he took a deep breath and nodded. He climbed out of the passenger side.

Rory got out and met him at the back of the Ford pickup. Together, they ran low back to the corner of the tree line. Not seeing anyone, Rory and Chet moved in a crouch to the dirt road off the main roadway and towards the left side of the rickety barn.

Reaching it, they pressed their backs against the old, weather-beaten boards.

Chet looked along the length of the barn and then whispered. "There's no door on this side of the building."

Rory nodded and waved him forward. They ran low across the front of the barn to the far side. Rory peeked around the corner and then whispered, "There's a window on this side and it looks like a door farther down." He looked towards the other buildings.

Chet moved up beside Rory and he stretched his neck, "I don't see anyone at the house. Or at those other buildings either."

"Does he live alone?" Rory asked.

Chet nodded and whispered, "His daddy died last year."

Rory waved the gun and they moved down along the side of the barn. They moved to a dirty window where Rory carefully peeked inside. He rubbed some of the dirt away with the side of his hand for a better view.

Moving up beside Rory's shoulder, Chet peeking through the window himself.

They could see the red, heavy-duty pickup truck parked inside, front end facing the barn doors. A man appeared beside it. He set something down on the barn floor and then disappeared off to the right. A minute later, the man came back and placed something else down before disappearing again.

Chet crept forward to get a better look and got up on his tiptoes, peering inside. He turned to Rory quickly and whispered, "It *is* Luther Ponder. And he's got some body filler and sanding equipment beside the truck...."

"He's going to cover over the evidence," Rory concluded.

"We have to stop him," Chet whispered urgently. "Right?"

Rory nodded and moved quickly towards the door at the far end of the barn. Reaching it, Rory tested the old handle. It squeaked a little as he pressed it down. Rory slowly pushed the door part way open and it groaned in protest. He stopped and listened.

They could hear Ponder shuffling back and forth over the barn floor, obviously in a hurry.

Rory slowly squeezed through the doorway.

Chet followed. He started to close the door and it groaned.

Turning quickly and shaking his head no, Rory put a finger to his lips.

Chet froze on the spot and listened.

Luther Ponder was still moving back and forth.

Rory turned and slowly crept past the old animal stalls. The barn smelled of old hay and dried manure.

Chet stayed close behind, creeping low. He wrinkled his nose, passing a hand under it.

Putting a hand up, Rory motioned for Chet to stop in his tracks.

Chet crouched and looked past Rory.

Luther Ponder was working with something on the floor beside the truck.

Rory started moving slowly again toward the Sheriff with Chet following closely behind. Twenty feet away from the truck, Rory rose to his full height and aimed his weapon, "Don't move."

Luther Ponder whirled around. He held a large sander in his two hands.

"Put it down. Now!" instructed Rory.

Ponder stood taller and puffed his chest out, sneering at Rory, "Do you know who I am?"

Chet stepped up beside Rory, "Yeah, you're the idiot Sheriff who's covering up evidence of a murder."

Ponder looked only half surprised to see Chet Calhoun standing beside the out of town stranger.

"I won't ask you again," Rory said as he motioned with the gun for Ponder to drop the sander.

Luther Ponder dropped it, wiping his hands on his pants. He gave Rory a half-smile, "What do you mean covering up a murder? You can't really prove that –"

Chet hitched up his pants, "Yes, we can." He pointed at the side of the red pickup, "Those paint markings on the side of that pickup will match the ones on the sides of Nora-Jane Jackson's Lincoln. You killed Nora-Jane. How could you? You knew her?"

Luther Ponder licked his lips and ran his hands through his brown hair. He looked panicky. "Look," he said. "I didn't kill her. I didn't really know what was going on until–"

Chet took a step and yelled, "Is that your truck or not, Luther?"

"Yes but–" Ponder looked this way and that again. "It must've been that stupid Buster Connor." He swore as he ran his hands through his hair again, "He borrowed my truck. And I didn't see the damage or the paint transfer until I was told to pick it up on the Clarkson Sideroad. Ask Buster–"

"Can't. He's dead," Chet said with finality.

"What? How–?"

Chet's words were hard and bitter, "My old *friend* followed me up towards Cherokee Ridge, thinking I was looking for the treasure. And he was going to *kill* me."

Ponder looked stunned. He looked at Rory and asked in a quiet voice, "You killed Buster Connor?"

"No," Chet said forcefully. "Somebody shot him between the eyes with a rifle from some distance away. Guess they didn't want him talking to us."

Ponder put his hands over his eyes and rubbed them, "This is going sideways," he whispered.

Chet bared his teeth in anger, "Didn't think you'd get caught because you're the Sheriff, right? You shoot Buster and then–"

Ponder shook his head no as he put his hands out, "Look. I'm being set up here. They asked me to pick up the truck on the Clarkson Sideroad. They said Buster had a job to do up on the Ridge. I didn't know they were going after you, Chet. I swear it."

"Who are 'they'?" Rory asked.

Ponder shook his head vigorously no, "I can't say."

Chet turned to Rory, "Can you get him to move away from the truck?"

Rory nodded and waved the gun at the Sheriff.

"Look," Ponder said as he stepped away from the truck, "You don't understand. You don't know who these people are. What they're capable of doing...."

Chet opened the passenger side of the heavy-duty pickup truck and looked inside. A moment later, he yelled, "You son of a bitch, Luther." He reached across for something in the truck cab, then stepped back, slamming the door hard, making both Rory and Luther Ponder jump. Chet held a large roll of yellow, tinted material and he began to unroll it. He looked at, flipped it around and examined it closer. It had old signs from the Knights of the Golden Circle sketched across it. He lifted his eyes, looking at the Sheriff with menace in his eyes, "*This* is the oilskin Corry Haney had hanging over the whiteboard in his house."

Ponder sneered at Chet and shook his head, "You can't prove that—"

Chet held the oilskin up and yelled, "See the torn corner on this side, Luther? Do you see it? Do you? *That* will match the torn piece that we found still attached to the whiteboard inside the Haney house."

Ponder licked his lips.

Rolling the yellow, tinted material back up, Chet's hard eyes remained on Ponder, "This is proof. Not only did you sneak into the Haney house to get this, it says *you* killed those kids!"

Luther Ponder shook his head vigorously again, "No. No. No. I didn't. You can't prove that."

"The authorities will," Rory said. "Once we show them this truck—"

Ponder snickered, "You idiot. Many of them *are* the authorities. You can't fight them. They're state troopers, they're FBI, Judges...they *own* the system."

Rory narrowed his eyes, considering what Ponder had just said. Then he took a deep breath, letting it out in a soft curse, "He's probably right, Chet. Probably get off somehow, with all the friends he has. So...as far as I'm concerned, this evidence is good enough for me." He extended his arm and aimed his Baby Eagle directly at the head of Sheriff Luther Ponder.

Ponder backed up a step, his hands out, "No, no, no, no. You can't just—"

Chet hitched up his pants, "Executing a child killer won't bother me either. Go ahead, Rory. Do it."

Ponder was frantic, "No please. You don't understand—"

It was Chet's turn to sneer and his voice was hard, "Did those poor kids plead like that before you killed them? Did they Luther?"

Ponder looked over at Chet, "You don't get it, do you? Those kids *ain't* dead."

Chapter 17

RORY AND CHET looked at each other in shock. Neither man had expected that. Both men looked back at the Sheriff, trying to figure out if he was telling the truth. Rory finally decided Ponder was lying. He gave the Sheriff a hard look as he shook his head and lifted the gun, aiming directly at Ponder's head again.

Ponder held his hands near his head and cringed, "I'm telling you the truth mister. Those kids *ain't* dead."

Chet cocked his head as he looked at Ponder. "So...if they ain't dead, where are they?"

Ponder screwed up his face, "If I tell you, I'm a dead man–"

Rory took a step forward, bringing the handgun closer to the Sheriff's head, "You can't lie your way out of this–"

Ponder took a step back, waving his hands in front of him, "I ain't lying. I mean it. They're alive. Isn't that good enough–?"

"No! And if you don't tell me right now, I'll consider you a child killer," Rory replied firmly. "And like Chet says, I have no problems executing a child killer." He took a breath, "Chet, count down to three."

Chet cleared his throat and hitched his pants up, "1...2 –"

Luther Ponder swore, "Okay, okay." He shook his head, took a deep breath and blew it out in frustration, "Okay...look...the kids are working on a big, old cotton plantation down in Mississippi. *All* the kids are down there. They're all working, okay. They're fine–"

Chet raised his arms and yelled, "They're on a plantation picking cotton! How stupid do you think we are, Luther? Huh? How stupid – shoot him, Rory. Do it–"

"No, no, no," Ponder cried. "The cotton picking is still done by machinery today. It would be cheaper, but we can't have the kids working out in the open like that. Not yet anyway."

"Talk sense, Luther," Chet yelled. He stepped forward, his fists in a ball, "Talk some damn sense."

Ponder swayed in anguish, pushing his fingers through his brown hair. "Look, it was old Tuck's idea–"

Rory glanced at Chet and back to Ponder, "Who?"

Ponder just pushed on as he looked at Chet, "You know about the Knights of the Golden Circle. How the Golden Circle was–"

"A ring of slavery states," Chet stated harshly. "The Southern States, Mexico, Central America, South America Cuba, the Caribbean islands, blah blah blah. We don't need a history lesson. Where are the kids," he yelled.

"That's what I'm trying to tell you," Ponder said as he held his hands out towards Chet. "The original Golden Circle was to have *black* slaves. The Southern slave-holding class would build an economy so big the government couldn't do nothing about it–"

"You can't tell me you're kidnapping *black* children. Corry and Emma were *white*," Chet yelled in frustration. "How stupid do you think we are?"

Ponder shook his head, "No, no, no. It isn't about blacks. It would be too difficult to hold them down today anyway. But think about it. Where's all our clothes from the big stores coming from? Who's building all the running shoes and the tennis shoes for the big sporting goods companies?"

Rory and Chet looked at each other, wondering where this was going.

Ponder ticked them off on his fingers, "Ethiopia, Pakistan, Afghanistan, the Congo, Somalia, Bangladesh, Mali and a whole bunch of other countries who use *children* in their factories. It's cheap labor that we can't compete with. You know that. All the good American jobs are disappearing and going over to those countries. And we don't do nothing about it. But the Knights of the Golden Circle did. We're doing something about it. Think about all the kids running around today, nobody taking care of them. We dug up a number of the smaller treasure caches and Old Tuck built a factory in Guatemala. That was the first one. There were others in places like El Salvador, Puerto Rico and Co-lumbia. The newest is in Mississippi. Your kids are there. But unlike those countries overseas, we're taking care of them. Hell, most of the families in Central and South America were happy to see them go—"

Chet Calhoun's voice was an incredulous whisper, "You have to be shitting me. You absolutely have to be—"

Crack!

Rory took two steps and dove behind the rear end of the heavy-duty pickup truck as soon as the rifle shot registered in his brain.

Chet was right behind him, landed heavily on the ground behind Rory.

Scrambling around to his knees, Rory used the wheel as cover. Chet scrambled around on his knees behind him, dust and straw from the floor leaving a trail in the air.

Crack!

A bullet pinged off a piece of metal somewhere behind Rory and Chet and both men ducked.

Silence.

Rory looked around behind him, whispering, "Chet?"

Chet was crouched over and he slowly lifted his head, "I'm...I'm okay."

Rory nodded and peeked around the side of the pickup, holding his handgun up and at the ready.

Chet moved forward on his hands and knees, looking over at the door and the window of the barn and then peering around the truck as well, "Where...where did those shots come from?"

"Looks like from the barn doors at the front," Rory said. He looked over at Sheriff Luther Ponder. "But just like up at Cherokee Ridge, the first shot wasn't for either of us."

Chet looked over, "Oh crap."

Ponder was lying on his stomach, head turned towards the red pickup. Half of his face was blown away.

"Shot in the back of the head," Rory said quietly.

A distant screeching sound was heard as a vehicle ripped away on the highway.

Rory was up quickly, heading for the barn doors.

Chet was right behind him.

The barn door was open about 6 inches. Rory pushed the big doors aside and ran for the roadway.

Running as hard as he could, Chet stayed close to him.

Reaching the highway, they both saw a vehicle disappearing in the distance off to the right.

Chet cursed.

"Yeah tell me about it," Rory said as he put his handgun back into the holster under his camouflage jacket.

"Now what?"

Rory looked down at Chet's hand, "You still have the oil-skin?"

Chet looked down to see he still had it in his hand. He had squeezed the rolled-up oilskin in his hand so hard it was bent in a U-shape. "Yeah, I guess I do."

Rory looked back at the partially open barn door. Then he gestured to their pickup just ahead, "Get in the pickup and get ready to leave. I'll be right back."

Before Chet could say anything, Rory was running back to the barn. Chet headed straight for the pickup and got in the driver's side. He gently unbent the oilskin and placed it across the back window ledge of the cab. The keys were still in the vehicle and he started it. His heart jumped into his throat when the passenger door was ripped open–

Rory climbed in, "Let's go."

"I almost peed my pants," Chet complained as he put the pickup into gear and drove onto the roadway. A moment later, he asked, "What did you do back there?"

"I wiped your prints off the pickup truck," Rory explained.

Chet's eyebrows went up in surprise as he pressed down on the gas, "I never thought of that. I guess I wouldn't make a very good criminal."

Rory smiled and looked across at Chet, "Are you saying I would?"

"Well...just better than me," Chet replied. He shifted in his seat, "Now what?"

"Do you have any idea who this Old Tuck is?"

Chet shook his head slowly, "I have absolutely no idea. I've never heard that name before. Ever."

Rory nodded his head slowly as they drove. "Okay. Let's take this pickup and the all-terrain vehicle back to your friend. We'll have to get out of here. If Ponder is half right, we can't trust the police around here, that's for sure."

"So we go on the run?" Chet asked.

Rory looked at Chet, "Or take a trip."

Chet nodded, and gripped the steering wheel tighter and accelerated, "Mississippi, here we come."

Chapter 18

MISSISSIPPI

"BUT MISSISSIPPI IS SUCH A BIG STATE. How do we even start to figure out where they are?" Donna-Lou Haney asked from the back seat of Rory's black Jaguar XKR-S. Chet had insisted they pick up Donna-Lou before they had even dropped off the pickup and the all-terrain vehicle. And Rory couldn't blame him. There was a good possibility the local Knights of the Golden Circle would go after anything else Corry might have in their house. And Donna-Lou Haney would be in the way. Better safe than sorry. Although, having her along might make it difficult if they did find the children. After a stop to sleep in Atlanta and a six-hour drive, they left the State of Alabama and entered Mississippi.

"I called my Uncle Murdoch in the New York office," Rory explained. "He and Avis, our computer wizard, are sifting through construction permits for factories in Mississippi going back ten years. They are cross-referencing each one with cotton farms to see what pops up."

"Would they be able to figure out if any of them are textile factories? Or clothing or shoe factories?" Chet asked in the passenger seat. "If that's what Ponder said they were making, then...."

"I would imagine so," Rory said in reply. "But not all the applications are computerized yet."

Chet shook his head in frustration, "It could be like looking for that old needle in a haystack."

"I still can't believe someone in America would kidnap children to work in a factory!" Donna-Lou exclaimed. "It doesn't make any sense."

Rory's cell phone rang. He hit the blue tooth button on the steering wheel, "Hello."

"Rory? It's Avis."

"Morning. You're on speaker-phone. What have you got for us?"

"Well, fortunately for us...and unfortunately for America...there weren't a lot of new factories being built in the last ten years in Mississippi," Avis answered. "And cross-referencing those with cotton still left twelve possibilities scattered across the state. But a little more research narrowed it down to Leflore County in the Mississippi Delta region, north of Jackson. Leflore County is one of the largest cotton producing areas in the country. I made a call to the chamber of commerce in Greenwood, which is the county seat, and they were quite helpful. They have a large, new factory that went up in the area three years ago. It added a lot of revenue to the tax base for the county, but it hasn't resulted in many jobs for the locals. The company says that's because they are highly automated. But the Chamber of Commerce is still very, very proud of this company."

"Why is that?" Rory asked.

"The factory has become one of the leading suppliers of cotton clothing to the top outlet stores in America. They're beating foreign countries in both quality and price," Avis reported.

Chet whistled.

"I hope that whistle was for me," Avis said with a smile in her voice.

"It couldn't be for anyone else," Chet said.

Donna-Lou Haney reached forward and hit Chet on the shoulder with the back of her hand.

Chet Calhoun clutched his shoulder in surprise and looked back at the Donna-Lou and mouthed Ow!

Donna-Lou crossed her arms and glared at him.

Avis chuckled, "I heard that smack. There must be a woman in the car."

Rory ignored the banter. "Do you have a name and address for the company for me?"

"Do you really have to ask?" Avis said.

Rory smiled and nodded, "Already on the way to my phone."

"You are correct, sir. The company name is Mississippi Castle," Avis said.

Chet looked up in surprise, "Did you say Mississippi Castle? Are you sure?"

"Yes. Uncle Murdoch had a lawyer pull the incorporation papers," Avis answered. "The official name is Mississippi Castle Incorporated."

"Why? Is the name important Chet?" Rory asked.

Chet held his hands out, "The Knights of the Golden Circle had local branches or lodges that they termed *castles*. That was the exact term they used. Castles. It can't be a coincidence."

Rory gave that some thought. "Avis, were you able to find a name for the main individual behind the company? Or was it all hidden behind shell companies and hidden corporations?"

"It *was* buried and that did take a bit more work. Uncle Murdoch had to call in a couple of favors," she answered.

They could hear the shuffling of papers.

"Here it is. The name is Tucker Watley Calhoun–"

Chet said as he sat up straighter in his seat, "Calhoun? The last name is Calhoun? Really?"

"Yes. The records show Tucker Watley Calhoun is 93 years old," Avis said. "With the help of those favors, we did some checking and the inquiries led us to the Bureau of Alcohol, Tobacco, Firearms and Explosives. The ATF is fully aware of Mr. Calhoun. They said he's the shadowy power behind a number of militant extremist groups in Mississippi, Alabama and South Carolina, all opposed to the federal government. The agent in charge of the case told us Calhoun is called 'Old Tuck' by his closest friends."

"Do you know this Calhoun, Chet?" Donna-Lou asked from the backseat.

Chet's brow furrowed and he was defensive as he glanced back towards her, "No. Why would I?"

"Just same last name is all," she answered quietly.

Chet looked sheepish, "You're right, sorry. No, I don't know him. Just surprised by the last name is all."

"Anything else to add, Avis?" Rory asked.

"No that's everything. You have the address of where your backup will meet you," Avis added.

"Okay, thanks," Rory said as he hit the disconnect button to end the call.

"Backup? We have backup?" Chet asked.

Rory nodded, "You'll see."

THEY REACHED A SIDE road west of Greenwood, Mississippi two hours before sundown. There were a number of vehicles in a flat field on the right. Rory turned right onto a short dirt road over a culvert, driving fifty feet over the short grass before parking.

Several men, dressed in dark-blue pants, shirts, and jackets, wearing bullet-proof vests and cradling rifles in their right arm, stepped out from behind a large van. They eyed the black Jaguar cautiously.

"Who's that?" Donna-Lou asked as she sat forward in the back seat.

"Should be the ATF," Rory answered. "They were interested in joining us once that Calhoun's name popped up."

"Do they have Corry?" Donna-Lou asked as she reached for the door handle on Rory's side of the car.

"No," Rory said as he opened his own door.

"Why not!" she exclaimed as she slammed her door shut. "Shouldn't they be doing something? Why are they just standing around? Is Corry close by–?"

Rory closed his door, turned and put his hands on her shoulders, "Be patient–"

"Don't tell me to be patient! I want my son *now*." She struggled to go around Rory.

Rory held her gently but firm, "We have to do this right."

Chet came up from behind the Jaguar and put his hand on Donna-Lou's elbow, "He's right. Don't worry, we'll get him back."

Donna-Lou whirled on Chet, anger in her eyes.

"Just be patient, okay?" Chet said gently.

Taking a deep breath, Donna-Lou gave Chet a nod, "Okay. But you better be right." She then turned back around, the look of anger still in her eyes.

Chet exchanged a glance of worry with Rory as he stepped up beside Donna-Lou.

Rory gave him a nod and then looked at Donna-Lou, "Let's go talk with them and see what they have to say. All right?" He turned and the three of them began walking towards the men.

Several other men came around the van, all of them armed. One of them looked back and said something to someone. A few moments later, the men parted to allow someone through.

A 6'-2" woman with a shapely figure and dressed in black leather jacket and pants strode cat-like around the van. She had green, sparkling eyes filled with confidence and her fiery red hair flowed off her shoulders as she walked across the short grass towards them.

Chet's jaw dropped and then he whispered, "Who is *that*!"

Donna-Lou slapped his left shoulder hard with the back of her right hand.

Chet held his shoulder, looked at Donna-Lou and mouthed Ow!

Donna-Lou glared at him, then looked back at the woman, crossing her arms over her chest.

"Ciamar a tha thu?" the tall woman said as she opened her arms and embraced Rory.

"Tha gu math, tapadh leibh," Rory said in return, hugging the red-haired beauty tightly. Seconds later, he turned to Chet and Donna-Lou. "Skye, this is Donna-Lou Haney. Her son Corry is one of the missing children. Donna-Lou, this is my sister, Skye Steele."

Skye Steele was three years younger than Rory and had start-ed working as a private investigator in the family business while her brother was still serving in the Canadian military. She was an expert in several martial arts disciplines, including Wing Chun, a form of Kung Fu, specializing in close-range combat and prac-ticed by proponents of the art like Bruce Lee, as well as more esoteric forms like Brazilian Jiu-Jitsu, a self-defense system that focuses on grappling and especially ground fighting. But despite Skye's core of steel, it was wrapped in a blanket of concern and she shook Donna-Lou's hand warmly, "I can't imagine what you're going through, Donna-Lou. We're going to do everything we can to get your son back."

"Thank you," Donna-Lou said quietly as she looked up into Skye's determined green eyes.

"And this is Chet Calhoun," Rory said.

Skye stepped over and shook Chet's hand, "Thank you for helping my brother, Chet. I appreciate it."

Chet looked a little tongue-tied, "Well...I really haven't done anything...it's been Rory who...."

"No. It takes people like you who are willing to stand up for what is right. Despite the odds."

Chet actually blushed at the praise. And then the redness went up a notch as Skye stepped forward and embraced him warmly.

Donna-Lou lifted an eyebrow as she looked from Chet to Skye Steele.

As Skye stepped back, Chet noticed Donna-Lou looking at him. What? he mouthed.

Skye turned and motioned to one of the men at the van. As he strode forward, she introduced him, "This is Special Agent Ryan Bowman of the ATF."

Bowman was in his 50s, built like a bodybuilder and walked with a military bearing. But the white, slicked-back hair and the good looks made him look more like an older runway model.

"This is my brother, Rory," Skye said.

Bowman held out a hand to Rory, "Very nice to meet. I've known Murdock MacLeod for years and he's told me all about you and your sister."

"Don't believe everything he tells you," Rory teased.

"I wait until we're at the bottom of the second bottle of scotch before I ask him the serious questions," Bowman replied with the hint of a smile on his lips.

Rory smiled in return and nodded.

Bowman turned serious. He pointed off to a tree line to his left, "The cotton farm and the factory you folks are looking for is just beyond those trees—"

"Then why haven't you gone in," Donna-Lou asked as she jumped forward. "We need to get my son out!"

"I understand. But if we go in full force, these are men who *will* fight," Bowman stated calmly in return. "We don't want your son or any of the other youngsters caught in a firefight. And I'm positive they have automatic weapons. It wouldn't be pretty."

Donna-Lou turned white when she realized what could happen before the day was over.

"Besides, I don't have a warrant," he said to Rory. "And from what I was told about these people, I didn't want to take a chance in asking a *local judge* to give me one and possibly have it leaked to anyone inside that compound."

Rory nodded in agreement.

Skye's green eyes had a sparkle to them as she said, "But a couple of citizens wandering around in there, coming across something, could always phone and report it to the ATF. Right?"

"I never suggested that," Bowman said seriously. "But it sounds like a workable plan," he added with a wink.

"Aaaand...he just happens to have unmarked vests and weapons for us," Skye said to Rory.

Rory nodded to Skye, "Okay. You and I can penetrate the perimeter to the cotton farm and–"

"I'm going with you," Donna-Lou interjected as she stepped up to Rory.

Rory shook his head, "No, you can't. It's too dangerous–"

"You'll have to tie me up to keep me from going," Donna-Lou stated emphatically.

Skye shrugged as she looked at Rory. "And she would probably gnaw through the ropes even if you did."

Chet stepped up beside Donna-Lou, "I'm going too. And I can watch out for her."

"I don't need you to watch out for me," Donna-Lou stated firmly.

"I was just trying to help," Chet said quietly.

Rory looked at them for a moment and then said, "I hope I don't live to regret this but I guess we're the four musketeers. Okay, let's get ready."

Skye put her hand on Donna-Lou's shoulder as she walked with her behind Bowman, heading to the ATF vehicles to get the weapons.

Rory followed behind them.

Check hitched up his pants as he walked behind the group, "I thought there was only three of them musketeers?"

Chapter 19

THE FOUR NOW STOOD on the other side of the tree line, each of them dressed in bulletproof vests, wearing headsets for communications and carrying a Heckler & Koch UMP submachine gun over their shoulder. That included Donna–Lou, who insisted she had shot rifles when she was a youngster and could handle herself. They were looking across a stretch of scrub grass at the enormous compound dead ahead. A ten-foot-high fence surrounded an immense cotton field and the smell of rich earth and green plants wrestled with the slight scent of a pesticide. In the far distance, in the middle of the field, they could see an immense building.

Chet looked along the fence line and hitched up his pants. "So how exactly do we get inside there?"

Rory shook his head as he considered the fence and the fields beyond, "Good question. I'm sure they'll be protecting the front entrance quite heavily, so that's out."

Donna-Lou shifted her bulletproof vest, muttering to herself, "Stupid thing."

Skye stepped over and adjusted one of the straps, "There you go."

"Thank you," Donna-Lou said. She gestured to the fence, "Why don't we just climb over that thing and get in there? I'm not interested in just standing here and talking. I want to get my son."

"I know you do," Rory said. He pointed up at some small black boxes on the top of the upright steel poles of the fence. "See those boxes up there? And those wires just running along the top the fence? If we touch that fence, we'll probably set off an alarm."

"So what do we do?" Donna-Lou said in frustration. "We can't just stand here all day—"

"Why don't we just borrow that?" Skye said as she pointed in the direction of the cotton field on the other side of the fence. A green machine, seventeen feet high, nineteen feet wide, and thirty-one feet long, sat one hundred yards into the field off to the left. It consisted of a large bubble in the front for driving and a large, square metal storage container behind that. A label on this side of the contraption designated it as a Case IH MODULE EXPRESS 625 cotton picker.

Chet looked at the machine and scratched his head, "But...it's on the other side. How do we do that?"

Rory smiled, wondering where his sister was going with this as well.

"Follow me," Skye said and she set off at a jog. The others moved quickly to catch up. In a few minutes, Skye reached a large tree, just on this side of the fence line. She slipped her submachine gun off her shoulder, turned and tossed to Rory. Then she turned back to the tree and began climbing.

"What in the world is she doing?" Donna-Lou asked as she watched Skye climb. Fifteen feet off the ground, she reached a large limb that extended towards the fence. She stood on it, her back against the tree.

Rory knew what she was thinking, "Are you sure you can make it?" he yelled up to Skye.

"What's she doing?" Chet asked.

Skye stepped out, flexing her knees and bouncing her weight to test the limb. She called down, "If I get enough forward momentum, I should be able to just roll safely on the other side."

"I would imagine she's going to run along that limb and leap over the fence," said Rory simply as he slung Skye's submachine gun over his other shoulder.

"But the limb is five or six feet short of the fence," Chet protested.

Rory shrugged.

Donna-Lou swallowed and looked at Rory, "You don't expect me to...to...?"

"Hopefully, you won't have to," Rory assured. "But you will have to do some jumping if she makes it."

Raising her eyebrows, Donna-Lou said, "If?" She shook her head and looked back up at Skye.

Skye placed her back against the tree again, took several deep breaths and then took off running along the limb. The limb bent downwards as she reached the end but she continued on, soaring like a broad jumper, feet running in the air, towards the fence. Her foot caught the top of the fence and she tumbled in the air. She came down hard on the other side of the fence and rolled several times over several rows of cotton plants.

Rory ran to the fence, stopping at the last minute. "Skye! Skye–" he yelled.

Skye Steele staggered to her feet, grimacing and holding a hip, "Next time, it's your turn, big brother."

Feeling the relief course through his body, Rory nodded, "No problem, little sister. But you better hurry. I don't think you triggered an alarm, but if someone comes along...."

"Ever the taskmaster," Skye grumbled as she turned and ran, her red hair flowing behind her. She stumbled a couple of times as she hopped over each row of plants, but it wasn't long before she was climbing into the large bubble of the 625 cotton picker's cab. It only took her a few seconds and the 365 hp engine started with a deep growl. Turning the huge machine right, Skye drove across the rows of plants, heading for the fence. Within 5 minutes, Skye parked the picker as close as possible to the fence and just across from the tree limb. She climbed out of the bubble and walked halfway to the back of the picker. From there, Skye climbed the seventeen feet to the top of the square metal container. "Who's next?" she yelled from the flat top.

Donna-Lou's voice was a fear-filled whisper, "You have got to be kidding me?"

"I don't blame you," Rory said, "You can wait here –" He never finished the sentence.

Donna-Lou quickly handed her UMP machine gun to Chet and began climbing the tree. Reaching the limb, she balanced herself with her back against the tree

"Just run hard and I'll catch you," Skye yelled.

"And what if you don't?" Donna-Lou asked in a scared voice.

Skye Steele just motioned with her hand to get moving.

Donna-Lou closed her eyes, counted to three, and ran hard. She took off from the end of the limb and screamed all the way over the fence. Her body hit the side of the metal container and nearly dropped. Skye grabbed her arm and pulled her up while yelling, "Next."

Chet looked white. He handed his submachine gun to Rory and began climbing. Like Donna-Lou, once in position on the limb, Chet had to take a few moments to work up his courage. Then he took off at a run, "Oooooooohhhhhhhhhh—" His feet hit the edge of the metal container on the other side of the fence and he fell forward, Donna-Lou and Skye each grabbing an arm to keep him from falling off.

"Skye. Drop down and I'll toss the guns over," Rory said.

"I'll go," Chet said as he rubbed his shins. He began climbing down the metal frame. His footing slipped halfway down and he fell hard onto the cotton plants on his back.

"Are you okay, Chet?" Donna-Lou called down with worry.

Chet got up with a moan, nodded his head once and limped over to the fence.

Rory tossed each submachine gun up and over the fence.

Chet caught each one in his arms and laid them down in the field, one by one.

It was Rory's turn and he hustled over to the tree and climbed to the limb. Without hesitation, he ran and jumped over the fence, landing hard on the top of the steel container of the cotton picker. Donna-Lou and Skye each grabbed an arm to help him stay on the machine. Then all three climbed down to meet Chet, who handed each person their submachine gun.

Rory shouldered his weapon and ran around to the back of the large cotton picker. He pounded on the large door in the back with the side of his fist, "It sounds empty back here."

Skye jumped up inside the driving bubble and looked over the controls, finally hitting a button. The hydraulics slowly lowered the back door of the metal container.

Rory waved his hand to the others, "Get inside. Hurry."

Chet and Donna-Lou climbed inside the empty steel container.

Rory put his hands to his mouth and yelled up to Skye "If you see any trouble coming, lower the back door." Then he climbed inside the container and pounded his fist in a signal against the side.

Skye hit the button again and slowly closed the door to the metal container. Putting the cotton picker in gear, she soon got up to 17 mph, heading across the field towards the back of the immense building in the distance.

AFTER A LONG, SLOW and bumpy trip across the rows of cotton, Skye could now see a large asphalt area at the back of the building and ten loading docks, with a set of metal stairs right in the middle of them. There were three gold colored transport trucks backed up to docks two, three and four on this side. A wide roadway ran around this side of the building to the front on the right. There, she caught a glimpse of another patch of asphalt that looked like a parking lot. But most of it was hidden from view by a low line of trees. She angled towards the transport trucks as the back of the building. As she came closer, she detected movement.

A man dressed in black, wearing a bulletproof vest and carrying a submachine gun, jumped down from the first empty loading dock. He cocked his head as the large cotton picker drove towards him, obviously wondering why it was there.

Skye kept driving, only stopping the big machine on the grass just before the asphalt. She hit the button to lower the rear doors, left her submachine gun on the floor and opened the bubble. Jumping to the ground she moved leisurely, giving the guard her best smile as they closed the distance between them, "Hi sweetie, haven't seen you around here before. Where have you been keeping yourself?" She unzipped her leather jacket.

The man's eyes immediately went to the swell of her breasts under the silk material of her black blouse. He slung the submachine gun over his shoulder, giving her a lecherous smile, "Actually, *you're* the one I haven't seen around here before. And why are you driving that thing here? The shed for the machinery is way at the back of the property."

Hearing the conversation, Rory put a finger to his lips to warn Donna-Lou and Chet. Then he slipped quietly out of the back of the vehicle.

Donna-Lou and Chet moved to the edge of the box and listened.

Skye closed to within a few feet of the guard, her hips swaying, "Weren't you told? Old Tuck himself asked me to come see you."

The man narrowed his eyes, looking at Skye suspiciously, "Why don't we go see him and check that out?" He moved to unsling his submachine gun.

In an instant, Skye did a complete spin and brought the heel of her black boot with force against the side of his head.

The guard dropped, his submachine gun hitting the ground just before he did.

Rory peered around the cotton picker and saw the body of the guard lying on the ground. He waved to Chet and Donna-Lou to move with him as he headed for the front of the vehicle.

Skye reached back into the driving bubble and picked up her submachine gun.

"What happened to him?" Donna-Lou asked in a loud whisper as they reached the front of the vehicle.

"He got fresh with me," Skye said simply.

Donna-Lou held up a finger to Chet, "Just you keep that in mind."

Chet mouthed 'what?'

Rory stepped up beside Skye, looking over at the truck docks, "Is he the only one you saw?".

Skye nodded and pointed, "He came out of the first loading bay."

"Probably more of them inside," Rory concluded. "But at least we have a way in." He shouldered his weapon and turned to the body, "Chet, grabbed this guy's feet and we'll throw him in back of the cotton picker."

Chet handed his own weapon to Donna-Lou and helped Rory to carry the unconscious guard behind the cotton picker and tossed him inside.

Skye went back inside the driving bubble and pressed the button to close the doors hydraulically, locking the guard inside. She closed the driving bubble and rejoined the others.

"Now what?" Donna-Lou asked as she gave Chet his weapon back.

Rory pointed at the empty loading dock beside the first truck, "We should be able to penetrate the building where that guard came out. I'll go first. Donna-Lou, you stay close behind me. Chet, you follow Donna-Lou and Skye can handle the rear-guard. Stay in line, no talking unless you see something. Ready?"

All three nodded yes.

Rory led them quickly across the grass and over the pavement to the first loading dock. Rory signaled for everyone to crouch down. Then he signaled for Skye to check the cabs of the three transports while they waited in position.

Skye nodded and moved to the cab of the first gold colored truck.

Donna-Lou and Chet looked nervous, checking around them constantly.

Rory couldn't blame them. No telling how many gunmen were here.

Skye quietly closed the door on the first truck and disappeared around the front to check the other two.

The next few moments were long and agonizing for Chet and Donna-Lou as they waited and watched around them.

Finally, Skye slipped back around the transport. "No one in the cabs or the sleeper berths," she said quietly.

Rory nodded, "Good. Everybody ready? Then let's go see what we can find."

Chapter 20

RORY HAD CHET give him a boost up into the open loading bay and he crouched low, looking over the large, open loading area. There were a number of large crates and pallets piled up, starting in a stack thirty feet away. Rory moved low, used them as cover and knelt by the right side of the stack. Straight ahead, beyond the crates, he could see a cement block wall and a set of double doors one hundred feet away. Looking off to the far left, he could see a single closed door. That door had a twelve button numeric keypad lock, which meant they couldn't go in that way. Curiosity kicked in and he checked the crate's manifest and saw it contained clothing. He dropped the manifest to the bare cement floor and listened. There was no sign of anyone. Everything was quiet. Rory looked back to the loading door and gave the go-ahead signal. Then he kept watch as the others helped each other up into the loading area.

Once they were all kneeling behind him against the crates, Rory spoke in a low voice, "There's a set of double doors about one hundred feet away on the other side of these crates. It looks to be our only way in." He looked at Skye, "Can you check the trailers of each truck? I can see a few crates are already loaded but we have to be sure no one is inside there and we get caught from behind."

Skye nodded and then moved cat-like across the cement floor to the first trailer, checking it. Then she moved inside the second, checking behind the loaded crates, and then disappeared inside the third one.

Rory checked on Donna-Lou and Chet behind him. They both looked concerned but not overly–

"Hey!"

Rory swung his head back and realized a guard, wearing a bulletproof vest, had come through the doorway with the numeric keypad lock. His submachine gun was up and pointing at Rory, Chet, and Donna-Lou in a heartbeat.

Rory brought his weapon up but he knew he had no chance....

Skye stepped out from the last trailer and fired a short burst.

Bullets ripped through the guard's throat. His mouth opened to scream but his vocal cords were gone. Falling slowly backward, his gun clanged to the floor just before he did.

Moving fast, Skye came back across the floor to the crates and pressed herself against one just behind Chet, putting the two between her and Rory as she watched in the other direction. There was silence as all four waited for an attack.

Donna-Lou was shaking and Chet put a comforting hand on her arm. But he looked scared himself.

After a few tense moments, Skye slid past Chet and Donna-Lou to Rory. "They must all be in a cafeteria or a lunchroom," she whispered.

Rory nodded, "Makes sense. Or they're just not expecting anyone to come in through the back to steal clothing crates."

Skye nodded as they both listened intently again.

The heavy breathing of Donna-Lou Haney and Chet Calhoun echoed lightly behind them.

"I'll get the body of the sight," Skye said in a low voice after a moment.

Rory nodded.

Skye turned and patted Donna-Lou on the knee and then looked at Chet, "Keep an eye out behind you while Rory watches the front."

Both nodded but looked very scared.

Skye shouldered her weapon and moved carefully across the open floor to the dead body.

Rory covered her as she moved.

Chet turned in the other direction and stood in a low crouch with his weapon up and ready.

Donna-Lou just sat with her back to a crate, still shaking at the close call.

Skye placed the guard's weapon on the dead body and then dragged it over to the nearest empty trailer, leaving a thin, dark trail from the pool of blood just outside the doorway. Leaving the body lying inside the trailer behind a crate she then moved quickly back to rejoin the others. Skye glanced at Donna-Lou and asked Rory, "You still think we should go inside?"

Donna-Lou turned her shaking head, "Please. We have to find Corry. I...I can do it."

Skye raised an eyebrow, "There *will* be more of them. If...when we find your son, he'll need a mother who is still alive–"

Her voice a harsh hiss, Donna-Lou said, "I said I can do it."

Nodding defeat, Skye looked at Rory, "I guess we keep going then."

"Yeah," Rory said, "but I've been thinking. That door where the guard came through has a twelve button numeric keypad lock to keep unauthorized personnel out. The double doors don't look to be locked. It makes sense that one with the lock *has* to be the one we should go through."

Skye gave it some thought, glancing over at the door and then nodded, "I think you're right."

"But how do we get in if we don't know the code?" Donna-Lou asked.

"Trial and error," Skye said. She turned and headed in a low crouch across the cement floor for the door.

Rory stood up, signaling to Chet and Donna-Lou to follow Skye.

Chet helped Donna-Lou to her feet but she didn't move a step, "But how long will that take?"

"Just let them do their thing," Chet whispered.

Donna-Lou's voice was harsh as she looked at Chet, "But if the double doors aren't locked, we should try that one first."

Taking her by the elbow, Chet moved her across the floor, "Just trust them. Okay?"

Shaking her head in frustration, Donna-Lou pulled her arm from Chet's grasp and glared at him briefly before heading across the floor.

Skye was kneeling in front of the locked door, looking it over as the other three knelt behind her, keeping watch. Skye pulled a small penlight out of a pocket and began examining each number on the keypad.

A frustrated Donna–Lou swiveled around on her heels, her jaw clenched, "This is ridiculous. What's she doing?"

"Figuring out which keys are being used to punch in the code," Rory said as he scanned the area for any movement.

"But –"

Rory put a finger to his lips to ask her to be quiet.

Skye looked at the keys from different angles. "Looks like 1...3...4...7 are the numbers used," she said in a low voice. "According to my understanding of permutations, we would have four...times three...times two...times one...that gives us 24 different combinations."

Chet raised his eyebrows.

Skye glanced at Rory, "Try and keep them in mind as we go through them."

Rory nodded. "Keep watch," he whispered to Chet.

Chet nodded but his hands shook as he raised his weapon to his shoulder. He scanned the loading area, trying to keep his raspy breathing down as he listened.

Skye punched in a set of numbers, repeating them as she did. They went through eleven combinations before the door clicked. Skye reached for the doorknob and turned it, pulling the door open a couple of inches.

Rory got up in a low crouch with his weapon at his shoulder. He nodded once.

Skye pulled the door open quickly.

Rory moved through quickly, weapon sweeping ahead of him. He found himself in a long hallway.

Skye held the door open with a foot and readied her own submachine gun for possible action.

Rory took a few quiet steps down the hallway. Then he made a motion for the others to follow him.

Skye motioned for the other two to move quickly through the open doorway.

Donna-Lou scrambled through the doorway, followed closely by Chet.

Skye moved quickly in behind them, closing the door softly as they began to penetrate the building, looking for the children but fully expecting to find armed guards along the way.

Chapter 21

THE MAKESHIFT TEAM of rescuers made its way cautiously file down the hallway in single. Rory kept his Heckler & Koch UMP9 submachine gun weaving back and forth as he advanced. He checked each door they passed by opening it quickly and stepping inside, ready to fire.

Chet and Donna-Lou kept pace, both of them still looking scared and out of their element.

Skye kept a watchful eye behind them.

"Freeze!"

"Don't move! Don't move!"

Three men filled the narrow hallway, two feet in front of Rory, submachine guns aimed directly at him.

A moment later, three men appeared in the hallway behind Skye, submachine guns trained on her as she stood sideways in the hallway.

Chet froze.

Donna-Lou sank slowly to the floor in fear.

Rory put his left hand up and slowly lowered his weapon towards the floor.

Skye put her left in the air as well, glancing towards Rory as she slowly crouched to lower her weapon to the floor.

Chet followed suit, crouching and placing his submachine gun on the floor.

As Rory was beginning to rise from placing this submachine gun on the floor, he kept his left hand up in the air. The guards didn't see his signal, a quick thumbs up to Skye.

Skye dropped and grabbed her weapon.

Rory thrust his right hand up towards the guard's face and moved to the right, crouching with his back against the wall.

The guard flinched and fired.

Donna-Lou screamed.

Bullets from the front guard ripped into the first man behind Skye and his weapon fired up into the ceiling as he fell backward.

Rory drove his left knuckles into the lead gunman's throat, then drove with his shoulder into his chest, knocking him into the other two behind him.

Skye spun around on the floor and opened fire. More automatic weapons fire joined hers as the two men danced like marionettes, bullets tearing into their bulletproof vests and ripping away their throats and faces. As the men were falling dead, Skye turned quickly.

Chet stood in a half crouch, his weapon smoking. His face showed the disbelief in what he had just done in taking down the two men with Skye.

Rory had the second man on his side pinned down under the dead body and they were struggling.

The third man had been knocked backwards and was now rising to his feet, weapon in hand.

Skye yelled, "Down."

Chet dropped to the floor.

Skye opened fire and 9 mm bullets passed over top of Rory and tore into the far gunman, killing him before he could get his weapon up to fire.

The gunman under the dead body swung his weapon out and fired. His bullets tore into the wall of the hallway just inches from Chet and Donna-Lou.

Donna-Lou screamed.

Skye leaped past them and stood just to Rory's left, firing a burst into the gunman's head.

"Thanks," Rory said as he reached for his weapon and turned to Chet and Donna-Lou, "Is everyone okay?"

Chet nodded.

Donna-Lou had her hands on her head, her weapon on the floor beside her, "I'm...I'm so sorry...I'm no good to you...I never should have...."

Rory motioned to Chet and they began working to pull each set of bodies into side rooms. Blood smeared the floor as they dragged the dead gunmen from the hallway.

Skye moved to Donna-Lou, bent down and picked up the H&K submachine gun. "It happens to everyone the first time they're under fire. Don't beat yourself up," she said softly. "Take your weapon and let's go find your son."

Donna-Lou nodded to Skye after a moment and took her gun.

"Okay. We're going to have to move fast," Rory said. "We may not have the luxury of being in tight spaces like this hallway again. Let's go." He turned and began moving up the hallway again.

Chet helped Donna-Lou to her feet and she moved woodenly in a crouch behind Rory.

Chet and then Skye followed behind.

After a few minutes, Rory came to a corner. He pressed his back against the wall and had the others line up against the wall behind him.

He peered around the corner.

He pulled his head back in quickly and put his fingers to his lips.

Sounds of a number of people walking in the distance reached their ears as they waited.

It took several minutes of tense waiting before the sound was replaced by the echo of a door slamming shut.

Rory peered around the corner again.

After a moment he turned and gave instructions in a low voice, "Okay, stay behind me, keep low and move fast."

He peered around the corner again, then moved quickly around and down the hallway.

Donna-Lou, Chet, and Skye moved around the corner and stayed in a line as Rory advanced quickly. His Heckler & Koch UMP9 submachine gun moved back and forth, covering the hallway ahead as he advanced. There was only a door on either side to check and he cleared each one quickly. Within moments they approached another door on the left with a numeric keypad lock

"They took a line of kids in here. Do your thing," Rory whispered to Skye. He readied his Heckler & Koch UMP9 submachine gun at his shoulder.

"Kids? Did you see Corry? Did you–?" Donna-Lou said loudly.

Chet jumped forward and put a hand over her mouth quickly

Skye raised her weapon and readied for an assault.

Donna-Lou's eyes were big as she realized what she had done. She listened intently along with the others.

Everything was quiet.

Chet took his hand away from Donna-Lou's mouth.

Skye slipped her weapon over her shoulder and knelt in front of the keypad. She pulled out the small penlight, knelt and began examining each number on the keypad.

Chet placed his submachine gun against his shoulder, guarding the rear.

"This one looks like...3...4...6...9 are the numbers used," Skye whispered.

Donna-Lou knelt beside Skye, her voice shaky but determined, "I'll try and help remember the combinations you try."

Skye nodded and they began going through each one. Their whispers echoed lightly off the walls. Failed attempt after failed attempt went by. Finally, a satisfying click sounded. Skye pulled the door open and placed her foot in the crack to hold it in place as she slipped the UMP9 off her shoulder.

Donna-Lou rose, holding her UMP9 in sweaty hands.

Skye whispered to her, "You open the door for me on three like we did back there. Okay? On three."

Donna-Lou nodded once, slipped her weapon over her shoulder and grabbed the handle. "1-2-3, " and she pulled the door open.

Skye slipped inside, followed by Chet.

Rory moved into the doorway and held the door open with his shoulder as Donna-Lou moved in behind Skye and Chet. Then he let the door slowly close to minimize the bang.

Skye, Donna-Loub and Chet lined up, crouching beside the left wall, waiting for Rory to take point again.

Setting his Heckler & Koch UMP9 submachine gun to his shoulder, Rory moved past them and led the way again, weaving the weapon back and forth as he advanced up the hallway.

Skye kept her eye on the door behind them as they moved.

Halfway down the hallway, Rory reached a door on the left. He raised a fist, the signal to hold and the others crouched behind him. The top half of the door was tempered glass and Rory slowly rose and took a peek inside. After a few moments, he crouched with his back against the wall. "It's a large cafeteria," he whispered. "There are a number of children inside, maybe one hundred–"

Donna-Lou began to rise and spoke loudly, "Can you see–?"

Chet immediately put his hand on her arm.

Donna-Lou stopped halfway up, looking down at Chet in anger.

Rory and Skye brought their weapons up and faced both ends of the hallway. If the guards heard her....

Donna-Lou's body relaxed after a moment. She nodded and whispered, "Sorry."

Silence ensued as Rory and Skye waited.

After a few tense moments, Rory turned and began whispering again, "There are guards on either side of the door just inside. Donna-Lou, you pull this door open. Skye and I will move inside and neutralize them. Chet, you move in through the middle. There are guards on a second level walkway looking down, one on each side of the room. You shoot up at them starting on the left. Donna-Lou, you have to come through and start shooting high up on the right. Can you do that?"

Donna-Lou licked her lips and she trembled but she nodded.

"Good," Rory said, "Once we get our two, we'll help you. But remember...both of you...*you can only fire high*...all of the children are dead ahead. Understood?"

Chet and Donna-Lou looked very nervous but they nodded their heads.

"Okay," Rory said. "Everyone keep low so they don't see us through the window."

Donna-Lou crouched low and moved passed Rory to the door, putting her hand on the doorknob.

Skye and Rory moved in position to move inside, with Chet ready to do his part, coming in behind them.

Rory counted down, whispering, "3-2-1-go!"

Chapter 22

DONNA-LOU PULLED the door open and held it against the wall to allow the others to move in quickly. The guard on the left was just beginning to turn to see who was coming in and she almost went into a panic. Her eyebrows shot up and she opened her mouth to yell a warning.

But Rory moved past her in a heartbeat and drove the side of his submachine gun's metal stock into the guard's jaw. As the man fell, Rory crashed the gun barrel into his skull to make sure he was down for good.

Skye moved in behind Rory, smoothly and efficiently taking down the guard on the right side with the butt of her weapon.

Chet moved through the open doorway, stepped between Rory and Skye as they did their work, and aimed upwards to the left. He caught sight of a guard and pulled the trigger. His submachine gun roared.

Donna-Lou hands were now shaking and she fumbled to get her weapon in hand, now positive she had messed everything up with the hesitation. Moving on legs of jelly through the doorway, she lifted her submachine gun up and to the right as she had been told. A guard was just reacting to the invasion from below. Donna-Lou began firing and filled the wall to the left of the guard with 9 mm slugs. He reacted by ducking the other way.

Children were screaming and scrambling for cover under the cafeteria tables and away from the gunfire. The smell of gunpowder battled with that of soup, sandwiches, pizza and soda drinks.

Rory moved forward quickly and spun, looking up for another target.

A guard was looking down and just bringing his weapon up.

Rory fired a long burst.

The guard danced a bullet jig, dropped his weapon and fell forward over the railing, his back hitting the floor as Rory began searching for other targets.

Skye lifted her weapon and took out the guard Donna-Lou was firing at. Then she reached out and placed her hand on Donna-Lou's arm, indicating they had got him.

Everything went quiet. And then a hard voice broke the silence, "Drop your weapons or the kid is dead."

Everyone looked towards the cafeteria tables. One of the guards held a young boy, left arm around his neck to hold him firmly in place while his right hand held a submachine gun pointed at his head.

Donna-Lou dropped her weapon and cried out, "Corry –!" The submachine gun clattered on the floor as she put her hands to her mouth.

Corry opened his mouth but the guard squeezed his arm around the boy's neck, cutting off any words. Emma Houston was on her knees under the cafeteria table behind Corry, shaking in fear and she let out a sob.

Rory, Skye, and Chet looked at each other. They had no recourse. They slowly lowered their weapon to the floor.

More silence ensued as the two sides eyed each other. Then a clapping sound came from the right. A tall, thin man with snow white hair was clapping slowly as he emerged from a side room on the far side of the cafeteria. He continued clapping as he walked slowly across the floor, a superior half-smile on his face, "I was told you folks were digging up things back in Golden. But I honestly didn't expect any of you to figure this place out. Or have the balls to infiltrate it." He looked to the guard holding the boy for a moment, "I've alerted the others," he said in a raspy voice.

The guard nodded, tightening arm left arm around Corry.

Corry winced.

Donna-Lou made a move forward, "Don't–!"

The guard tilted his arm up, emphasizing the gun he held against Corry's head.

Chet reached out and stopped Donna-Lou's movement.

Donna-Lou ripped her arm away from Chet, giving him an angry look. She looked back at the guard holding Corry and then took a step back, fear for him registering on her face.

The tall, thin man continued walking slowly across the floor, his eyes darting to each intruder, measuring them up. He walked to within twenty feet and then stopped. His eyes scanned down Skye's body for a moment and then he turned his head and looked right at Chet, "Hello, cousin."

Chet looked surprised and then shaken.

Donna-Lou's moist eyes looked to Chet, "D-do you know him, Chet?"

Unable to find his voice, Chet just shook his head no.

"No, he doesn't know me," the white-haired man said. "But we *are* family. Goes back a long ways. I've been watching him for some years now–"

Chet had a surprised look on his face, "Watching *me*? Why?"

The white-haired man's eyes narrowed, "To see what you knew. To see what you may have been told when you were younger." His eyes studied Chet's face and reactions. Then the man gave a derisive snort, "The fact you're here proves you're no better than your kin folk–"

Chet's voice was a hoarse whisper, "You killed them, didn't you? You killed them."

The white-haired man never answered and the superior half-smile stayed in place.

"You must be Old Tuck," Rory said.

The white-haired man quickly looked at Rory, the half-smile leaving his face. "That's right." He took a step forward, his eyes studying Rory, "Few people know of me. You seem to be a man with deep contacts. Just keep in mind we don't like people who pry onto our affairs...."

"Why did you kill my daddy and my grand-daddy?" interjected Chet in a low, strained voice. "Everybody loved them. They were great people–"

"Great people? They were traitors to the cause," spat Old Tuck. "Traitors against those who would see the old South rise against the tyranny of the North. *Your* family didn't have any honor–"

"Honor!" Donna-Lou exclaimed. "You kidnap children and put them to work in a factory and you talk about honor?"

"Ye,s I do," Old Tuck said matter-of-factly. "The honor of the old South runs through my veins. And because of that, we took care of these children. For many of them, they're from the poverty-stricken inner cities with their drug-addled parents and it was better care than they received from their own families–"

Donna-Lou bared her teeth, "You still don't have the right–"

"I *do* have the right," Old Tuck stated firmly. "We're building something. Something important–"

"Not important enough to involve *my* son," Donna-Lou snapped.

A look of sheer contempt crossed Old Tuck, face, "Fine. He's proved to be of no help to us anyway." He looked towards the guard holding Corry, "Kill the boy."

The guard grinned and he looked at Corry's head as his finger tightened on the trigger.

Chapter 23

EMMA HOUSTON SUDDENLY scrambled to her feet."You leave him alone!" she cried as she dove across the floor, wrapped her arms around the guard's lower leg and bit hard into his calf.

The guard howled. His gun came away from Corry's head as he pulled the trigger, the slugs hammering into the epoxy floor to his right, ripping up chunks of material that exploded into the air.

Young Corry Haney dropped to the floor and scrambled back towards the cafeteria tables. Children were screaming again.

Donna-Lou Haney dropped to her butt, picked up her weapon in one motion and fired up into the guard. Bullets ripped into his bullet-proof vest and then his throat, face, and skull, making him dance. His arm came up in a spasm and bullets ripped in a line across the floor.

Emma emitted a squeaky scream and scrambled away across the floor and under a cafeteria table next to Corry.

Rory, Skye, and Chet all dove for their weapons. Chet spun around on the floor and let a burst go in the direction of Old Tuck.

But Old Tuck was already running. He moved faster than you would expect an old, white-haired man could.

Chet's slugs ripped into the wall just to Old Tuck's right as he pushed open a door and disappeared. Chet continued to fire, filling the frame and the slowly closing door with 9 mm slugs before Rory's hand on his gun told him to stop.

Donna-Lou stopped firing as well.

The body of the dead guard fell backward into the floor, his weapon clattering beside him.

Dropping her submachine gun, Donna-Lou scrambled to her feet and ran for Corry.

Corry saw her coming, scrambled out from under the table and they wrapped their arms tightly around each other.

The smell of gunpowder was heavy in the air and everything was suddenly quiet. Chet looked around and then scrambled to his feet, his eyes wild and his chest heaving, "W-what do we do now? Old Tuck said other guards were coming. We can't stay here. What do we do?"

Rory had his cell phone out and hit speed dial as he held a hand up for Chet to calm down.

Skye moved to Chet and put a hand on his arm, "You cover that door and I'll watch this one. Okay?"

Chet looked at her and then nodded, "Yeah, yeah, Okay." He raised his weapon and aimed at the door where Old Tuck had disappeared.

Emma moved out from under the table and ran to Donna-Lou and Corry, joining the hug. Donna-Lou kissed her on the forehead, "Thank you, sweetie."

"You were badass mom!" Corry said.

"Language young man," Donna-Lou replied with a smile.

"Okay, listen up," Rory said in a loud voice. "It will take a few minutes for the ATF to crash the front of the compound and enter this building. We could get caught in the cross fire if we stay here. Let's take the kids to the back doors where we came in. The ATF will meet us there. If they don't get around there in time, we can use the trucks to get away."

"Good idea. I'll take the lead," Skye said and she was already moving to the door.

Rory nodded. He then turned to all the kids that were hiding under the cafeteria tables, "Okay, kids. The police are coming. We're going to the back of the building to meet them. Let's go." Only a few started to move, the rest obviously scared with all that had happened. Rory moved closer to the youngsters, "It's all right. We're going to take you home. Do you want to go home?"

A number of the kids nodded and they all began to move, scrambling past the cafeteria tables, fifty to sixty scared youngsters eager to get home.

"What do you want me to do?" Chet asked in the chaos.

"Go with Skye," Rory said. "I'll protect the rear."

"What about me?" Donna-Lou asked as she picked up her weapon.

"Help me keep the kids moving back to where we came in," Rory instructed her. "Work in the middle and I'll work from the end of the line."

Corry looked at Rory, a cheeky grin on his face, "And she should be a badass and shoot more bad guys when they show up. Right?"

"Yeah, what he said." Rory tousled the boy's hair, then gave Emma a wink.

Skye already had the door open and she stood in the doorway, watching both ends of the hallway. As the kids approached with Chet, she held a hand up for them to stop and then said to him, "Hold the door open while I go check the hallway down there."

Chet nodded, holding his weapon at the ready as he watched Skye move down the hallway. He glanced back at the scared kids and gave them a nod of assurance, even though he didn't feel too confident himself. A few moments later, Skye motioned for him to follow with the kids. Chet nodded, took a deep breath and stepped into the hallway, looking back at the youngsters, "Okay, kids. Follow me."

As they filed out, Donna-Lou helped herd the youngsters out as Rory acted as the rear guard.

At the first doorway, Skye had Chet watch the hallway to the left while she moved right, towards the back of the building. Chet waved for the kids to follow Skye and then turned to watch. Only half the kids were through the door when several guards burst into the far end of the hallway. Chet opened fire.

Two guards went down, their weapons firing into the ceiling. The remaining guards pulled back through a door for a brief moment.

Screaming filled the air as youngsters flattened to the floor and against the walls.

Skye turned but she couldn't do much with the possibility of hitting the kids or Chet.

Fighting her own fear, Donna-Lou kept Corry and Emma moving towards Skye and then she worked with the other kids, urging them to keep moving.

As the youngsters approached her position, Skye turned and moved low towards the back again, waving for them to follow.

Back down the hallway, one of the guards jumped out from the doorway, firing his submachine gun at Chet.

Chet dropped to a crouch, opened fire again and took out the guard.

More screaming erupted and the kids hit the floor.

Rory came out into the hallway behind the last youngster.

Chet opened fire as more guards appeared in the hallway. The two-way gunfire in the hallway was deafening.

Rory moved beside Chet, adding his own gunfire, cutting down at least a dozen men.

Chet made a grunting sound and his right hand dropped away from his weapon.

Rory looked quickly to see Chet had fallen to a sitting position, a dark wet spot showing he had taken a bullet to his right shoulder.

Chet kept firing with his left though, struggling to keep the weapon on target.

Rory looked behind them. The last youngster disappeared around the far corner. He tapped Chet on the knee and indicated he should get moving.

Chet nodded, struggling to his feet and running down the hallway, his right arm hanging.

Rory began backing up, laying down cover fire as they all headed for the back of the building.

Skye finally led the way through the last door. There was a slight movement on her left. She turned and took out two guards with a steady burst of 9 mm shells. Staying low, she waved the youngsters towards the transport trucks at the loading docks and then lifted her weapon to her shoulder, watching towards the double doors for more guards.

Donna-Lou rushed out of the hallway along with the kids, weapon at the ready.

"Get the kids in the back of the truck," Skye instructed, "I'll cover you."

Just as Donna-Lou moved, half a dozen men burst through the double doors.

Skye dropped to one knee, bullets passing over her head and burrowing into the wall behind as she opened fire.

Donna-Lou turned and began firing past the line of crates at the men.

The youngsters screamed and flattened to the concrete floor as bullets ripped into the walls behind them.

Chet came running out of the doorway along with more youngsters. He ran low to the left, his right arm dangling. He dropped to his knees and one-handed he added his own bullets to the thousand flying back and forth.

The guards were bunched together and the two in the front went down under a savage hail of bullets. The other four men turned, only to be cut down by Skye and Donna-Lou.

Rory was out behind the last of the youngsters and he knelt beside Skye and Donna-Lou, "I'll work with Chet to cover you. Get the kids into the trailers."

The two women immediately went to work to get the youngsters inside the trailers.

Chet kept his submachine gun trained on the double doors with his left hand. The barrel began dropping, along with Chet's head and then it snapped up as he fought to keep from passing out.

Rory glanced over at him, "Just hold on, Chet."

Chet nodded and grimaced in pain as he leaned back in his effort to keep the submachine gun up and aimed at the doors.

Black SUVs suddenly screeched around the back of the building. Men in bullet-proof vests jumped out before the vehicles had slid to a stop.

Donna-Lou turned toward them quickly and brought her weapon up.

"Don't," Skye yelled as she placed her hand on Donna-Lou's weapon. "They're ATF."

ATF personnel began climbing into the loading bays, scrambling into position to cover the doorways. One of the agents yelled out, "Everyone okay? Anyone need medical help?"

Rory got up and went to Chet as he yelled, "Just one. Chet's been wounded."

Donna-Lou turned and immediately showed concern.

Helping Chet to his feet, Rory moved with him towards the trailers as the agent talked into a mic at his shoulder.

As Chet came close, Donna-Lou cried out, "You're hurt!"

Chet's face showed agony and pain but he said, "I'm fine. It's okay–"

Donna-Lou dropped her weapon. As it clattered to the cement, she threw her arms around Chet's neck, hugged him and then planted a big kiss on his lips.

Chet's eyes stayed wide open in surprise and he turned bright red.

Donna-Lou broke off the kiss and she turned bright red herself. She withdrew her arms, looking sheepish as she whispered, "Sorry about that."

Corry was standing beside his mother, "Ewww, I like the badass stuff better than the kissy-face stuff."

Chapter 24

RORY'S CELL PHONE RANG as they entered the highway heading back to Golden. Donna-Lou was in the back seat with her son Corry and Emma on her left. Chet was sitting in the passenger seat. He was half asleep from the pain killers the paramedics had given him when they patched him up and the smell of antiseptic was still evident. He had refused to spend the night in the hospital, preferring to get away from the area as soon as possible with the others.

Rory hit the answer button on the steering wheel, "Hello? You're on speaker."

"Rory? It's Ryan Bowman of the ATF."

"Yes sir, what can I do for you?"

"I just wanted to thank you and the rest of the folks for cracking this kidnapping ring," Bowman said. "You were fortunate, we found out they had moved nearly two hundred kids from that factory to a new one in Louisiana and were probably about to ramp up more kidnappings. We have FBI agents on the way there now. Hopefully, they didn't get wind of what happened in Leflore County."

Rory glanced into the rearview mirror and saw the look in Donna-Lou's eyes. She was partly happy but also showed the torment at the mere thought they might be still looking for Corry if they had moved him.

Bowman continued, "The other good news is, we were able to find addresses in foreign countries where other kidnapped children are being held. These folks had quite an extensive organization. The government had already opened up talks with several foreign governments right now to send in police and free the other children."

Donna-Lou spoke up loudly from the back, "But what about the rest of it? They were killing people. These people are talking about rising up against the government—"

"Yes, I'm aware of what was alleged along those lines—"

"Alleged! These people are killers," Donna-Lou expressed loudly.

"I can understand your anger," Bowman said. "But all the evidence we've come across so far only pertains to the kidnappings—"

"What about that Old Tuck guy?" she said angrily. "Why aren't you making him talk?"

"There's no sign of him anywhere," Bowman said. "We found an extensive network of underground tunnels and it—"

"You let him get away? I can't believe it—"

"Do you have a lead on him?" Rory asked.

"No," Bowman said. "And no one is talking. We'll work on them but these men are extremely loyal to their cause, no matter how misguided it is. I doubt very much if anyone we have in custody will co-operate in any significant way. I have to go. I'll let you know if we learn anything more. Thanks again."

The call ended.

Donna-Lou crossed her arms in a huff, "I can't believe it. What if this Old Tuck or his men come after us again?"

Chet stirred in his seat, his voice groggy, "If he's on the run, I doubt he's gonna take time to go on a treasure hunt."

"You don't know that," countered Donna-Lou angrily. "The man's a nut case. Kidnapping children, killing people. And all over a treasure that probably doesn't–" She cut herself off and said in a huff, "I don't want to hear any more talk of that stupid treasure, Chet Calhoun. You hear me?"

Opening his mouth, Chet shut it instead of arguing and the next several miles were ridden in silence by everyone.

It was finally Corry who spoke up, his voice quiet, "But...we *do* have to go find the treasure, mom."

"Oh, no, no, no, no, no, no," Donna-Lou firmly said, wagging a finger at him. "That *isn't* happening young man. Your treasure hunting days are over."

"But we have to, mom. We *have to*," Corry insisted.

"I said *no*," repeated Donna-Lou.

"But they're going to buy an atomic bomb," Corry said.

Shock and silence filled the car.

A moment later, a shocked Donna-Lou sat up straighter, "Where in the world did you get such an idea?"

"Because I overheard them talking about it," Corry said.

"Yep, I overheard them too," Emma confirmed with a nod. "That was when they first took us there."

Rory sat up straighter in his seat, adjusting the rearview mirror so he could glance into the back as he drove, "Are you sure you didn't hear it wrong, kids?"

Emma shook her head firmly, "No. They said they already made a down...a down...?"

"A down payment?"

"Yeah, that's it...a down payment," Emma confirmed with another firm nod. "They used the money from the clothing they sold to make a down payment on an atom bomb. But they need to dig up the treasure to finish paying for it."

"That can't be," Donna-Lou insisted. "Why would they need a bomb−?"

"They're going to attack the White House, mom. We have to stop them," Corry insisted.

Chapter 25

THE TALK OF USING an atomic bomb against the White House hung heavy in the car. Chet swore and asked, "Are you sure Corry? I mean, that's movie type stuff and...."

"Yeah. I'm sure. That's why they took me down there," Corry explained. "They wanted me to help them find the treasure."

"Yep. They called him treasure boy," Emma added. "He didn't have to work like the rest of us."

"That's right. They kept me in a room and they kept talking to me over and over and over again," Corry said.

Chet twisted in this seat, groaning a little at the pain, "Why would they need *you* to find the treasure? They're KGC. Don't they know–?"

Corry shook his head, "Nope. Me and Emma heard them talking. Some of the members of the Knights of the Golden Circle decided to move the treasure for some reason a long time ago."

"The men we were listening to called them traitors," Emma added.

Corry nodded and he sat forward, eager to tell the story, "There was a big fight and some of them were killed over it."

Emma nodded, "Yep. And then they found out the ones who buried the treasure made up signs to the new spot."

"And they fought over that too," Corry added.

"And then some more were killed," Emma said.

"But they found out someone kept the stuff to find it. But the others didn't know where it was and then they found out–" Corry's voice suddenly cut off and he looked stricken like he had said too much.

Donna-Lou looked at her son, realization suddenly dawning on her, "And that...*stuff*...they were looking for...? You found it in our attic, didn't you?"

Corry lowered his eyes

Emma jumped in, "Corry told some of the boys at school about a skin he found in the attic. A skin that can lead to the treasure. And those men found out."

Corry nodded, "The men kept asking me where I got it. I told them...I found it..." His voice trailed off again and he sat back and didn't seem to want to say any more.

Donna-Lou glanced at Rory and Chet. Then she shifted slightly in her seat towards her son, "Corry, where did you say you found it? Corry? You have to tell us. It's important."

Corry's head hung down, "I didn't want them going to our house, mom. So...I told them I found it in the old house over on Carmichael Street."

Donna-Lou put her hand to her mouth in shock.

"I... I didn't know who lived there before," Corry said. "It's really, really old and...I'm sorry...."

"Whose house are we talking about?" Rory asked.

"That's where Jesse Flint's family lived," whispered Chet.

Rory wasn't sure who they were talking about until it dawned on him, "You mean Jesse...from the diner?"

Donna-Lou nodded, "She was raised by her grandparents. They were very poor and that house was almost unlivable, even when she was there as a little girl."

"They're gonna go after Jesse because of me, mom," Corry blurted. It looked like he was about to cry.

They rode in silence for a few moments, everyone digesting the information.

It was Chet who spoke up, "Corry, is the treasure up near Cherokee Ridge?"

Well, I'm pretty sure we have to start up there."

Chet shook his head, "But...how can anyone find the treasure now, when at least two of those signs no longer exist up there? We saw the photocopies of the signs you had on that whiteboard. But...we have no way of knowing where they were—"

"I do," Corry answered, suddenly eager again. "One of the signs was on a tombstone. Someone was building a dam and other buildings up there and one of the things they removed was the graveyard."

"They said the Knights of the Golden Circle tried to stop them from doing that and there was some more killings over it," Emma added.

"Yeah," Corry said. "But a photographer recorded each grave because they were moving it."

"That's fine and all but you still don't know the direction, Corry," Chet countered.

"I could tell which direction the sign was pointing from the old picture they sent me from the Historical Archives in Atlanta," Corry explained. "I could see the western part of Cherokee Ridge in the background."

Rory and Chet looked at each other.

"I guess we didn't ask enough questions," Rory said.

Chet nodded, thinking some more. Then he turned with a grimace from the pain and looked over the seat at Corry, "Okay. But that still leaves one sign...."

"I think the photographer was a treasure hunter too because he took a photograph of that one as well," Corry said.

"Or he was a member of the Knights of the Golden Circle too," Emma added.

Corry nodded, acknowledging the possibility, "Anyways, it was on an old tree that was removed. And you can tell which direction it's pointing in, too. All we need to know is *where* the tree was growing when they cut it down and removed the stump."

Rory and Chet looked at each other again. Rory then looked into the rearview mirror at Corry, "Okay, I'll bite. How exactly do you figure that out?"

Corry shrugged, "That's how you find any of the signs. You find two or more signs, and they point to a spot where you find another sign. That's what I was doing when they kidnapped me. I was trying to figure out the spot where that last sign was located."

Chet shook his head slowly, "Told you the kid was better than any of us."

"The only problem is that I heard them say they got the skin," Corry said. "I think I can remember the layout but—"

"Rory and I got the skin back," Chet said. "Well... Rory mostly..."

A big grin split Corry's face, "Cool. So now we can go up to Cherokee Ridge and I'll help you to find out where the last signs are—"

"Let somebody else do it," Donna-Lou insisted. "I'm not losing you again."

"But I know which signs are false and which are real. And I can help find it faster," Corry insisted. "And if we don't, they could buy a bomb. And if they go after Jesse...."

"We can protect her," Donna-Lou replied. "We'll keep her safe—"

"When daddy died you said that sometimes bad things happen to good people. That we can't always keep them safe," Corry said. "I don't want bad things to happen to Jesse...or you...."

Donna-Lou put a hand to her mouth and shook her head. Now it looked like she was about to cry.

"We got to go help her first, mom," Corry whispered. "And then...."

Finally, she said, "Okay. Maybe we can call Jesse and have her leave Golden—"

"I'll make a call and see if Skye can go up there to take care of her," Rory said. He hit the call button on his steering wheel, "If she can catch a plane, she'll be there quicker than we can."

"Oh, thank you, Rory," Donna-Lou said in relief. "She's always been good to Corry and me."

"And then we can go and find the treasure. Right, mom?" Corry asked.

"I'm going too," insisted Emma as she crossed her arms. "I have to protect my boyfriend."

Corry Haney rolled his eyes.

Chapter 26

SKYE STEELE CIRCLED GOLDEN, trying to orient herself in the darkness. After she had received word that the office still had not been able to contact Jesse to alert her, she had decided a change of plans and a more aggressive approach was in order. Besides, it gave her an opportunity to fly the Air Tractor 501 crop duster she had spotted back at the cotton farm where they found the kids. The 1100 hp Pratt + Whitney turboprop engine purred as she climbed back around for another pass. If her recollection of the Google map she had looked at before take-off was accurate, she had only one choice.

Swinging the aircraft around, Skye began a quick descent. Street lights flashed below her. She banked right and swung lower. Skye wasn't an adrenaline junky but she had to admit it, there was a thrill in what she was about to do because someone was in danger. She passed just over an old barn, aiming for the old road on the edge of Golden, one street over from Jesse Flint's house. The crop duster had a wingspan of 48 feet and should fit between any poles on the road's edge. Should being the operative word. The crop duster dropped lower, then hit the pavement with a slight bounce. The low wing aircraft tilted up on one wheel and then she brought it back down and braked hard, bringing it to a quick stop.

Skye was out of the cockpit and running within seconds. Slipping through the darkness between two old houses, she found herself on the sidewalk, looking at a dark street lined with old, two-story houses. The smell of a backyard barbecue hung on the air. Just as she was about to start looking for house numbers, Skye spotted two state trooper vehicles and a large, dark sedan parked in front of a house at the far end of the street. She paused and checked on the nearby house numbers. She concluded the vehicles were parked right in front of the house she was looking for. She was either too late and the troopers were working a crime scene...or they were members of the Knights of the Golden Circle gang she was told about.

Jogging casually along the sidewalk toward Jesse Flint's house, Sky kept an eye out for any attacks from the darkness around her. Reaching a spot just across from the police cars, Skye bent over, hands on her knees, pretending she was resting. But her eyes were scanning for any movement around her. No one would be expecting her but she couldn't afford to take any chances. Not detecting anyone, she slipped leather gloves out of her pocket and put them on. Then, turning on her toes, Skye ran low and quiet across to the dark sedan in front of Jesse Flint's house. She wanted to know who this vehicle belonged to, who she was up against, besides state troopers. There was a South Carolina government parking sticker on the windshield on the passenger side. She spotted a few folders in the backseat. Pulling a small penlight out of her pocket, Skye flashed it over the folders. A label on the thick top folder identified the contents as trial papers for a Circuit Court Judge, The Honorable Vernon P.

Teague. Interesting. Why would a circuit court judge be visiting Jesse Flint along with state troopers late at night? She couldn't see any lights on in the house at all. Everything was dark. If they were working a crime scene you would expect lights on everywhere. Something else was happening inside.

Skye slipped across the lawn to the side of the house. She moved slow, watching the darkness around her as well as each dark window she passed. Reaching the backyard, she waited, listening. Everything was quiet. Moving to the back door, she gently turned the knob. Locked. She moved over to the far side of the house. There were definitely no lights on downstairs. Moving further into the backyard and away from the house, Skye turned and looked up. The windows above her were dark but there was a light glow. A light was on upstairs in one of the inner rooms. She wanted to see inside before she penetrated the house. There was a cast drain pipe running up the back wall to the roof. It ran past a second-floor window on this side of the house. Skye moved to the bottom of the pipe, tested it and then began climbing hand over hand, using her feet against the old boards where she could. She reached the window, braced her feet against the house while holding on with one hand, and reached over. The window was not locked and she slid it up and open enough to get inside. She placed her hand inside the window frame and swung herself over. Slithering through the open window on her stomach, Skye found herself in a bedroom. She knelt on the floor and listened. She could hear low voices. Moving to the bedroom door, she reached up to the doorknob and opened it a crack. A light spilled into the hallway on the other side, from an open doorway about 20 feet away on the left.

"C'mon Jesse," said a deep voice with a southern drawl, "this will go much better if you tell us where the other items are."

"And I keep telling you, I have no idea what you're talking about," a female voice said. The voice sounded both frustrated and scared.

"Jesse, Jesse, Jesse," chided the deep voice, "you disappoint me—"

I disappoint *you*," the female said with anger in her voice. "We went to school together, Vern. I thought I knew you—"

"I know how loyal you were to your grandparents," continued the deep voice as if the woman was never even talking, "and I admire that loyalty. But we're on the same side. We've also been protecting the knowledge and information—"

The door exploded in on Skye Steele, knocking her backward. She rolled over smoothly and to the side as a large form filled the open doorway. The light glinted off the barrel of a handgun.

Chapter 27

A LARGE STATE TROOPER had burst into the bedroom, using his shoulder as a battering ram. Fortunately, he was right-handed and he had used his left shoulder to bash his weight against the partially open door. The handgun was in his right hand, so the gun had been pointing away from Skye. But now he was swinging it around towards her.

Skye had a brief opening to act. She sprang forward from her crouch, her own right shoulder catching the state trooper in the stomach and knocking him hard back against the door frame.

But he was a big son of a gun and he stayed upright. His gun hand moved towards her again.

Reaching out, Skye placed her right hand on his elbow, pulling it up as her own weight pressed his hand downward.

The big state trooper grunted in pain.

Skye heard the weapon hit the floor and she looked down, trying to see it in the semi-darkness

But the big state trooper grabbed Skye's red hair with his left hand and tried to yank her away from him.

Grimacing in pain as her hair was yanked backward, Skye grit her teeth and threw her weight against his lower hand, jamming the elbow again.

The trooper grunted in pain and released the grip on her hair.

Dropping to the floor, Skye swept her arm out, sending the weapon sliding across the floor before she rolled away and then came up in a defensive stance.

The trooper stumbled forward and bent over, reaching for his weapon on the floor.

Sky moved to the right, grabbed a lamp from a small dresser and threw it at his head.

The lamp smashed to pieces over the trooper's head and he yelled in pain as he stumbled to his knees. A moment later, he came up in a rage, forgetting about the gun and moved quickly across the room after her.

Moving aside nimbly like a matador, Skye used his momentum against him - placing a hand on his back and pushing.

The big trooper smashed into the small dresser, turned and came back after her again, growling in anger.

Skye knew she had to end this quickly before reinforcements for the trooper showed up. She took a calculated step back and then moved deftly to the left as the trooper lunged. She used his momentum once again to push him past her.

The heavy bulk of the trooper's body easily smashed through the wooden frame of the window and he screamed all the way to the ground two stories below.

Skye was on the move quickly, rushing to the open bedroom door. She looked into the hallway, wary of other troopers. The hallway to the left was empty. A set of attic stairs was just off to her right. She could hear heavy boot steps in the attic. Someone up there was heading for the stairs, no doubt alerted by the screams of the falling trooper. Black boots and gray trooper pants appeared on the top step. As the trooper started down the stairs,

Skye made a quick decision. She ran for the foot of the stairs and lifted them. She had just enough leverage to lift them 6 inches off the floor.

The state trooper grabbed for something to hold onto, dropping his weapon in the process.

Skye let the stairs go and they hit the floor hard under the weight of the trooper, throwing him backward and tumbling down the steps.

The state trooper hit the floor hard, landing flat on his back. He groaned as he sat up, then turned and reached for his weapon on the floor.

Skye kicked the trooper's handgun away. It spun like a pinwheel as it slid all the way down the hallway and stopped at the top of the stairs to the first floor.

The trooper cursed at Skye as he rose to a crouch, preparing to attack.

"That's not very nice talk," Skye said.

He lunged at her.

She turned sideways on her left foot and buried the heel of her right foot into the state troopers face, knocking him cold.

The trooper's body thudded face down to the floor.

Skye automatically went into a defensive crouch, alert to another attack.

Nothing happened.

She moved quickly but quietly down the hallway towards the open door where the light was coming from. Placing her back against the wall, she peered around the door frame into the room.

A woman sat in a chair in the middle of the room facing the door. The ropes around her chest told Skye the woman wasn't there by choice.

Behind the woman stood a tall, thin man with salt-and-pepper hair and a white mustache and goatee. He held a handgun against the woman's head.

"Welcome to the party," the man said. He had a very smug smile on his face like he was in total control of the situation.

Skye imagined the woman had to be Jesse Flint. That should only leave one player if she was right. "Hello, Vernon," purred Skye.

The smile left the man's face, replaced by a startled look. He narrowed his eyes and looked at Skye.

"Strange situation for a judge to be in," she said.

That comment unsettled him as well. This was definitely Judge Teague. And he appeared to be a man used to being in charge...a man who knew and presided over every player in his courtroom. And right now, that wasn't the case. He didn't know who this player was and he looked uncomfortable with the situation. "If you know who I am, then you know how powerful I am," Teague said as he tried to regain his composure.

Skye looked at the woman, "He's right, Aunt Jesse. I know that you trained me to take care of the–" Skye stopped talking and looked up at the man as if she had said too much.

Teague's eyes lit up, "You know where the items are?" He pressed the gun barrel hard against Jesse's head, making her wince. "I want them *now*."

"Not if you hurt her–"

"This is not up for debate," Teague said harshly. He pressed the gun barrel harder.

Jesse tilted her head, crying out in pain.

"They're hidden," Skye said quickly, "and you won't ever find them if you hurt my Aunt Jesse."

"Tell me where they are. Now!" Teague bellowed.

Definitely a man used to being in charge, thought Skye. "And if I tell you where they are, you kill us both. I'm not that stupid."

Teague considered what she was saying. He blinked as if he couldn't figure a way out of this stalemate.

"Why don't you let her go and I'll take you to the items," Skye offered.

"And if I leave her behind, she warns the rest of your friends," Teague reasoned. "You see, I'm not stupid either."

Skye nodded. She couldn't stretch this out much further here. She had to get them all out of the house, in case the judge had more state troopers coming. "Then how about we all go for a drive," she offered. "Once we're in a secluded spot, you can let her go...."

Teague narrowed his eyes as he considered his next move. "Okay," he finally said. He waved the handgun at Skye, "Move back down the hallway, away from the stairs, and don't do anything stupid." He reached down and made a tugging motion. The ropes loosened around Jesse Flint's chest. "Up," Teague said.

Skye backed quickly away from the doorway and back down the hallway. She had to trust Judge Teague wouldn't simply shoot her as she stood exposed since he needed her alive. She glanced at the fallen trooper to make sure he was still out and then waited.

Jesse Flint appeared in the doorway, her face a mask of fear. Her feet shuffled as Teague pushed her out, hiding behind her like a shield.

As Teague move backward towards the stairs, pulling Jesse with him, Skye began to move forward, following them. She had to keep his attention on her and hoped this worked.

Teague had the gun up near Jessie's shoulder, but as Skye moved forward, he placed the gun against Jesse Flint's temple, "Don't do anything stupid. I'm warning you."

"All I'm doing is going with you, right?" Skye asked. She placed her hands up in the air and stopped for a moment as well.

Teague started backing up again, glancing behind him.

Skye began moving forward again, a little faster this time and to the left side of the hallway to attract his attention.

Putting his eyes back on Skye, Teague shook his head as he moved with Jesse backward and to his right to counter her move and maintain the woman as a full shield, "No, no. Take it nice and slow–" He took another step backward and emitted a cry of surprise. He had stepped on the trooper's weapon that Skye had kicked down the hallway to the top of the stairs. The Judge's arms flailed as he tried to catch his balance. His weapon fired into the ceiling as he fell backward, pulling Jesse Flint with him.

Skye shot forward and reached out.

Jesse Flint made a cry as she reached out for something to hold onto.

Skye and Jesse locked hands and Skye was pulled forward by the other woman's momentum.

Teague fell backward, tumbling down the staircase.

Skye and Jesse Flint's weight countered each other and they fell safely to the floor at the top of the stairs.

The sound of Teague's body rumbled down each stair to the floor below.

Skye pulled Jesse quickly to her feet, "There's no time to wait. Let's go." Not waiting for a reply, Skye led Jesse down the stairs.

At the bottom they found The Honorable Vernon P. Teague lying very still. His open eyes stared vacantly up at the ceiling. His head was bent at an awkward angle.

"Couldn't happen to a nicer guy," Jesse hissed as she jumped over the body

Skye pulled Jesse Flint out of the house and down the street, running as quickly as she could go.

"Who are you?" Jesse asked. "And do you have any idea what Vern was after back there?"

"I'll explain everything I know once we're away from here," Skye said.

Jesse shook her head, "Vern was talking stupid nonsense about me and the KGC treasure."

"Shhhh. There might be more after you yet."

Jesse went quiet suddenly and stayed that way as she was led through the houses to the backstreet.

"What the–" Jesse stood still in shock as soon as she realized what was parked on the street. "You have got to be kidding me," she whispered.

"Welcome to Golden Airlines," Skye said as she grabbed Jesse's hand and pulled her towards the plane. She helped the woman to climb onto the wing and into the second seat. Then she scrambled into the pilot seat and started the engine. The sound of the 1100 hp Pratt and Whitney turboprop engine cut through the night air as Skye swiveled the plane around on the roadway to give her a longer take-off area. Pushing the throttle forward, they began rumbling down the road. They gathered speed quickly. The crop duster vibrated, then the nose pointed upwards just slightly as the wheels left the ground.

Skye pulled back hard on the stick.

"Oh, mercy," Jesse Flint said as a line of trees suddenly loomed dead ahead.

The aircraft shuddered as it clipped the top branches but cleared the trees.

"Woo-hoo! Crop dusting, tree trimming, and rescue work. We do it all." Skye yelled.

Jesse Flint began to laugh, relief very apparent in her voice.

Chapter 28

IT TOOK FIFTEEN LONG HOURS of driving before Rory pulled to the curb in front of Donna-Lou Haney's house. Donna-Lou had taken turns with Rory in driving back from Mississippi but right now she was in the back seat, asleep with the kids. Rory wanted to sleep as well but there was no time. The threat of an atomic weapon being used on American soil was just too serious a matter. He kept the car running as he leaned forward over the steering wheel and examined the windows of the dark house. Everything looked quiet.

Chet had been sleeping and he now stirred in the passenger seat. Stretching his good arm, he yawned and looked out the passenger side window, "Are we there?"

"Yeah," Rory replied. His attention was focused on a couple of cars parked further down the road under the street lights. Neither looked like a police car but they couldn't afford to be caught off-guard.

Chet turned in his seat, reached over and placed his hand on Donna-Lou's knee, shaking it gently and whispering, "Donna-Lou. Donna-Lou."

Rory looked in the rearview mirror, then the side mirror, checking the street behind them for police cars or anything else suspicious.

Donna-Lou stirred, "Hmmmm?"

"We're here," Chet said in a low voice.

Donna-Lou wiped the sleep from her eyes and sat up, glancing out the side window, "What time is it"

Chet glanced at the car's clock, "It's just after five. We have an hour or so before sun-up. And just so you know, Rory got a call from his sister Skye two hours ago. She's taken Jesse to Greenville. Apparently she found her tied up at her house by a couple of state troopers. And guess what? Circuit Court Judge, The Honorable Vernon P. Teague was *also* there with the troopers."

"What?" Donna-Lou sat up wide awake. "You mean Teague is KGC?"

"Looks like he was."

Donna-Lou swore, "No wonder he wouldn't help much with finding the kids. He was part of it."

"I know. But he's dead."

Her eyebrows flickered at the news and then she leaned forward, dropping her voice, "But how many others are involved, Chet? That's the question. I mean...are we surrounded by them?"

Chet nodded and shrugged, "I don't know. But at least there's one less."

That didn't seem to offer much comfort to Donna-Lou. She glanced at Corry, sleeping beside her, and she frowned, her jaw clenched in anger.

Chet decided there wasn't much more he could offer and he turned back around, opened the glove compartment and pulled out a pair of Glock 19, 9mm semi-automatic pistols. He looked across at Rory, "Are we still going inside?"

Rory took another quick look down the street ahead of them. Then he took another look at the dark house. Finally, he nodded, "Yeah. Hopefully, nobody's broken in to get the flag or anything else we need. You up for it?"

Touching his wound gingerly, Chet, nodded, "Yeah, I guess I have to be."

Nodding in return, Rory looked over the back seat, "You should get the kids up."

Donna-Lou reached out and gently brushed the hair off Corry's forehead. She smiled. Corry and Emma had fallen asleep against each other and they looked so cute. "Can't we let the kid sleep a little longer?"

Rory looked over at the seat at the kids, "I'd like to, but we don't have any time to spare. And it's definitely not safe to leave them out here alone. If any members of the KGC show up before we get back out here...."

Donna-Lou nodded, "You're right." She shook her son, then Emma, "Wake up you sleepy heads. C'mon, wake up."

The kids stirred, stretched and sat up, yawning. Instead of saying anything, both of them rubbed their eyes, looked at the darkness outside the car and then plopped their heads against the seat and closed their eyes again.

Rory pulled his Baby Eagle handgun from his shoulder holster and looked across at Chet, "I think it's best if you and me check around the outside of the house first. Just to make sure before we all go in."

Chet nodded, "Okay, that sounds good to me."

Looked back over the seat, Rory asked Donna-Lou, "Were all your doors and windows locked when you left?"

Donna-Lou nodded, "Yes. We always make sure to do that when we leave." She shrugged, "We don't have much but...."

Rory looked at Chet again, "Okay. Watch for unlocked or open windows. Same for the doors. Donna-Lou, I want you to get behind the wheel and be ready to drive the kids away from here and to safety if anything happens."

Donna-Lou nodded and got out on her side as Rory and Chet opened their doors and got out.

Chet handed her one of the Glocks, "Be careful out here."

Donna-Lou took the gun and whispered, "Uh...about that kiss back there...."

"It's okay. It was the heat of the moment and all that," Chet whispered. He waved a hand, "I've already forgotten about it—"

"You have, have you?" Donna-Lou replied tersely in a low voice. She snorted, "I guess you're not as smart as I thought you were, Mr. Calhoun." With that said, Donna-Lou marched in a huff around to the driver's side.

Chet stood there, blinking, embarrassed and feeling a little foolish.

Donna-Lou got in the driver's side, setting the pistol on the seat beside her.

"You leave the minute you even suspect trouble," Rory told her and then he closed the car door. There was a clunking sound as Donna-Lou locked the doors.

Rory took a look in both directions down the street, making extra sure there was no police car or any other suspicious vehicle in sight. So far so good. He walked around the front of the Jaguar to Chet, "Okay, let's go check the yard and the house. Keep your eyes and ears open."

Chet took a deep breath and nodded, following behind as they headed for the house.

Rory moved to the left of the house while he indicated he wanted Chet to check out the right side. Moving slow, Rory held his Baby Eagle in both hands as he swept it back and forth, peering into the darkness of the yard. He reached up and checked the first window. Locked. He moved further down to a smaller window and found it locked as well. Skirting some bushes, Rory moved carefully to the next window. He reached up and checked. Locked. Reaching the corner of the house, Rory peered around into the dark backyard. He spotted movement on the far side of the house. Dropping to a knee, he brought the Baby Eagle up and then realized it was Chet.

Chet was moving low in the dark, his Glock held in both hands. He swung around to his left when he detected movement.

"It's me," Rory whispered.

There was a visible drop of relief in Chet's shoulders and he nodded.

Rory moved out from his position, gesturing towards the back door as he knelt and kept his gun trained on the darkness around them.

Chet tip-toed to the back door, reached out and turned the doorknob. He looked back over his shoulder and whispered, "Locked,"

Rory nodded and indicated for Chet to move back around the right side of the house. Rory kept his eyes trained on the darkness behind them as they moved back to the front of the house. Standing at the bottom of the front porch, Rory indicated for Chet to go check the front door while he kept alert for movement in the surrounding darkness.

Chet walked softly onto the porch, reached out and checked the door. He quietly and quickly moved back to Rory. "Locked," he whispered.

"Okay," Rory whispered, "You stay here and keep your eyes open. I'll go get the others."

Chet tiptoed back up on the porch, holding his Glock 19 in two hands as he kept an eye on the darkness around him.

Rory went back to the sidewalk beside the Jaguar. He looked up and down the street in both directions again - he brought his weapon up when he caught movement down the street. Every muscle was tense, ready for battle. But after a few moments, everything stayed quiet, the only sound his own breathing as he watched, listened and waited. Rory slowly let his breath out and he lowered his weapon. Finally, he tapped lightly on the vehicle and motioned for Donna-Lou to bring the kids.

Donna-Lou looked back over the seat and called to the kids. They had fallen into a slumber and she had to reach back and shake them both. Then she grabbed her pistol, jumped out and ran around to the passenger side back door. She looked at Rory and whispered, "Did you see something? It looked like you did...."

Rory shook his head, "Probably just a cat."

Donna-Lou licked her lips, nodded and then opened the back door, urging the two sleepy heads to get moving.

The two kids slid across the seat, grumbling and got out.

Rory stood on the sidewalk, his head on a swivel as Donna-Lou got the kids moving towards the house. Then he followed, constantly keeping an eye peeled for any sign of an attack.

Donna-Lou fished her key from a pocket and unlocked her front door.

"Let us go in first," Rory whispered.

Nodding, Donna-Lou stepped aside, standing with the kids, holding her Glock low in both hands.

Rory moved quietly ahead, slipping inside the house, followed closely by Chet. Rory gestured for Chet to check the living room on the right while he slipped into the kitchen.

Donna-Lou and the kids stepped inside behind them, closed the door and waited.

Meeting Chet back at the front entrance, Rory whispered to him, "I'll check upstairs while you check the sitting room and the closets down here. Come up to the top of the stairs when you're finished."

"Okay."

Keeping close to the wall, Rory crept slowly up the stairs. The stairs squeaked softly despite his best efforts to tread lightly. Once at the top of the stairs, he moved from room to room, checking the closets and under the beds, clearing each. Last was Corry's treasure room. He opened the door carefully and slipped inside. It was empty and quiet in here as well. Moving back to the stairs, he found Chet just coming up.

"Everything is clear downstairs," Chet said.

"Only one other place," Rory said as he holstered his weapon. He walked over, jumped up and pulled the attic stairs down.

Chet kept watch as Rory climbed the stairs into the attic.

Rory cleared the attic quickly, checking behind all the boxes and every possible hiding spot. He went back to the top of the attic stairs and called down to Chet, "Okay, everything looks good.

I'll get the stuff from the trunk. Send Donna-Lou and the kids up and then you get what we need out of the car."

"Okay." Chet headed back down the stairs.

Chapter 29

AS CHET REACHED the bottom of the stairs, he found the kids leaning against each other and the wall beside the door, eyes closed. When they heard his footsteps, they opened their eyes, wondering what was going on. Donna-Lou stepped out from the kitchen area, "Is everything okay?"

"Yeah. Everything is fine. Rory says to go on up and help him gather everything we need."

Donna-Lou nodded in return but still looked nervous and concerned, despite his assurance, "Okay."

Chet held his hand out, "While you do that, I'll need your house key and the car keys."

Pulling them from her pocket, Donna-Lou passed the keys over to Chet, "What are you going to do? You're not going out there again, are you?"

"Yeah. Rory wants me to bring in the oilskin. It's in the Jaguar's trunk." Chet turned and placed his hand on the front doorknob.

"Chet?"

He turned back, "Yes?"

Donna-Lou took a step forward, looking into Chet's brown eyes, "You be careful out there, okay?"

Chet gave her a sheepish smile and nodded. He turned back to the door and opened it, "Lock the door behind me."

"Chet?"

He turned back again, one foot out the door.

"You don't still have a thing for Josie McDaniel, do you? I mean...she's divorced and you're single and...."

Chet had a surprised look on his face, "Uh...no...."

A small smile played on Donna-Lou's lips, "Okay, so we just have more work to do." She gave him a gentle push with both hands to get going.

Emma looked at Corry, "That's what mama always says, we always gotta work on our men."

Corry rolled his eyes.

Chet had a confused look on his face as he slowly closed the door.

With the door locked again, Donna-Lou slipped the Glock 19 into the waistband of her jeans at the back. She walked over to the telephone by the stairs and quickly dialed a number.

"Who you calling?" Corry asked.

"Emma's mother. The police said they couldn't get hold of her from Mississippi. They were supposed to let her know and she would call us but –" She got a voice message and cursed under her breath as she listened. Then she left a message of her own, "Charlene, it's Donna-Lou Haney. We have Emma with us. She's fine. Call us as soon as you can." She hung up, "For some reason, your mother went to Mississippi to get you. I guess you'll have to stay with us–"

"All right!' Emma said as she gave a fist pump.

Donna-Lou had to smile and shake her head, "Okay. Let's go upstairs kids."

RORY WAS JUST COMING back down the attic ladder as Donna-Lou and the kids reached the second-floor hallway. "Corry," he said, "we need to through everything about finding the treasure before we leave here and head up to Cherokee Ridge. Can you to set up things in your room back there and fill us in?"

Corry nodded eagerly and ran to his treasure room, followed closely by Emma.

Rory handed the folded Confederate flag, the stag hat and the Confederate uniform to Donna-Lou, "I just have to get the gun and I'll join you."

Donna-Lou took the items and followed the kids into Corry's treasure room as Rory hustled back up into the attic.

Rory retrieved the gun, climbed back down to the hallway, then pushed the attic ladder back up into the ceiling. He listened for Chet but didn't hear anything. He moved to the top of the stairs and listened. It was quiet. He stepped to the left and walked down the short hallway to the second story window overlooking the front yard. He saw the trunk of the Jaguar up and someone bent over, looking inside. "C'mon Chet," he whispered to himself. Turning, he walked back to Corry's treasure room.

"The slicker thing is gone," Corry said excitedly as soon as Rory stepped into the room. He pointed at the whiteboard, "It was on there–"

"Somebody broke in to get it after you were taken but we got it back. Remember? We told you that in the car on the way back."

"Oh, yeah."

"Chet has gone out to the Jaguar to get it."

Corry looked at his mother, a concerned look on his face, "I'm sorry. I guess I shouldn't have brought it home."

"You didn't know what would happen. And I wasn't here when they came in," reassured his mother. Then she pointed to the items she had just set on a small table, the folded Confederate flag, the stag hat and the Confederate uniform, "And they didn't get all that stuff."

"Or this," Rory said as he handed her the gun case.

Corry looked relieved for a brief moment and then he turned quickly and went to the large whiteboard in the center of the room, "But they took the photocopies of the signs we need to–"

"Do you have other copies?" his mother asked as she set the gun case on the table.

"Uh, yeah...maybe...I...I think so," said Corry. He headed to the desk at the back of the room. Emma joined him to help look. Corry shuffled through some papers until he finally held two up, "Here they are." He handed them to Emma, "You hold those and I'll take the map." Corry reached down to a long, rolled up paper leaning against the side of the desk and put it under his arm. He took a couple of hand spring-clamps from a drawer and then led Emma back to the whiteboard. Unrolling one end of the long paper, Corry clamped it against the right side of the whiteboard with one of the spring-clamps.

Rory went over and helped Corry unroll the paper across the whiteboard.

Donna-Lou moved closer, "What is that?"

"It's a topographical map all around Cherokee Ridge," Corry said. "We learned about these in school last year and the teacher sent away for this for me." He clamped the other side of the map at the top and bottom so it wouldn't curl up. "Now we just need the slicker and we put it over top of this."

Rory nodded, "I'll go see what's keeping Chet. He should have been back up here by now."

Donna-Lou nodded, then listened as her son explained the topographical map to Emma. After a few moments, she began to worry about Chet herself. She left the kids behind and headed for the window overlooking the front yard.

RORY OPENED THE FRONT door and stepped out onto the porch. He could see the dark outline of Chet standing by the side of the Jaguar. He walked across the porch to the edge of the top step and called softly, "Chet? Everything okay?"

Chet stayed silent. Then his form seemed to grow taller.

Rory cocked his head. It looked like Chet had two heads. He looked down to the top step–

"Crack!

The bullet hit Rory square on the heart. His body slowly fell backward and bounced once on the old boards before coming to rest on the wrap-around porch.

Chapter 30

TROOPER BUCK WALKER HARRISON kept his hand firmly over Chet's mouth, "See what happens when folks don't listen? I told that man to leave. Now he'll be doing it in a pine box."

Chet twisted his head, trying to get the big man's hand off his mouth.

Harrison put the still smoking Glock against Chet's temple, "Now why don't you tell me who else is in the house? And keep in mind, if you make any attempt to warn anyone, I'll kill you and then everyone else in the house. Of course, if that sweet Donna-Lou Haney is in there, I'll have a little bit of fun with her first. Know what I mean?" A moment later, he took his hand off Chet's mouth, Now who's in there–?"

"You touch Donna-Lou and I'll–" Chet winced as Harrison pressed the end of the gun barrel hard into his temple.

"You'll do what?" Harrison asked smugly. "You always were a little piece of–"

A light flashed in the window on the second floor, catching Harrison's attention.

Chet looked up as well and fear registered on his face. Flames were climbing the drapes on the second-floor window.

"Are you people crazy?" Harrison hissed. "That house is a tinderbox and we'll lose anything of value in there–"

Chet struggled to free himself.

Harrison smashed the Glock against the back of Calhoun's head.

Chet's world exploded in a mass of stars and pain as he fell to his knees. He clutched the back of his head and groaned, his eyes squeezed shut. A moment later, he looked towards the old house and his heart skipped a beat.

Buck was running for the porch, the weapon in his hand swinging back and forth.

Chet desperately bought a foot up, wanting to give chase but his legs betrayed him. They were jello and his hands clutched desperately for something to hold onto as he fell face down, landing hard on the sidewalk.

Harrison ran up the two steps to the porch, leaped over Rory Mack Steele's body and barged into the old house.

As soon as the trooper disappeared inside, Donna-Lou appeared at the side of the house, running ran low in the darkness, the Glock 19 in her right hand. She carried the Confederate flag, folded around the gun case in her left hand.

Closely behind her came Emma and Corry. Emma carried the stag hat and the Confederate uniform, while Corry had the topographical map along with his photocopies. They all ran for the Jaguar, with Donna-Lou dropping to her knees beside Chet, laying the flag and gun case down, "Chet, Chet! Are you okay? Speak to me. Chet?"

Chet rubbed the side of his head as he rolled over on the sidewalk, "Yeah...yeah... I think I'm okay–"

Donna-Lou kissed him squarely on the lips, "Thank God, I saw someone with you and I heard a shot...."

Blinking for a moment at the kiss, Chet then said, "Uh, yeah. It was Buck Harrison—"

"Buck Harrison! Is he part of the KGC too?"

"Yeah...looks like it...."

"Where's Rory?" asked a very worried Emma.

Chet's head snapped up and he looked at the house. "Oh, no!"

Whirling around on her knees, Donna-Lou brought the gun up, looking for a target, "What's wrong, Chet? Who is it?"

Chet pointed a shaky hand to the house, "No, no. It's Rory. Buck shot him when he came out of the house. I think...he's dead."

Donna-Lou put a hand to her mouth as she looked at the house. Flames were leaping out of the second-floor window now and a body could be seen on the porch in the flickering light. She got to her feet, running for the porch.

Corry and Emma dropped everything and ran for the porch as well.

Chet tried to rise, moaned as he put a hand to his head and collapsed, hitting his head on the side of the Jaguar.

Donna-Lou bounded up onto the porch and dropped to her knees beside Rory.

Corry and Emma jumped onto the porch, crying as they got on either side of the body.

"Rory, Rory," Emma cried as she shook his shoulder.

Donna-Lou lay the Glock down beside her knee and placed her hands on Rory's head, searching for an injury. Then she slid her hands to his chest, feeling for a bullet wound.

Rory's head snapped up, "What–?"

Startled, Donna-Lou pulled back, "Chet said Buck Harrison shot you! Where are you hit?"

Rory coughed as his hands went to his chest. His fingers fumbled for a moment and then held up a flat metal object.

"Is that a bullet?" Corry said in amazement.

Rory's voice was hoarse as he nodded, "Yeah, I'm still wearing my bulletproof vest the government guys gave us."

Tears of relief flowed from Donna-Lou's eyes.

Corry tugged urgently at his mother sleeve, "Mom, mom. Look!"

Donna-Lou grabbed the Glock as she looked at her son and then realized what he was pointing at. Through the crack of the still open door, they could see flames engulfing the main floor of their house. Donna-Lou spoke urgently as she slipped the Glock into the back of her jeans, "We have to get out of here, Rory. Help me get him up, kids."

Rory grunted in pain as he struggled to get to his feet with their help. But his body was still weak from the force of the gunshot and he fell over with his first step, taking everyone down with him, the old porch boards rattling and groaning under the force.

Donna-Lou, Corry, and Emma scrambled back to their feet, all three of them nervously eying the open door and the flames beyond as they worked to get Rory back up.

Rory shakily got to his feet again, his legs rubbery as they helped him down the stairs. "Where's the guy who shot me?" he asked, his voice raspy.

"He ran into the house," Donna-Lou said as she and the kids helped Rory move away from the burning structure.

Glancing back, Rory looked at the dancing flames as the fire intensified, "What the hell happened?"

"That was me," Donna-Lou said. "I looked out the window and saw someone had hold of Chet. Then I heard a gunshot. I figured it was the KGC after us again and I panicked. I didn't know what to do so started a fire to distract them. Stupid, I guess...."

"No, not stupid at all. You did what you had to do," Rory said. "But we should get out of here before that guy comes back out."

As they approached the vehicle, Chet had struggled to his feet and he leaned against the Jaguar, confusion written on his face, "Rory, I saw Buck shoot you. I thought you were–"

A man's scream tore through the air.

Everyone looked to the Haney house to see a figure, completely on fire, stumble out of the front door. Buck Walker Harrison screamed and beat at the flames that engulfed his body. He took one step off the porch and collapsed on his face, flames and sparks from his body dancing with the force. Behind his burning body, flames tore through the house, the old boards and timbers snapping and crackling. Black smoke began to creep through the door and the strong smell of burning wood filled the air.

"Mom, our house," Corry whispered.

"It's okay, sweetie, we can always get a new house. It's people that matter."

The black smoke crept across the yard and swirled around them and Corry and Emma coughed.

"We have to get moving," Rory said urgently, "the fire will bring people. And if other KGC members show up...."

"You're right," Donna-Lou said. "Emma, get the car doors open. Corry, help me get Rory up."

Emma waved swirling smoke away and pulled on the passenger side door beside Chet. "It's locked!" she cried.

Chet swore, "I...I had the keys when Harrison jumped me." He placed a hand against the Jaguar, holding himself steady as he looked around on the sidewalk, "I think I dropped them...."

Emma spun around, frantically looking for the keys p she pounced to the side of the Jaguar just behind him, "Here they are." She aimed the key fob at the Jaguar and pressed the button. There was a slight thunk as the doors unlocked and then Emma opened the passenger side door.

"Good girl," Donna-Lou said as she urged Rory to get up.

Rory groaned in pain as he slid into the car and sat heavily on the passenger seat.

Corry pulled open the back door, helping Chet to slide inside.

Donna-Lou slammed the passenger side door shut, took the car keys from Emma and ran for the driver's side, yelling to the kids, "Get all the stuff and put it in the car. Hurry."

Corry and Emma gathered up all the dropped treasure items, along with Chet's dropped Glock and threw them into the Jaguar. Then the two kids ran around the car and jumped into the back seat, slamming the door shut behind them.

Donna-Lou started the Jaguar and looked at Rory "Where do we go?" she asked desperately.

"Just drive," Rory said as he winced in pain. "We can't stay here in town. Head towards Greenville and we'll find a hotel along the highway. We don't know if any other troopers are members of the KGC, so you need to keep your speed down–"

"Like that's going to be easy," Donna-Lou complained as she stamped on the gas pedal and the Jaguar squealed away from the corner, leaving behind the heavy smell of the house burning and the smoldering body of Buck Walker Harrison.

Chapter 31

DONNA-LOU DROVE for half an hour along I-85, trying hard to keep her nerves under control and not speed away from Golden as fast as possible. The sun was up and she felt exposed in the daylight, her eyes constantly moving back and forth, watching for any signs of a state trooper. There was no telling where a member of the Knights of the Golden Circle could show up.

Chet and the two kids were dozing in the back seat while Rory was slumped in the passenger seat, leaning against the door and trying to keep watch with her. As they passed a highway sign, Rory pushed himself up in the seat, groaning as he did, "Okay. I want you to take the next cut-off. The sign back there said there's a town twenty miles to the south."

Shaking her head, Donna-Lou said, "But we're still half-hour at least away from Greenville. I thought that's where you wanted us to go to get away from them?"

"I know," Rory said. "But I've been thinking. We can't stay in this car. Harrison pulled me over when I was going back to Golden and any of his state trooper buddies could have the make, model, and license number and be watching for us. Especially after finding Buck's burned body and his car at your burning house by now–"

Donna-Lou voice rose an octave in fear, "I know. I've been watching. But if we don't get far away, if they see us–"

Rory held a hand up to calm her, "I know. I understand your fears. But we can't take the chance on staying in this car. Besides, we have to find the treasure before they do–"

"We just call the police," Donna-Lou stated firmly. "They can take care of it."

"I thought we had agreed–"

"I've changed my mind," she shot back. She glanced into the rearview mirror at the kids in the back seat, "After what happened back there at my house...at what's left of my house...I can't take the chance."

"Okay. So which police do we call?"

There was a moment of silence and then Donna-Lou's jaw clenched and rippled with anger.

"Which ones can you guarantee won't be members of the KGC?"

More tense silence.

"Are there more judges like the one that was at Jesse's house? Which members of the–"

"Okay, okay. I get your point." Donna-Lou cursed under her breath.

"Just trust me on this. Okay?"

Licking her lips and working to push her fears back down, Donna-Lou finally gave him a nod, "Okay." Her hands gripped the steering wheel hard, "But if something happens, so help me...."

"I understand."

In five minutes she took the next off-ramp and drove south for another twenty minutes before finally reaching the outskirts of a small town.

The kids stirred in the back seat, rubbing the sleep from their eyes as they sat up to see where they were.

"Okay, here's what we need," Rory said as he pointed ahead on the left. There were three car dealerships. Rory leaned ahead and examined the signs coming up. "Turn off at the second dealership," Rory said.

Donna-Lou nodded, turning off the road into the dealership's lot, driving between two lines of cars that stretched to the left and right.

Rory pointed off to the left, "Okay, park over there."

In a moment, Donna-Lou pulled the Jaguar to a stop on the left of the large garage for the dealership.

Rory peeled off the bullet-proof vest off, groaning in discomfort as he did. "Do you still have your weapon?" he asked Donna-Lou.

She nodded, reaching under the seat and pulling out her Glock 19 handgun, showing it to him.

"You're bad ass mom," a proud Corry said from the back seat.

"Language young man," she chided with a half smile.

Chet stirred in the back, where he had been lying against the door, holding his head as he slept.

"Here's your gun, Mr. Calhoun," Emma said as she handed Chet his Glock from the floor of the back seat.

"Thank you, sweetie," Chet said. "Now, does anybody have any aspirins? I'm not sure what hurts worse, my arm or the back of my head."

"We'll get you some as soon as we can," Donna-Lou said as she looked back over the seat with concern.

Rory removed his shoulder holster containing the Baby Eagle and set it on the floor in front of his seat. "I'll be back in a moment. Keep an eye out," he said as a got out.

HALF AN HOUR LATER, Rory was driving towards the Jaguar in a large Land-Rover Range Rover. He parked to the left and rolled down his window, calling over to Donna-Lou, "Let's transfer everything to this vehicle."

Donna-Lou nodded and it wasn't long before everyone and everything was transferred to the Land-Rover Range Rover. Rory drove the Jaguar towards the back of the dealership and then came back a few minutes later, holding a hand against his chest.

"Are you okay?" Donna-Lou asked as Rory jumped into the driver's side.

Rory nodded, "Just a little sore, is all."

"Do you want me to drive?"

"No, it's fine," Rory said, "I've had some driver training in evasive maneuvers and if someone tries to stop us...."

Donna-Lou nodded in understanding, "What did you do with the Jaguar?"

Rory glanced at the building, "I didn't tell the dealership, but I parked it in the back lot with a bunch of other vehicles. It should be some time before anybody finds it." He put the Range-Rover in gear and they left the lot behind.

Ten minutes later, they were parked in front of a Best Western Inn and Suite and Rory took three adjoining rooms. Everyone enjoyed room service and several hours of sleep before they got up just after noon and began to plot out their next move.

Chapter 32

RORY GATHERED EVERYONE in the living area of the central suite and they were all sitting in front of a large whiteboard he had borrowed from the hotel. Standing next to the board, he began by gesturing to the pile of items set up on a folding table he had borrowed as well, "Okay, Corry. Chet and I brought everything up from the Range Rover. Before we make our way up to Cherokee Ridge–"

An eager Corry bounded up from his chair, "We're really going?" He looked at his mom, "Yeah?"

Donna-Lou still looked conflicted but she nodded, "Yeah. We're going." She looked at Rory, "And nothing better happen."

Corry pumped his fist, "All right."

Rory gave Donna-Lou a nod and then said, "Why don't you set everything up on this board, Corry and show us what we're going to be looking for."

"Okay." Corry said as he looked towards the table, "I'll need the topographical map of Cherokee Ridge first."

An equally eager Emma bounded up from her own chair, "I'll help." She ran over and picked up the map, unrolling it as she brought it over to Corry.

There were a number of spring clamps set along the edges of the board and Corry took one in hand, waiting for Emma to place the unrolled map across the whiteboard.

"Explain what you're doing and *why* you're doing it," Donna-Lou said, "for us uninitiated treasure hunters."

Nodding and smiling, Corry said, "Okay, this is a topographical map. It gives us a lot of detail for the area, including hills and lakes and stuff like that." He worked with Emma to clamp both sides of the map as well as the top and bottom to the whiteboard. When they were finished, Corry pointed to several spots on the map, "What I did is I used a magic marker to put a small black dot on this map *exactly* where I found each sign."

"You mean each treasure sign? Like the one we have on the tree in the backyard?" Donna-Lou asked.

"Uh huh, I borrowed Ronnie Gentry's cell phone," Corry said. "He had a free app on the phone that he used for geocaching and it gave me the exact coordinates for the map."

"You mean you used the exact longitude and latitude for each sign? That's smart," Rory said.

Donna-Lou looked a little sad, "I'm sorry you had to borrow a phone, sweetie. I know you wanted one like the other kids, but we just didn't have the money...."

"That's okay," Corry said. He shrugged it off as no big deal. "Okay. Now we need the slicker to put it over top of the topographical map."

Rory had the oilskin in hand and Emma darted over, taking it back to the whiteboard. She placed the oilskin against the map and began to unroll it, "Like this, Corry?"

"Yep," Corry said. He and Emma unrolled the oilskin completely, each holding an end. "This slicker has most of the signs that we need on it, Corry explained. "We just...place the center of each sign on the skin...over the dot on the map where I found it...."

Emma worked with Corry to shift the oilskin around, looking at each black dot, getting it just right. "There," Corry said finally. "Can someone put clamps to hold it?"

Rory stood up and placed spring clamps carefully in place to hold the oilskin in position.

Donna-Lou and Chet stood up, both of them moving closer to the whiteboard.

"This the first time I've really had a real chance to look at this oilskin," Rory said.

"Me too," Chet said quietly as he leaned over, narrowing his eyes, examining the skin in detail.

"I'm not really sure what I'm looking at," Donna-Lou said.

Corry and Emma gave her a rundown of how it worked and what the different features of the topographical map showing through the skin meant.

After a few minutes, Rory pointed to the left of the oilskin, "Two of the signs on the left side here are faded so badly I can't really make them out. That one on top of those two is readable but...."

"That's why I needed these two photocopies of the signs," Corry said as he retrieved them from a coffee table. "This is the last one I found," he added as he tapped on the oilskin on a black dot on the topographical map underneath, "it's exactly here." He placed one photocopy on the skin and directed Emma to put a piece of scotch tape to hold it. He went back and got the next one.

Donna-Lou stepped closer to Chet, looking closer, watching in fascination as the treasure map was built by her son.

"I think this sign is the *distance* sign," Corry added as he placed the next one. "I *think* the number of feathers shows how far we have to go to find the next sign - or maybe the treasure."

"Are you sure?" Donna-Lou asked.

"Pretty sure," Corry answered with a shrug.

"Does the number mean a distance in feet? Or in number of miles?" Chet asked.

Corry shrugged again, "I'm not really sure. But this is the last one...it was on the tree they cut down at Cherokee Ridge." He held the last paper over the spot on the map and had Emma tape it in place. Corry then said, "We still have to figure out *exactly* where it was, though. That's the other problem...."

Rory placed a finger on a photocopied sign, "So...if *this* feather sign is the distance one...and we figure it out...how do we know which direction...?"

"That's where the flag comes in," Chet said. He turned to get it but Donna-Lou put a hand on his shoulder, "You just stand there and I'll get it. You're still a bit unsteady on your feet."

Chet blushed a little at the attention.

Donna-Lou got the old Confederate flag and handed it over to Chet, along with a brief smile.

Chet took the flag in hand and folded it carefully along the seam in the flag. Then he held it against the oilskin, "From what I know...if we just align this repaired-looking star...over this star on this sign...."

Corry moved in and helped to adjust the star on the flag over the star on the sign.

"And you follow the direction of the seam?" Donna-Lou asked as she moved closer.

"Yes and no," Chet said in a distracted his voice. He readjusted the flag.

"Yes and no?" Donna-Lou repeated. "You're confusing me."

Chet looked at her, "Remember what I said about the guide when we found the flag and the other items up in the attic?"

Donna-Lou made a grimace, "Not really. Sorry."

Chet looked at Emma, "Would you hold the flag for me, please?"

Emma eagerly moved in and took up Chet's job in holding the flag in place.

Stepped back beside Donna-Lou, Chet said, "Okay. The signs were set up as a treasure map that could be rebuilt. In order to find the treasure again years later, any KGC member could go back to the signs and copy them back onto a slicker in the exact pattern in which they're found in the area. In our case, we have what might be the original oilskin that set up all the signs in the first place–"

"So they would rebuild the treasure map, just like we just did," Donna-Lou said.

"Right," Chet said.

"But two of the signs are too faded to read on this oilskin," Corry added. "So I added the two photocopies."

Yes, I can see that," Donna-Lou said. She winked at Rory, obviously proud of her son's abilities.

Chet continued, "So the slicker they draw on would be placed over top of a topographical map scaled to fit the area where the signs were found. Which is what we have here.

Now...here's the tricky part...one of the signs in the area was *the keystone....*"

"That's the sign with the star on the oilskin...and you aligned the star on the flag on top of that," Donna-Lou interjected, eager to understand the whole thing.

"That's right," Chet said.

"You're getting it, mom," praised Corry.

Chet held up a finger, "But...remember what I said before. One of the signs was *the guide.* Which means one of these signs on the oilskin...matches something *on the flag.* You line up those two - like we did with the stars - and you now have the exact direction to go in."

"Got it," Donna-Lou said. "So...which of the signs is the guide?"

Chet scratched the back of his head as he looked at the oilskin, "I have no idea."

Donna-Lou moved in next to her son as she looked at the flag and the oilskin, "Any ideas, Corry?"

Corry shook his head, "No. But I think we'll know once we go up to Cherokee Ridge and find out *exactly* where that last sign should be on the map."

"Okay," Donna-Lou said slowly. "But...what if we *can't* figure out exactly where?"

Giving it a moment's thought, Corry then shrugged, "Then we're F'd."

Donna-Lou's eyebrows rose abruptly, "Language young man, language!"

Corry gave her a big belly laugh.

Chapter 33

THEY LEFT WELL BEFORE SUNUP the next morning. Rory drove north and then took the Old Greenville Highway west before working his way back south towards the Golden area. The sun was just peeking through the trees when Rory came to a stop on a narrow back road in the middle of nowhere. He hit his power button and let his window roll down. The air was warm and carried the rich scent of pine trees. The twittering of birds competed for his attention with the chattering of squirrels.

Despite the pleasant atmosphere, Donna-Lou went on alert and sat up in the back seat, "Why are we stopping here?"

Rory looked over his seat, "Everything is fine, don't worry. From here, we're going to head cross-country to Cherokee Ridge."

Chet had been dozing in the passenger seat and he stirred with the conversation, sitting up as well and looking around at the surrounding trees, "You want us all to get out here and walk now? I have no idea where we are, but...I think we're still a long ways away yet, Rory."

Corry stirred in the back seat as well and set his forehead against his window, "Yeah. I don't know where we are either."

Emma kept her eyes closed and moaned, "I'm too tired to walk."

Rory shook his head and patted the steering wheel, "No, Emma, we're not walking. That's why I rented this Land-Rover Range Rover. It's the biggest and baddest for cross-country trekking." He jerked a thumb over his shoulder, "I had the dealership put a big cooler back there when I rented this thing. And before we left, I got that place across the road from the hotel, to fix us up a whole bunch of sandwiches and cool drinks. We're all set."

Corry sat forward and eagerly put his hands on the back of Rory's seat, "So we're staying in this?"

"Yeah, it's an off-road vehicle so...."

Pumping his fist, Corry said "Cool beans." He looked at Emma and gave her a big grin, "We're in the biggest and baddest."

Emma gave him a sleepy return grin and two thumbs up.

Donna-Lou leaned forward, "Well, I sure hope you know where you're going, cause, like Chet here, I'm lost."

Chet nodded as he looked at their surroundings again, "She's right. I've never been up in this area."

Corry set his chin on the back Rory's seat, "So...if we don't know where we are...how do we get to Cherokee Ridge?"

"Some treasure hunters you guys are." Rory pointed to the GPS console screen, "We have a navigation system, don't we?"

Raising an eyebrow, Chet said slowly, Okay. But...?"

Rory shook his head, "Corry? You have that topographical map back there, right?"

"Yeah?"

"Can you get it?"

Corry scrambled around in his seat to look into the storage area behind the back seat. All their items were sitting on top of the fold-down seat. He grabbed the rolled-up map and turned back around, holding it up, "Okay, I got it. Now what?"

Rory pointed to the GPS console, "Can you and Chet figure out where we are using the GPS and the map coordinates?"

Corry and Chet looked at each other for a moment and then Chet reached for the map, "I guess we can try. Right?"

Shrugging, Corry stood on the back seat and leaned over and watched as Chet unrolled the topographical map.

Emma squeezed her way up beside Corry.

Rory sat waiting for five minutes as Corry and Chet discussed where they were and how to use the navigation system.

Chet finally said, "Okay. I *think* we have it figured out. I'm not sure how to set the system but...."

Rory hit the power button and his window rolled back up, "Just do your best. I'll concentrate on the driving, so we don't get stuck, and you guys keep me heading in the right direction. Sound good?"

"Sounds good," Chet said as he looked at Corry and Emma, who both looked eager to get going.

Rory pulled his Baby Eagle and placed it on the dashboard in front of him, "And let's keep an eye open for anybody suspicious as well. Everybody ready?"

Chet scrambled to get his Glock 19 out and placed it on the dashboard in front of him, "Ready."

Donna-Lou picked up her weapon from where it was at her feet and placed it into the pocket at the back of Chet's seat. She glanced through her window nervously, "Okay. I'm ready...I guess."

Rory nodded, "Okay. Let's go." He put the Range Rover in gear, applied gas and steered slowly off the road. The wheels bumped their way over several rocks as he drove between two bushy pine trees and headed up a slight incline of grass.

Corry and Emma were already discussing the treasure signs they should look for.

Chapter 34

SEVERAL HOURS LATER, after weaving across fields, between trees and around rocks and bogs, they approached the eastern side of Cherokee Ridge. Rory pulled to a stop just inside a clearing. Undulating, forested hills lay ahead of them in the sunshine. He glanced at Chet, "How are we doing? We should be getting close."

Chet stirred in his seat. The topographical map was resting on his lap and he brought it up to look at it.

Corry leaned over the seat, looking at the map. He and Chet discussed it, using the GPS and the map coordinates to orient themselves.

Finally, Chet shifted around in his seat, looking at their surroundings. Then he pointed a little to the left of the Range Rover, "We should swing a little more south that way, so we can skirt the high ground."

Corry nodded, "Yep. We should do that. And once we get on the other side of that hill, we should at the place where the signs are at the top right side of our map."

Rory looked at him, teasing, "Should?"

Corry shrugged and then grinned.

Donna-Lou leaned forward, putting a cap back on the bottle of water she was drinking, "How much farther do we have to go to find the area for the missing signs?"

Corry gave her a serious look, "Oh. we still have a looooong way to go yet, mom."

Chet turned in his seat, "Yeah. This map extends–"

Crack!

The rifle shot was followed by a metallic ping.

Donna-Lou screamed. So did little Emma.

Rory floored the gas pedal.

Crack!

Chet yelled as he looked around frantically, "Who's shooting at us?"

The tires on the Range Rover tore into the grass, kicking dirt and grass out in a rooster tail as Rory steered towards the trees on the right. The vehicle fishtailed. "Everybody down!" he yelled as he let up on the gas to control the skid.

Crack!

Another metallic ping.

As the Range Rover straightened out, Rory hit the gas again and the tires ripped through the grass and dirt before it gained traction and darted between two large trees.

Crack!

Bark exploded off the tree on their left.

The Range Rover dipped into a depression and Rory steered to the left to keep the slight incline on their left between them and the shooter. The vehicle bounced up and down as Rory drove over rocks and fallen tree limbs.

The Glock19 on the dashboard in front of Chet bounced up and down with the jostling of the vehicle and Chet reached for it. He fell back into his seat twice before he was able to snag it. Holding onto his seat with one hand, Chet held the Glock19 with his right and kept a watch as best as he could on all sides.

Rory's Eagle was bouncing up and down as well and he steered with his left as he reached for it with his right. It bounced off his fingers. Rory slapped it down with his hand and dragged it off the dashboard. He slipped it gun-barrel-down into a cup holder in the center console. "We're going to come out of this low spot in a minute," Rory said. "Chet, keep an eye out. Everybody else stay down. Got it?"

There were murmured responses all around and everyone in the back seat got lower.

Rory slowed the Range Rover, steered to the right and floored it up a smooth incline. "Here we go." The vehicle climbed the slight hill eagerly and then shot over the ridge into another stand of trees.

Crack!

Another scream came from little Emma.

Rory hit the gas hard and the Range Rover soared down the other side of the hill and across an open clearing. Tree branches began whipping the side of the vehicle as Rory pushed it through a tight stand of pine trees. He slowed down and began to weave back and forth, driving the Range Rover through a dense grove of trees, branches slapping and scraping at the sides, "Everybody okay?"

"I think so," Chet said as he turned to look into the back seat.

"Yeah, I think we're okay," Donna-Lou said as she looked at the kids.

Emma nodded but she was crying.

Corry put his arms around her as she leaned against him, "You did real good Emma," he said.

Rory braked to a crawl and steered around a large boulder, "Did anyone see who was shooting at us? Anyone see anything?"

"It was a man on a horse," Corry said, "I saw him on a rise–"

"A horse? Are you sure?" asked his mother.

Corry nodded vigorously, "Yep, positive."

"Does that make sense?" Rory asked Chet in a low voice.

Chet gave a slight nod of his head, "I used to see that from time to time when I was a kid. Men with rifles on horseback." He chewed on his lower lip for a moment, "Remember what I told you when we were back at Martha's Diner? About tourists who were treasure hunting around here and claimed they was run off by men on horseback?"

Rory glanced over at Chet and nodded, "Yeah, I remember." He shrugged, "I guess it does make sense. It's an easy way to travel through this terrain, keeping an eye on people who get too close to something."

Chet nodded his head thoughtfully, "I always thought it was just people making up stories to impress their friends or something. But actually shooting at people...?"

Rory steered around a fallen tree and then pulled to a stop.

"What's wrong?" Donna-Lou asked as she sat forward. "Did you see someone?"

"No," Rory said as he opened his door, "I just want to see what they hit. You could hear the pings and I hope it's nothing vital. Everyone keep an eye peeled while I check."

Donna-Lou pulled the Glock19 from the pouch on the back of Chet's seat and turned to watch out the back window.

Chet sat up straighter as he gripped his weapon and watched the front and sides.

Rory left his door open and slid low towards the front of the Range Rover. He found a bullet hole on the front fender. It was just above the tire and angled slightly downward. "Bullet hole in the front fender. Nothing vital hit," he said as he slipped back past the open door. He slid back along the side of the vehicle, looking for another bullet hole.

"See anything?" Chet asked Donna-Lou in a low voice.

Donna-Lou just shook her head no as she maintained vigilance.

Rory slipped low to the back edge of the Range Rover and found another hole in the fender. It was exploded out so it was an exit hole. He moved along the back and found a bullet hole in the rear door. It had gone through at an angle. A bullet hole in the fender on the far side caught his eye. Three shots had hit them. He moved low back towards the driver's side and then crouched beside the open door, "Looks like they were trying to take out the tires. I'll double check them to make sure we're okay."

Donna-Lou leaned over to Emma, "See? They weren't aiming at us–"

Crack!

A bullet passed through the back window, sending fragments of glass over the back seat and penetrating out through the front windshield.

Donna-Lou screamed and threw herself on the two kids.

Chet slid down on his seat, weapon up, "Rory...?"

Rory jumped quickly into the driver's seat and put the vehicle in gear. He pulled the door shut and slumped down in his seat as he floored the gas pedal. The tires spun in the dirt and then grabbed, vaulting them forward, Rory steered hard right, driving between two large trees and across a clearing.

Crack!

There was a ping off the back bumper.

Chet hit the down button on his window and struggled to turn his body to the right, looking back behind them as Rory began weaving through trees again. Chet switched the Glock19 to his left and got his arm out the open window. He looked back and fired twice "That might make him think twice."

Rory kept the pedal down, sitting up a little higher in the seat to watch for big rocks. They couldn't afford to get stuck on top of one–

Crack!

A bullet pinged off the right front fender.

Rory steered left and plunged into another stand of trees, looking for any kind of cover, "That one seemed to come from a different direction."

Chet swung around in his seat, looking off to the left, "I don't see anyone. There's too many damn trees." Then he gestured with the gun, "Wait...there's–"

Crack!

Another ping sounded off the back bumper.

Chet struggled to turn back to his right. He stuck the Glock out the window, aiming towards the back again and fired twice more. Then he glanced towards Rory, "I just saw a man on a horse back there just like Corry said. I *think* he's starting to fall back behind us." A moment later, he said, "But I saw one on your side through the trees. There's two of 'em."

Rory cursed under his breath, "Two? Are you sure?"

"Yeah. Pretty sure."

Shaking his head, Rory considered his next move. Then he cursed again and slowed the vehicle to a crawl.

"A-are you sure you should be going slower?" Chet asked, his eyes filled with concern.

"I've got no choice," Rory said as he shifted higher in his seat to look at the ground ahead.

Chet looked ahead of the vehicle, "Oh, crap." Dead ahead were several thick, fallen trees crisscrossed over their path.

Rory looked left and right quickly and then swore again.

"The ground looks wet and soft on this side," Chet told him.

"Yeah, I can see that. Okay. We've got no choice. Let's see what this baby can do. Hold on."

Chet grabbed the dashboard with his free hand and then glanced behind them. Everyone was quiet and on edge as the vehicle climbed higher, then bumped and rocked as it moved over the wooden obstacles. A few moments later, the vehicle tipped forward slowly as Rory carefully worked to bring Range Rover safely back down on the far side. As soon as the back tires hit the ground with a jolt, he floored the gas. Grass, damp earth, leaves and twigs were spit out behind the vehicle. The engine growled as he maintained his speed, controlling a fish-tail as the vehicle eagerly climbed the side of a hill. Reaching the top, the vehicle suddenly soared into the air. There were gasps and squeals of surprise from the passengers and then grunts as the Range Rover hit the ground hard on the down-slope of a gully. The big vehicle skidded sideways twenty feet, leaving huge gouges into the soft earth before Rory straightened it out and then turned left. He drove along the bottom of the gully for a few moments before turning right again. A thick stand of trees forced him to the right and they ended up driving along the side of a hill, the Range Rover tilted dangerously to the left.

Everyone struggled to stay upright as Rory concentrated to keep them from sliding sideways.

"Crap!" Chet said

"Sorry. I'm doing the best I can," Rory said as he fought with the steering wheel.

"No, it's not that," Chet said. "I know what they're doing." He banged his fist against the seat and cursed.

The ground started to level out and Rory floored it. A moment later they were heading down another hill and he glanced at Chet, "What do you mean you know what they're doing?"

"They're herding us to the Money River."

"And...?"

"There's no way across without a boat," Chet said. "We'll be trapped."

Chapter 35

RORY HELD ONTO the steering wheel tightly, focusing intently on the terrain ahead as he drove down the hill. He considered what Chet had said and pulled himself upright, "Are you *sure* there's no way across this Money River?"

"Positive," Chet said. "There's no ford, no low spot, no shallows. And it's probably too wide for *me* to swim across, let alone the kids."

Rory gave it some thought. Okay. So how about a bridge? There has to be one close by?"

Shaking his head Chet said, "No. You got to drive north to take the bridge. And that's maybe...I don't know...maybe 25 miles away? And once we head that way, we'll be in the open."

Cursing, Rory banged his fist on the steering wheel.

Donna-Lou sat up in the back seat, "But we have to do something. We can't just wait for them to catch up."

Chet went to say something and instead ran his hand through his hair. He had no answer.

Rory slowed to go around a line of low bushes, then accelerated up over another rise, half expecting another rifle shot. It didn't come and he skirted several large trees and then drove down into another low gully. He turned to the left and rode the bottom of the gully, using it as a shelter from the riders for ten minutes before it became too rough. He turned right and over the brow again and along another ridge, keeping a dense line of trees on their right between them and where the horsemen should be. An idea came to him, "Corry, you mentioned some of the treasure signs were removed during construction of a dam in 1880 or so?"

Corry was still holding Emma and he nodded, "Uh, huh. It was for a sawmill, I think."

"Do you know if the dam is still there?"

Corry shrugged, "I never got up that far. I was going to but they took me before I did."

Chet looked across at Rory, "What are you thinking?"

Rory was quiet for a moment, thinking. Then he asked Chet, "Do you think you and Corry could use the topographical map and the GPS to figure out the approximate spot where they put the dam on the river. And then get us there from here?"

Chet held up the rolled up map and looked over the seat at Corry, "I guess we can try, right?"

Corry nodded, "Yep." He Leaned over the front seat as Chet unrolled the map again and went to work. Ten minutes later, Chet looked at Rory, "Okay. We can't be 100% sure but...."

"Well, I'm 100% sure I don't have a plan, so give it to me," Rory said.

Chet nodded and pointed off to his side, "We got turned around a bit with that chase and we'll have to angle back that way. It will put us closer to where I think those horsemen are, but we'll hit the river in the area where it should be...emphasis on *should*."

Rory gave it some thought. Finally, he nodded, "Okay, good enough for me. I want everyone to hang on tight and stay low. I'm going to drive as fast as I can, but we'll probably be a nice target for their rifles before we can get far enough away."

"Hopefully, they don't have a vehicle to chase us," Chet said.

The silence from the others said they were hoping the same thing.

Rory took a deep breath to prepare himself and then said, "Okay. Hold onto your false teeth Emma."

Emma laughed, "I don't have false teeth, silly."

Rory slowly pressed down on the gas pedal. The Range Rover picked up speed. Rory watched for a break in the tree line on the right that they could pass through. It took several minutes before he spotted a break coming up. Applying more gas, he steered in a half circle to the left, then floored it as he aimed the hood up the slight incline towards the trees. The Range Rover's 510 horse-power supercharged engine growled as they shot into the gap, the trees becoming a green blur on both sides of the big vehicle as their speed increased. Minutes later, they emerged from the trees and bounced into the open.

"Rider on the right," Chet yelled as he bounced up and down in his seat.

Rory steered hard left and the big vehicle fish-tailed. Rory didn't let up on the gas though. Slowing or stopping would make them an easy target. Instead, he wrestled with the steering wheel, bringing the 7000 lbs. back under control.

Crack!

"I don't think he hit us," Chet yelled. He lowered his window and turned in his seat, firing a left-handed shot. Bouncing up and down, Chet fired another shot. He nodded to himself, yelling, "That one made him pull up."

The Range Rover began vibrating as Rory kept his speed up over the uneven ground littered with rocks, roots, and twigs. There were a few screams of surprise as they slid sideways for a moment as Rory steered around a large boulder. He straightened the bug vehicle out and accelerated again.

Crack!

Chet looked over at Rory, "That shot sounded further away."

Rory nodded as he concentrated on the terrain ahead. The shaking lessened as he drove across a grassy field. He looked up in the rear-view mirror and noticed Corry's head looking at the side window. "Keep your head down, Corry, we're still in the open," he warned.

Emma's arms reached up and pulled Corry back.

A boggy area appeared ahead and Rory had to steer to the left to go around. He slowed to make sure he didn't make a mistake and put the tires on soft ground where they could get stuck. He held his breath, expecting a rifle shot. But nothing came. Finally skirting the area, Rory floored the gas again and shot across the undulating field on the other side. One hour later, the Range Rover crested a hill and Rory slid to a stop.

Donna-Lou was up quickly in the back seat, looking around, "What's wrong?" The kids were up and beside her, looking around as well.

Rory's voice was quiet as he looked ahead, "Well, Chet and Corry got us to the right spot...."

Through the front windshield, everyone could see the Money River, stretching across the horizon in a wide ribbon of blue below the hill. And straddling 300 yards across the river was a weather-beaten structure.

"Is that thing made of wood?" Donna-Lou asked in a low voice.

"It is," Rory said. "It's what's called a flat plank dam. That 45-degree slope on the left side, where the water is flowing over, that's made from flat boards."

Chet sat up straighter, "It's wide...but...it's full of holes...."

"It's a freakin' 1880 *wooden* dam! With a whole bunch of boards broken away? That's where you want us to cross?" Donna-Lou shook her head forcefully, "No. No way. We can't go across that."

Corry looked at her, "What do we do then, mom? If those men with the rifles catch up to us...."

Chapter 36

RORY DROVE DOWN the hillside with caution, riding over or around small logs and boulders and avoiding any depression that looked too deep, conscious that the least slip-up could hang them up and leave them vulnerable to the pursuing riders. Finally reaching level ground, Rory accelerated, heading towards the edge of the river. The area to the left of the old wooden dam was littered with traces of gravel and the decayed remnants of timbers and planks. The low remains of a wooden foundation were the only evidence of a long-gone and forgotten building.

Corry sat forward and pointed at the foundation, "That's where the old sawmill was, I bet."

"I think you're right," Chet agreed. "Boy, I wish we would have made it up this far when I was a kid. Would have been great to explore up here."

Rory turned left, moving them closer to the bank of the river and the dam. A moment later he stopped and put the Range Rover in park. The upper platform of the dam was thirty feet wide and it was very apparent there were a large number of boards missing in spots as the dam spanned across the river. In addition, a large number of the old boards were twisted and several of them looked rotten. The square timber beams that braced the upper platform were cracked and warped as well. Water flowed freely under the upper platform and down over the angled flat planks of the water chute, plunging far below to a series of rapids. The roar of the water was steady, loud and ominous.

"I thought a dam stopped the water?" Emma said. "How come this one doesn't?"

"I'm not positive," Rory said, "but I think they had boards attached to those square beams that formed the wall under the upper part at one time. That would hold the water back. And it looks like the wall was angled so the water would be pushed this way through an opening to run a waterwheel for the sawmill."

Emma nodded as she leaned over the back of Rory's seat. "So where are all those boards now?"

"Long gone," Rory answered.

"And long gone is *exactly* what will happen to anyone trying to drive across that rickety thing," Donna-Lou said.

No one contradicted her.

Chet looked over the seat at her, "But what else can we do? Those riders are bound to catch up before long—"

"Why don't we just follow the river north?" Or head south into town?" Donna-Lou asked. "Wouldn't that make more sense than this?"

"I'm sure those riders chasing us will be thinking the same thing," Chet said.

Donna-Lou blew out a hard, frustrated breath. She knew he was right.

Rory nodded as he looked at the situation, "I know how you feel. But we have no choice. And we're going to have to act fast. They can't be far behind us." He contemplated the river and the dam for a few moments and then he said, "Tell you what, Chet.

Why don't you and Donna-Lou take the kids and walk across? That should be safer. I'll drive across after–"

"Why don't we all just walk across?" Donna-Lou said in alarm. "Why risk your life for a stupid truck–"

"Because we need it to keep ahead of the KGC," Rory said. "They're on horseback and may even have vehicles of their own. They tried to put their bullets into the tires back there to stop us. They want the treasure and we have the information. Or should I say...we have *someone* they might feel might still have the information...."

Donna-Lou glanced at her son.

"They won't just give up because we're on the other side of the river," Rory added.

Donna-Lou grimaced with worry as she looked at the kids. She was torn between staying and having to confront members of an organization that had already kidnapped her son and having to take two kids across a rickety dam.

"But how do we find the treasure signs if we cross the river?" Corry asked. "They're all on this side."

"We can worry about that later," Rory said. "We need to stay alive and out of their hands so we can find it."

Corry looked disappointed, "I guess so..."

"Don't worry, we'll find them," Emma said to Corry.

Nodded reluctantly, Corry hung his head.

"Why don't we grab all the treasure stuff and get going?" Chet said as he looked back over his seat.

"Yeah. I guess we should go, mom," Corry said. He turned and reached into the back storage area for the items.

Donna-Lou's nodded her head with little enthusiasm. But within moments they were all standing in the warm sun at the edge of the dam's upper platform. The sound of the roaring water was louder and even more ominous.

Chet and Donna-Lou each placed their Glock19 handguns in the back of their jeans, ready to pull them and fight if necessary.

As they were preparing, and without a second thought, Corry was the first one to set step onto the upper platform, where he began bouncing on his feet to test it.

Donna-Lou reached for her son, "Careful–!"

"It's okay, mom," Corry said and he was beyond her grasp in a heartbeat. But twenty feet across the old upper platform he came to an abrupt stop.

Donna-Lou recognized the tension in her son's body language and knew something was wrong. Ignoring her own safety now, she bounded up onto the old wooden dam and headed for her son, "Corry? What's wrong?"

"M-my foot...went through," Corry said. He stood there frozen, with his foot sunk through a rotten board to his ankle.

Chet hitched up his pants, jumped onto the old boards and got there just as Donna-Lou grabbed her son's arm. "You hold on to him tight," he said, "and I'll see what I can do." He bent down slowly, examining the situation. Then he put his hands around Corry's ankle, "You just hit a rotten spot. Just pull it up carefully, so you don't get any splinters."

"O-okay, "Corry said.

Emma was right there as well, "Can I help–?"

Donna-Lou grabbed her arm quickly, "Be careful you don't go through, sweetie."

"S-sorry," Emma said as she stepped back.

With Chet's guidance, Corry pulled his foot up slowly, freeing it from the jagged edges of the old board. He let his breath out once he set foot on solid wood again.

Chet stood up and pointed out spots ahead, "Okay, everyone. Just avoid those wet looking spots as you go across and we should be okay."

Corry nodded.

Emma moved up to Corry and took his hand, "We can do it together. Okay?"

Corry nodded his okay and they began picking their way across the old dam.

Donna-Lou started walking behind them, whispering harshly to Chet as she passed him, "Just avoid the wet spots and we *should* be okay? And how exactly is Rory going to *drive* across if we can fall through just walking on it?"

Chet opened his mouth to reply and then grimaced. He glanced back at Rory, standing beside the Range Rover and wondered the same thing himself. Then he took a deep breath and turned back to the task at hand, getting Donna-Lou and the kids safely across first. He moved fast, avoiding those wet spots and soon caught up with the others, keeping an eye on everyone. There was no doubt the slightest misstep could plunge someone into the deep, fast-moving river and then tumbling them over the rapids to their death.

Back on the bank, Rory kept one anxious eye on their progress and one constantly looking behind him for any sight of the KGC riders. His Baby Eagle lay on top of the Range Rover, ready for battle if danger presented itself.

Two hundred yards across the old dam, Donna-Lou yelped as her foot went through a board. Sections of it fell away, tumbling into the river below and creating a larger opening.

Chet caught her arm just before she went down through the large gap created in the platform. She swung around and gratefully wrapped her arms around Chet's neck, "Thank you. I thought...."

"It's okay, I've got you," Chet whispered.

Corry turned and looked back, "Mom...?"

Donna-Lou released Chet and cleared her throat, nodding, "I'm...I'm fine, Corry." She turned, "Just keep going." But she was shaking and kept Chet close to her the rest of the way across.

As soon as they stepped onto the far shore, Chet turned and waved at Rory.

Opening the door to the Range Rover, Rory pulled his gun off the roof and slid in behind the steering wheel. He lowered all four windows for a quick escape, in case he went into the river, and slowly drove to the edge of the wooden dam, where he stopped. Taking a deep breath, Rory had arrived at the moment of truth. Could he really make it across? Putting the Range Rover in gear, he gently applied gas and put the front wheels onto the old wood. So far so good. He kept going. But once all four wheels were on, the dam swayed, the creaking and groaning very evident above the roar of the water.

Rory stopped. He waited. The swaying and the ominous sounds of imminent collapse stopped. The only noise remaining was the call of the roaring water.

Rory pressed down on the accelerator gently and began the journey across the upper platform of the 1880 wooden dam. There were creaks and groans of protest from the old wood as the immense weight of the vehicle passed over them. A gap in the planks appeared ahead and Rory steered to the left. The platform swayed and tilted slightly.

Rory stopped. The sway stayed but the platform didn't fall over. That was good. And despite the gap, he had all thirty feet of platform width to work with.

Applying the gas again softly, Rory leaned his head against the window frame, watching intently as he steered slowly around the gap, then steered back towards the center. The platform leveled out, then began tilting the other way. Rory quickly steered to the left to compensate. The platform again leveled out but began to sag. Rory gave it some gas and moved faster away from the sag and the platform came back to level.

But one hundred yards across, the swaying and tilting to the left returned. Rory swung gently to the right and almost went too far as the tilt the other way was more pronounced. The wood groaned heavily. Gripping the steering wheel like his life depended on it, and it did, Rory rolled the big vehicle back the other way, far enough to offset the right tilt. The boards moaned as the platform began tilting to the left and Rory took the vehicle to the right again. From that point on, he just kept weaving back and forth enough to keep the platform level.

But with just under one hundred yards to go, the upper dam platform not only tilted but began to vibrate. Rory's felt his heart leap into his throat as he compensated for the tilt by swinging the vehicle to the left, to try and bring the platform back level. It worked. But the dam's old boards continually moaned and groaned, cracked and rattled as Rory advanced over the river.

After another fifty feet, the dam suddenly tilted to the left and the vehicle suddenly began sliding to the edge. Rory gunned the engine and steered right. The bridge leveled out but shuddered violently. Rory heard a loud snap of wood and then felt the right front wheel drop through a plank with a bang. He hit the brakes and stopped. The shuddering continued for a few seconds and Rory could hear the clatter of boards falling away to the river below. Then the shuddering stopped.

Rory realized he had been holding his breath in and he let it out. He flexed his hands, sore from gripping the steering wheel tightly, and then put the vehicle in reverse. Applying the gas gently, he slowly drove back to pull the wheel out of the hole in the dam and back onto a solid plank. Then he put the vehicle in park and got out to take a look. The supporting timbers under this section had fallen away, taking every board with it to leave a twenty-foot gap. The only structure left was the heavy framework on the front and back edges of the dam and three boards side-by-side, just off to the left. He could see the loud, water rushing below. If those three boards held, Rory could walk across, but the vehicle wasn't going anywhere.

Chapter 37

ON THE FAR RIVERBANK, Chet and Corry stood watching and waiting as Rory stood in front of the Range Rover, still fifty yards from safety. Donna-Lou stood further away, her hands on Emma's shoulders and keeping her away from the rushing waters. Donna-Lou became agitated as she watched Rory just standing there. She shielded her eyes from the sun, "What's he doing? Doesn't he know we have to get away from here? Like *now*?"

Chet didn't answer right away. He looked at the fast-moving river, carrying fallen planks over the rapids to the right, and he wondered what he could do. He put his hands on his head, "A whole pile of the boards across the dam just fell into the–"

"I told you! Look."

Chet glanced back at Donna-Lou and then across the river to where she was pointing.

The dark outline of a horse and rider was very evident against the skyline at the top of the hill.on the far side of the river. The horse and rider were turned sideways, the horse pawing at the ground, ready for the chase and the outline of a rifle resting across the shoulder of the rider casting doubt he was here to help.

Chet put his hands to his mouth and yelled, "Rory. Behind you. Run." He waved his arms over his head.

But Rory was looking down at the gap and didn't hear them above the sound of the roaring water below him.

Corry took a step and pointed across the river, as well, "Look. There's another rider over there."

The second outline was about one hundred yards to the left of the first. Horse and rider turned a circle on the top of the ridge, pawing up clouds of dust. A moment later, the rider urged the horse down the slope. The outline of his rifle, resting butt end on the back of the horse as he rode, was very evident and menacing.

Corry tugged at Chet's sleeve in alarm, "They'll catch him, Chet. He has to hurry or they'll catch him. Or...or shoot him."

Back behind them, Emma put her hands to her eyes and began crying.

Donna-Lou put her arms around the little girl and yelled at Rory, trying desperately to be heard above the roaring water. Suddenly, her heart stopped. A mother's fear filled her and she screamed, "Corry!"

Corry was running across the old wooden dam towards Rory, his arms pumping hard as he moved across the rickety boards without a second thought.

Letting go of Emma, Donna-Lou put her hands to her mouth and took a step, "No! Corry, come back. Corry, come back here *now*." Emma darted past her but Donna-Lou took two quick steps and snatched her back, "No. You can't go out there. It's too dangerous."

Emma fought to free herself, "But Corry needs my help. I *have* to go."

Hands on his head, Chet twisted back and forth in agony, cursing as he watched Corry running across the aged structure. It had been dicey enough when they had moved slowly. But running headlong across there? He stopped moving when he saw Corry stop in his tracks, bend over, pick up the end a twenty-four foot long, loose board and then struggle to try and carry it. But the thick board was heavy and he had to turn and drag it towards the gap. It was then that Chet realized the kid had a plan. A plan that might work. He looked back at Donna-Lou and hitched up his pants, "You two stay here. I'm going to help."

Donna-Lou yelled no but Chet was already running for the wooden dam.

RORY COULDN'T SEE ANY way to get the Range Rover across. He took a deep breath and let it out in frustration. Time to go – he heard a faint yell above the sound of the water below and he looked up. Across the gap, Corry was running awkwardly towards him. And right behind him was Chet. He realized they were both carrying long, loose planks, struggling to get any speed as they carried them across to the opening. He put his hands to his mouth, to call out to tell them not to bother–

Crack!

The ping off the roof of the vehicle made Rory duck. He crouched and looked back along the side of the vehicle. Two riders! They were about one hundred yards apart and kicking up clouds of dust as they galloped towards the far end of the dam.

Crack! Crack!

Rory ducked again but realized those were shots from a handgun and not rifle shots. And they had come from behind him. He whirled around, fearfully expecting to see more riders.

Donna-Lou had her Glock19 in both hands, aiming across the river at the riders. She pulled the trigger again and again.

Crack! Crack!

Rory turned back and looked in the direction of the riders. They had turned their horses quickly and were heading back to the top of the ridge.

Behind him, Chet yelled, his voice still faint over the roar of the river, "Rory, get in and drive."

Rory spun back on his heels.

Corry and Chet were kneeling on the old dam boards and working to extend a long wooden board across the gap towards the Range Rover. There was another loose board lying beside them. He realized what they were doing. They were estimating the width of the Range Rover and setting the board in place opposite the three boards that were left. They were creating a ramp for the tires that he could drive across. Getting the first board in place across the gap, Corry and Chet began pushing the second board across the gap, next to the first.

Rory took in a deep breath and let it out slowly. *Maybe* he could drive across. But there was only one way to find out. He climbed back into the Range Rover and backed up slowly, the old dam creaking in agony. Back far enough now, Rory cranked the wheel, the boards under the tires protesting, and he drove ten feet to the left and then straightened the big vehicle out.

As Corry used hand signals to help him position the tires, Chet worked to slide the two boards a little closer to the other three. A moment later, Corry began waving him forward.

Rory did his best to stay calm. It was all up to them–

Chet jumped up into his view and put up his hand to stop.

Rory applied the brakes and rocked forward from the force.

Corry and Chet disappeared for a brief moment to reposition the boards. Then they popped up again, waving him forward.

Rory held his breath as he applied the gas slowly. He felt the front tires bump slightly as they climbed on top of the boards. Inching forward, he felt the back wheels bump up. He was now on the boards. Which meant he was on the gap and *over* the water below.

He was waved forward again.

Rory applied the gas slowly, watching Corry and Chet intently for the slightest sign he was not straight enough. He could hear the rushing waters of the river below. The slightest mistake would put him at the bottom.

The shuddering of the platform started again. The boards under the tires began to bend under the weight of the Range Rover, threatening to crack in the middle and send vehicle and driver into the river.

Clenching his jaw, Rory maintained his focus, shutting out the sounds of the old wood groaning and the rushing water calling from below. He couldn't afford any distractions.

Crack! Ping.

Rory swore. The riders back on the ridge held the range, accuracy and power advantage with their rifles. Rory had no choice. He gunned the engine and pushed the vehicle across the gap. The front tires bumped down and then the back wheels. He slowed just enough to let Corry and Chet jump in.

Chet yelled even before the pulled the door shut, "Hurry, hurry, we gotta go."

Rory gunned the engine, rolling fast across the clattering boards.

"You two are crazy," Rory yelled with a big smile on his face.

"I almost peed myself," Corry said from the back seat.

Chet bounced in the passenger seat and looked back, "Almost? I did."

Corry let out a big belly laugh.

Rory kept his speed up, the engine growling as they shot across the shuddering platform.

Crack!

Crack! Ping.

Chet swore and ducked down.

"Hurry, hurry, hurry," Corry yelled from the floor behind Chet's seat.

Planks and supporting beams fell away behind them, plunging into the river below.

The vehicle came off the old boards of the dam and hit the bank on the other side of the river with a thud.

Rory swish-tailed to a stop in the dirt.

Donna-Lou and Emma jumped in the back doors and were thrown against the seats as Rory accelerated away from the river and the armed riders on the other side.

"You better not do that again, young man," Donna-Lou yelled.

"But we had to do something, mom," Corry protested.

"You're my hero," Emma said to Corry.

Corry rolled his eyes.

"What about me?" Chet asked as he looked back over the car seat.

Donna-Lou shook her head, "Okay, you're *my* hero."

A big grin lit up Chet's face.

Then the grin was gone as the sound of a deafening rumble roared in pursuit the vehicle.

Chapter 38

RORY KEPT THE GAS PEDAL to the floor. The growl of the Range Rover's 510 horsepower, supercharged engine could barely be heard above the immense roar that felt like it was engulfing them from behind. The big vehicle fishtailed but Rory brought it back under control and the Range Rover bounced hard twice before it began climbing the steep hill and away from the river bank. At the top of the rise, Rory hit the brakes and slid to a sideways stop.

Everyone in the Range Rover turned to look back down at the river. Hundreds of broken boards and heavy timbers tumbled over the rapids.

Chet stretched to take a look, "The upper part of the dam is gone on this side. That's what that noise was."

The two riders appeared on the top of the ridge again on the far side of the river. The horses pawed the ground anxiously as the two riders surveyed the damage to the dam below.

"The loss of the dam will slow them down," Rory said, "but I have a feeling it won't be long before more of them are chasing us on this side."

"Maybe they'll have their horses swim across," Emma said.

Corry shook his head, "No, I think that's too far for them."

"Let's not wait around to find out," Rory reasoned. He took his foot off the brake and applied the gas as he steered to the right. The 7,000-pound vehicle moved over the ridge, out of sight of the riders, and then smoothly across a grass field as they headed south.

Donna-Lou sat back against the seat, pushing the hair back from her face, looking relieved, "What are we going to do now?"

Rory didn't answer right away. "That's a good question," he said after a few moments of thinking. "I'm open to suggestions. I'm not sure we can go back to Golden right now. I guess we could go to Atlanta and regroup. Come back at another time."

Corry leaned forward, "But what about the nuclear weapon they want to buy?"

That sober thought made everyone go quiet. They all knew the consequences if the Knights of the Golden Circle found the treasure first. But what else could they do right now? Rather than steer into the heavy forest ahead, Rory steered to the right and stayed in the open, hoping to put as much distance between them and the pursuing riders. The terrain became more rugged as Rory steered to the Southwest but the Range Rover handled it easily. It smoothly climbed a hill, skirting the forest as it bounced over rocks and fallen branches.

Corry suddenly began yelling, "Stop, stop, stop."

Rory slammed on the brakes and they shuddered to a stop.

Donna-Lou shot forward from her seat, putting her hands on her son in alarm, "What's wrong, Corry? What's wrong?"

But Corry didn't tell her. Instead, he turned in his seat, his hand windmilling frantically as he yelled, "Back up, back up, back up."

Rory looked to the back, put the big vehicle in reverse and began to back up. He glanced at Chet, wondering what had Corry so animated.

Chet shrugged and looked back, "What's wrong, Corry? What is it?"

Corry didn't say anything. His hand just continued to wind-mill, urging Rory to continue backing up. Then he put his hand up, "Stop, stop, stop!"

Rory slammed the brakes on and the big Range Rover slid to a stop on the grass.

The vehicle had barely come to a stop before Corry was out the back door and running towards the trees on the left.

Emma jumped out behind him, running hard through the half-foot of grass.

"Corry! Emma!" Donna-Lou exclaimed. She climbed across the seat, jumped out the open door and ran after the kids.

Rory put the car in park and jumped out, shielding his eyes from the sun as he watched the kids run across the grass, chased frantically by Donna-Lou.

Jumping out, Chet ran to the end of the vehicle and stood there, "What in the world is wrong with him?"

"I have no idea. But he sure is in a hurry."

As soon as Chet took off at a run, Rory did the same.

Corry didn't stop running until he reached a large, southern red oak tree. He ran his hand over the old, rough bark.

Emma and Donna-Lou stopped a couple of feet away from the tree, looking at Corry. Chet and Rory stopped just behind them and they all exchanged glances, still unsure what this was all about.

A moment later, Chet stepped forward and looked at the section of bark that Corry was concentrating on, "What did you find?"

Pumping his fist, Corry said, "Yeah. It's a treasure sign."

Carved into the bark was the image of an upside down cross.

Chet placed his hand almost reverentially on the carving, "He's right. I've heard of this one...but I've never seen one before."

Emma ran up and looked at Corry, her eyes shining with excitement, "What does this sign mean, Corry? Huh? What does it mean?"

Corry ran his hands over the carving, "It's a direction sign. It means, if we go ahead in the direction the top of the cross points to, that means back towards the river, we'll find another sign." Corry stepped back and took a look along the tree line to the south and then turned in a circle, "We'll probably find other signs around here somewhere, too."

Donna-Lou crossed her arms at the mention of more signs, looking uncomfortable.

Rory looked at Chet, "Is he right about that?"

Chet nodded as he backed up a step, hitched up his pants and looked along the tree line himself, "He's right. Two or more signs usually converge on a point." Chet took a few more steps and then turned, put his hands in his pocket and looked like he was doing some serious thinking. A moment later, he shook his head softly, "Although, I have to say, Corry...I've *never* heard *any-body* ever talk about treasure signs on this side of the river."

Corry looked at Chet and shrugged, "Maybe nobody ever looked."

"Maybe," Chet conceded. "I know I never came on this side of the river."

"Me neither," Corry said. "But we are now."

Rory stepped between them, looking from Chet to Corry, "Are you two positive enough that these *are* treasure signs? Are you sure enough, that we take the time to look for the other signs—?"

Donna-Lou threw her hands in the air, "Oh come on, people. We have men chasing us, trying to kill us and we're going to stop and look for treasure signs?"

Corry held his hands out to her, "But we have to mom—"

Shooting him a stern look, Donna-Lou said, "No. We can get to safety and then *Rory and Chet* can come back."

"But mom—"

"I don't want you hurt. And I don't want Emma hurt," Donna-Lou added emphatically.

"And I don't want anybody hurt if they blow up a bomb," stated Corry with firmness.

Donna-Lou crossed her arms as she looked at her son. Then she looked at Chet for help.

Chet put his hands in his pockets and he shrugged, "Sometimes doing the right thing isn't always the easy thing."

Donna-Lou bit her lip and closed her eyes in frustration.

"Please, mom."

Donna-Lou blew a strand of hair away from her face and finally nodded.

Corry pumped his fist, "All right." He looked at Chet, "Let's go and see if we can figure out where this spot is on the topographical map. We can get the exact longitude and latitude for each sign from the GPS in the Range Rover. Right?"

Chet nodded and then looked at Donna-Lou as her son ran for the Range Rover.

Donna-Lou just gave a sharp gesture with her head and her voice was quiet, "Get going. You boys have work to do."

Chet looked like he wanted to say or do something but he just stood there awkwardly for a moment. Then he turned and followed Corry to the vehicle.

"Still gotta work on your man," Emma said.

Donna-Lou nodded, "Both the big one and the little one."

Rory shook his head, "This is getting too complicated for me."

Emma giggled.

Chapter 39

USING THE GPS SYSTEM and the topographical map, it didn't take long before Chet and Corry were able to mark the exact location of the cross carved into the bark of the tree. They also marked a line with the direction it was pointing in. Then everyone piled in, Rory put the Range Rover into gear and they began searching for additional signs. Rory drove slowly between the trees and everyone kept an eye out on the front, back and sides. The windows were down and the scent of pine mixed with the smell of the rich earth. Dry leaves crunched under the tires, songbirds serenaded their passage and chipmunks chattered, telling them they were trespassing on their domain. It took twenty minutes of slow, methodical driving in patterns back and forth before the treasure hunters found something.

It was Emma who yelled, "There's one."

Rory quickly pulled to a stop and everyone piled out.

"It's an arrow," Corry yelled back over his shoulder as he ran hard for an old, Red-Maple tree. His hand caressed the carving in the bark.

Chet stood back, looked at the sign and stuck his arm out, "It's pointing in that direction. And it looks like it's going to cross with the direction line of the other one we found."

Corry nodded eagerly, "You're right. Let's mark this one on the map and see if it does. Or where else it goes."

Chet agreed. Back at the Range Rover, he worked with Corry to mark the exact location of this new treasure sign on the topographical map. Chet drew a line across the map.

Emma jumped up and down in excitement, "It does cross the other one. It's almost like an X on a treasure map."

Rory looked at Chet and Corry, "Emma is right. Should we head for that spot where they intersect?"

Corry didn't hesitate and he shook his head no, "Nope. I think we should go look for another sign."

"I agree," Chet said. "Even though we're getting the exact longitude and latitude for each sign, the lines we're marking are still fairly approximate. The more signs we can find that converge on a spot, the more accurate an area we have to search."

"Okay, then lets all climb aboard and start looking again," Rory said.

IF WAS THIRTY MINUTES before another sign popped up.

And again it was Emma who yelled, "I see one. I got another. We just passed it."

Corry quickly looked to where she was pointing. "Yeah, I see it. And I think it means we have to go back," Corry said to Rory.

Rory stopped, reversed and drove backward.

"Stop," Emma yelled. She jumped out with Corry as soon as Rory applied the brakes. Together, they ran eagerly back to another Red-Maple tree.

Chet and Donna-Lou jumped out to join the kids with Rory not far behind.

Everyone spent a few minutes feeling the carving in the bark.

"That one looks like a backwards three," Donna-Lou murmured as her fingers followed the indentations.

"It is," Chet confirmed. "And Corry is right. It means we have to go back, we missed something back there."

Rory looked surprised, "I thought you just meant you wanted me to back up to the sign. You mean we really have to backtrack?"

"Yep," Corry said. "We missed a sign or signs back there somewhere."

"Okay," Rory said, "we can do that. Do you want to mark this one down first?"

Chet nodded his head, "We should. We can always start back here if we don't find something."

Corry and Chet marked the spot for the sign on the map then everyone climbed back into the Range Rover.

"Head back that way," Chet instructed as he jerked his thumb over his shoulder.

Rory nodded and he turned the vehicle in a circle around the Red-Maple and headed back through the trees. He went slower this time, threading his way through and around the trees. Everyone was quiet as they all intently focused on every possible mark in the bark on every tree they passed.

"I see one," Donna-Lou yelled after 10 minutes. She was looking out the window and towards the back of the vehicle.

Rory stopped and everyone turned, looking at where she was pointing.

"Where mom?" Corry asked as his head swiveled back and forth.

"I see it," Chet said and he was instantly out of the vehicle.

"Oh yeah, I see it too," Corry said finally. "Good eye, mom," he said as he sprang from the vehicle and ran for the tree.

Everyone else piled out of the vehicle and joined Chet and Corry as they examined the image carved into the bark of a large, old tree.

"That one is pointing back away from the river," Donna-Lou said. "We have to go back again?"

Corry looked at his mother, shaking his head with a big grin on his face.

"Why not?" Donna-Lou asked. "The arrow is pointing back that way–"

"That's what they *want* you to think," Corry said.

Chet looked at Donna-Lou and nodded his head, a smile on his face as well, "Remember the other arrow didn't have the tail like this one?

Donna-Lou looked at the sign for a moment and then nodded to Chet, "Okay...?"

"That means *this one* is a reverse sign. When you first go looking for treasure, the other kids who know how they work, they usually have a great time watching you going in the wrong direction."

"Mom. There are other ones, like the turtle one that's also a reverse sign," Corry said. "You just have to know these things."

"Even I know that one," Emma announced.

Donna-Lou looked at Rory, raising her eyebrows, "Did *you* know that?"

Rory shook his head, "Nope. Not a clue. Not...a...clue."

"So, I'm not the only one," Donna-Lou said and she stuck her tongue out at Emma.

Emma giggled.

Chet hitched up his pants, "Let's get this one marked on the map and see what we have." He and Corry determined the coordinates for the sign, placed it on the map and then they drew another line.

Donna-Lou was watching them work and she said, "All three signs cross and make a small triangle on the map."

Corry gave her a confident nod, "And *that* is the area we need to search for another sign."

Looking over at Rory, Donna-Lou gave him a playful smirk, "Another one I figured out."

Rory just held his hands out and shrugged, "I'm just the driver so I don't have to have a clue. Right, Emma?"

Emma put her hands to her mouth and giggled.

Chapter 40

CHET AND CORRY guided Rory as he drove through the forest and back towards the river. Everyone had their weapon out now and the tension was high as they kept a continual watch for the slightest sign of a rifle-carrying horseman or any other armed threat. It took several hours of weaving back and forth to cover the area of the forest contained within the triangle of the three converging lines, formed by the three treasure signs. There were a number of false sightings before something significant appeared.

"I see something dead ahead," Rory said as he pointed over the steering wheel. Everyone leaned forward, eager to see what he had spotted. Rory pulled to a stop twenty feet away from a huge maple tree.

"Wow," Corry said. He was out of the vehicle in a flash and ran for the tree, stopping dead in front of it.

Emma was out running hard right behind him and came to a stop on his left.

Chet ran but slower, struggling to keep his pants up so he wouldn't trip over his droopy pant legs. He stopped on Corry's right.

Rory and Donna-Lou met at the front of the vehicle and gave each other a shake of their head at the enthusiasm of their fellow treasure hunters.

"I know that one," Donna-Lou said as she walked up to stand behind her son. He was now tracing the sign in the heavy, rough bark with his fingers. She put her hands on her hips, "Okay. That's a turtle sign. Which means it's a reverse sign. We go in the opposite direction of the head."

"You got it, mom," Corry said proudly.

Chet put a hand on Corry's shoulder, "Notice something else about it, Corry?"

Corry nodded as he touched the head carved in the bark, "Yep." He looked up at Chet, "And *that's* why they can't find the treasure."

Chet gave him a return nod of affirmation.

Donna-Lou moved to the side of the others to get a better view, crossed her arms over her chest and cocked her head this way and that as she looked at the carving.

Rory moved up behind her, trying to get a better view as well and a better understanding of how the signs worked.

Glancing back at him, Donna-Lou gave a slight shrug and then looked at her son, "Okay. For us *rookie* treasure hunters, what do you mean *that's* why they can't find the treasure?"

Emma looked from Donna-Lou to Corry, giggling and tugging at his sleeve, "Go ahead, tell them."

Corry looked at his mother, pointing to the sign, "Do you notice how the head is broken in the center?"

Reaching out, Donna-Lou traced the carving's head, "It's not a complete circle, you mean?"

"Right. That means the treasure was *moved* by someone to a new location."

Donna-Lou considered that stunning revelation for a moment. Then she gestured in the direction of the river, "You mean someone actually moved the treasure over there...to another location?"

Corry nodded, "Yep."

She narrowed her eyes, thinking for a moment. Then she shook her head, "But I don't get it. Why would the Knights of the Golden Circle be guarding this entire area, running people off if it wasn't here anymore? Wouldn't they know that?"

Corry looked at Chet, unsure.

Chet only blinked his eyes. Then he said, "Maybe...maybe they're just guarding the signs?" He looked less than convinced, though.

Silence ensued as everyone gave that some thought. Finally, Rory shifted on his feet, scratched the stubble on his face and spoke, "Chet?"

Looking over his shoulder, Chet said, "Yeah?"

Chewing on his lower lip for another moment, Rory then said, "Remember the conversation you had with that guy with the rifle? When you were hiking up to the ridge?"

Chet nodded, "Yeah. Buster Connor." He glanced at Donna-Lou, "I told you about that when we was goin' down to Mississippi. Remember?"

Donna-Lou nodded, "Yeah, you said he was going to kill you."

Looking back at Rory, Chet nodded, "Yeah, what about it...?"

"What did he say about your family? About the killing? And the treasure?"

Looking down for a moment, Chet thought back, "He said...your family said there was too much killing. And...they were in charge of caring for the treasure and–" He looked up, "He said they were going to turn it over to the government. But...."

Rory nodded, "But they obviously didn't. Because the Knights of the Golden Circle are still looking for it. I could be wrong...but...." He glanced at the sign. "That sign says the treasure was moved. He looked at Corry and Emma, "And these two overheard the conversation about a feud, about someone wanting to move the treasure. About traitors who were killed...?"

Chet's face slowly showed the realization of what Rory was saying. He nodded his head slowly, "I bet you're right. And it was *my* family that was involved. That's why momma didn't want me looking for the treasure. My daddy and my granddaddy were not killed in an accident...or because they were looking for the treasure. *They* were the ones who moved it." He blinked his eyes for a moment and then looked at Donna-Lou, "Your granddaddy...and all the stuff you had in the attic...the slicker...."

Donna-Lou's hand went to her mouth, "Oh, my. My grandfather died just after yours. He...he must have been working with your family...."

Chet nodded solemnly.

Corry's eyes were big, "Really? He was one of them? The Knights of the Golden Circle? That's why we had that stuff in the trunk?"

Donna-Lou nodded her head softly, still having a hard time taking it all in, "It looks like it."

"Cool beans," Emma said. Then she turned serious, "But...if they moved the treasure, where did it go?"

"*That* is a good question," Rory said.

"Well, there is another clue," Chet said, his attention going back to the tree, "Do you see the sign under the turtle?"

"You mean the thick circle?" Donna-Lou asked. She stepped forward and traced the circle in the bark with her fingers, "What does this one tell us?"

Chet looked at her son, "Corry?"

Corry looked at the circle, running his fingers into the carving in the bark as well. After a moment he shrugged, "I should know this one...but...."

"What would it be if it was a circle with an X in it?" Chet prompted.

Corry answered instantly, "A mine."

"Okay. So what's this one, then?"

Looking at the sign again, Corry shook his head, "I'm...I'm not sure."

"This one is the sign for...a cave," revealed Chet.

Corry snapped his fingers, "Right, I forgot that one." He pointed at the turtle, "That one means they moved the treasure...and the circle tells us they moved it to a cave."

"Okay, then," Rory said. "If we follow in the direction opposite to where the head is pointing, we find the treasure?"

Chet and Corry looked at each other for a brief moment. Then both of them shook their heads no.

"Why not?

"Because it's pointing *away* from the other signs across the river," Corry answered. He looked at Chet, "Right?"

Chet nodded.

Rory and Donna-Lou looked at each, confused.

Chet hitched his pants up, "Okay. Keep in mind all the signs in an area work together. Remember how all the signs worked together over on the other side of the river, to show us which sign was the keystone?"

Rory nodded, "That's the one that lined up with the star on the flag, right?

Chet nodded in confirmation, "That's right. And the reason we came on this trip was to figure out exactly where the tree was that had the last sign on it."

"Right," Donna-Lou said, "we needed to find it to figure out where the guide was."

"Exactly. But these signs on the tree aren't pointing to the set of signs over there, so they don't fit in with them," Chet reasoned.

Corry looked around at the trees and then looked at Chet, "The turtle that's over the circle...telling us where the treasure is hidden...that's a reverse sign. That means there must be a complete set of signs on this side of the river that goes with it."

Chet nodded in agreement, "Someone moved the treasure and then created a whole new set of signs on this side. All we have to do is find them and—"

Donna-Lou interrupted him with an angry, concerned tone, "But we don't have the time to look for a whole new set of signs over here. Those riders and anyone else working with them will eventually come over here to find us and...." She didn't want to say it and then it erupted, "Make no mistake. It will be just like what happened to our *grandparents,* Chet. Those men will hunt us down. Those men will kill us."

"She's right, I'm afraid," admitted Rory.

Chet cursed. "Okay, you're right. But we probably just led them right to the signs that will help *them* find the treasure."

"And buy the bomb," Emma said in a quiet voice.

No one contradicted her.

"So," Chet said slowly, "what do we do?"

There was a long silence.

It was Corry who spoke up, "Maybe we should just set fire to the forest here and burn up all the signs. That will stop them, right?"

Rory, Donna-Lou, and Chet all looked at him with a resigned look on their faces. It was the only thing that made sense.

Chapter 41

RORY MASSAGED THE BACK OF HIS NECK, contemplating the possibility of setting fire to the Carolina woodland around them. Looking out through the trees, he wondered how far a fire would go, once they started it. Who would be in danger? The cheery songbirds, flitting through the trees, caught his attention and he looked up, wondering what it would be like for them if they had babies in the nests up there. He shook his head. It seemed unfair. Saving lives from an atomic bomb against–

"Hey. Look at this. Hey." The voice was faint, calling to them from farther away.

Everyone looked around. It was Emma. She had called to them, hands at her mouth, from nearly one hundred yards away.

Donna-Lou put a hand to her forehead, concern etched on her face, "How did she get over there?"

Seeing she had caught their attention, Emma turned and ran several feet to a tree and stood there examining it closely, running her hands along the bark.

Donna-Lou called out to her, "Emma. You shouldn't be so far away from us. Come back here."

But the little girl was too mesmerized by whatever she was looking at.

"I'll get her," Donna-Lou said and she took off at a jog. Moving over the grass, she called out to her again, "Emma. Remember the men on the horses, sweetie."

Corry looked at Chet and Rory and then was off at a run, followed by the two of them.

Emma never turned as Donna-Lou reached her. It was evident the little girl hadn't even heard the warnings from Donna-Lou; she was so preoccupied with what she had found.

Donna-Lou put a hand gently on her shoulder, "Emma, you have to be careful–"

Emma glanced at her and pointed at the tree, "I just followed the tail of the turkey back there and look–"

"Turtle," corrected Corry as he arrived beside her.

Emma made a face, "Okay, turtle. Anyway, I found this." She grinned at Corry.

Corry's eyebrows shot up as he put his hands on the carving in the bark.

Chet arrived a moment later, looking at the sign, leaning his head in closer.

Rory caught up and stopped just behind Chet, looking over his shoulder, "What is it–?"

Throwing his right fist in the air, Chet yelled, "Wahoo!"

Donna-Lou looked puzzled as she glanced at Rory, who only shrugged. She looked back at Chet and then at the sign, "Wahoo? Wahoo what, Chet Calhoun? What does that even mean?"

Chet hitched up his pants as he looked at her, his eyes filled with excitement "Don't you get it?" He pointed at the sign, "Look at it, Donna-Lou. Look at it."

Donna-Lou made a face, "Chet Calhoun, if I *got it*, I wouldn't be asking about it now would I?"

Corry turned to her, just as excited as Chet, his hands out and pleading with her to understand the thrill they were feeling, "Mom, that turtle, and the cave sign back there pointed *here*. Right here to *this* spot. And the rider on the horse on this sign is looking back across the river to the other signs. Don't you get it?"

Donna-Lou gave it a moment of serious thought. Then she looked at her son, "So...that means...this sign...and that turtle and the cave sign over there...*are* part of the signs over there? On the other side of the river, I mean?"

Corry gave her a big smile."You got it, mom. You got it." He held up his hand for a high-five.

Donna-Lou smiled and slapped her hand against his.

"And I found it," Emma said proudly, holding her hand up.

Donna-Lou slapped her hand in a high-five as well, laughing.

Emma turned and held her hand up to Corry.

Corry slapped her hand...and then gave her a big hug.

As he let her go, an excited Emma jumped and pumped her fist in the air, "Wahoo!"

Donna-Lou smiled and laughed. Then she turned deadly serious and put her hands on her hips, "Hold on. Are you telling me we have to go back on the other side of the river?" She waved her arms and said emphatically, "No, no, no. That's *not* going to happen. I am not taking my son back over there with those madmen looking to kill us."

Chet put his hands up to her, "Hold on, hold on–"

She folded her arms across her chest, "Chet Calhoun. Don't make me hurt you."

A sheepish grin crossed his face, "Just hear me out. Okay? Just hear me out."

Donna-Lou's jaw worked away as she stared at him but she didn't say anything.

Chet pointed to the sign on the tree, "Take a look at the sign that Emma just found. Take a good look at it."

Grudgingly, Donna-Lou looked at it. She shrugged, "Okay. I'm looking. It's like in our yard. A horse and a rider. Both looking ahead."

Nodding, Chet said, "Right. But...we also have *a star*. Just like the star across the river...?" His eyes were sparkling as he looked from person to person, wondering if they would get it.

Chapter 42

THE BIRDS AND SQUIRRELS sang and chattered as the group stood around, trying to figure out what Chet was talking about. There was a lot of head scratching until it finally hit Rory and he snapped his fingers, "I've got it. We just found *the guide*."

Chet grinned and hitched up his pants, "Yes, sir. Looks like we did." He looked at Donna-Lou, "And if this works out like I think it will, we may *not* have to go over there."

Donna-Lou shook her head softly, still not understanding what they were talking about. And then it dawned on and her eyes lit up, "The sign back there indicates all the signs on this side of the river work with all the ones on the other side." She looked at Emma and gave her a smile, "And the sign that Emma followed over here, led us right to the guide."

Emma beamed at her own involvement.

Chet nodded, smiling broadly himself.

Let's test out the theory," Rory said. "I'll go get the Range Rover and bring it here."

A few moments later, Rory drove up beside the tree.

Chet opened the door and reached in for the map before Rory had even stopped. Everyone crowded around as Corry and Chet placed the topographical map on the hood of the Range

Rover and added this latest sign from. Then they carefully placed the oilskin over top and added the photocopies of the other signs. Donna-Lou and Rory helped align the Confederate flag over the first star.

"Look," Corry said, "if we move the flag this way...this line of stars on the flag points right to where we just found the rider with the star. And this star fits over the top of the one here on the tree...."

"That's it!" Chet said.

Donna-Lou looked over what they had, "So...if we follow the seam...that's the direction there. It angles northwest and over Cherokee ridge on the other side of the river."

Corry nodded eagerly, "You got it, mom. So, according to the distance sign, that's the bird with the six feathers on it ...we have to go six...somethings...."

"Six somethings?" Donna-Lou asked. "What does that even mean?"

"Well," Chet said slowly, "it could be six miles. Or maybe some other old measurement, like chains, rods or sections that they used to use."

Rory pointed to the bottom of the topographical map, "Okay, the legend here on the bottom of this map gives us a scale for 5 miles." He looked at Emma, "Can you grab the pencil and the magic marker in the Range Rover?"

Emma scooted off and quickly returned.

Rory took the pencil and laid it on the scale. Then he used the magic marker to put a line on the pencil, "This gives us the length of five miles." Laying it on the slicker, he said, "So...six miles would put us about...here. Anyone know what's there?"

Donna-Lou shook her head no.

Chet rubbed his chin, "I've been up there a few times. There are a lot of trees up there but it's basically flat country. Hardly a place for a cave."

"Maybe it's buried?" Rory suggested.

Chet shook his head, "No, that would be a different sign." He looked at Corry, "Right?"

Corry nodded, "Right. Different sign."

"Maybe it's in the side of a hill, then?" Donna-Lou asked.

Chet ran his finger over the area and shook his head, "No. The elevations on the topographical map don't really show much in the way of any hills up there."

Emma poked her head between Chet and Donna-Lou, "What about the hat? Or the gun?"

Donna-Lou looked down at her, "What you mean, sweetie?"

"Well, we used all the stuff you got from your house, except the hat and the gun," observed Emma. She ran to the back door of the vehicle and retrieved the Confederate stag hat. She pointed to the emblem, "What about the eight? Maybe it's eight somethings."

Chet shook his head, "No, that insignia refers to the 8th Cavalry."

Rory took a step forward, "Maybe she has something."

"How do you figure?" Donna-Lou asked him.

Taking a moment to think, Rory finally said, "Just think about it. Pride in their past may have been the reason your grandfather put the hat and the gun in the trunk. But it could also be part of the clues to the treasure." He scratched his stubble again, "A serial number from the gun wouldn't make sense. But...."

Donna-Lou gave him a few slow nods, giving it some serious thought as well, "Everything else pertained to the hidden treasure cache. Maybe the hat does too. What do you think, Chet?"

Chet took the stag hat and looked at it, thinking.

Rory placed the pencil against the map again, "The problem is...even if we go 8 miles...we still have nothing of any significance."

"Add them together," Donna-Lou said quickly. "Try 14 miles."

Chet looked at her, "Why?"

"Cause it's the only thing that makes sense," Donna-Lou reasoned. "We only have two numbers to work with, so add them, multiply them, whatever it takes."

Rory used the pencil to estimate 14 miles along the line, "That puts us...right on the edge of this topographical region."

Chet looked closer at where Rory was pointing. He straightened up, "That's the edge of the Blue Ridge Mountains."

"That's where it is!" Corry said in excitement. "They moved the treasure to a cave in the Blue Ridge Mountains."

Everybody stood there leaning over the map looking at each other.

Chet looked at Rory and then Donna-Lou, "What do you think?"

Donna-Lou shrugged, "You guys are the treasure experts."

"It makes a lot of sense to me," Rory said. "All the clues seem to point to that conclusion." He looked at Corry, "What do you think?"

Corry nodded, "I think so, too. He looked proudly at Donna-Lou, "You're a real treasure hunter, mom. You did it."

Chet gave Donna-Lou a big grin, "Yeah. He's right. You're a real keeper."

Donna-Lou crossed her arms over her chest, "Sure took you some time to realize *that*, Mr. Chet Calhoun."

Chet blushed and looked uncomfortable.

"Why don't we just head up there and take a look? That's the only way we'll know for sure," Rory said.

Chet looked relieved with the change in topic. He nodded eagerly, hitched up his pants and looked around, orienting himself and pointing, "Well, if we head directly west that way, we'll catch a highway that heads north. If the KGC is looking for us along the river, they won't expect us to be going west and then north."

Rory nodded, "That sounds like a workable plan."

Donna-Lou gave a subtle shake of her head as she eyed Chet and then turned to Rory. "There's a nice inn up there too. We can stay overnight. And then we can take The Blue Ridge Parkway. It runs across the foot of the Blue Ridge Mountains to that area on the map."

"So what are we waiting for? Let's pack up and get going," Rory conceded.

Emma pumped her fist, "Yeah."

"Oh, boy," Corry said with enthusiasm, "we're going to find the treasure of the Knights of the Golden Circle."

Donna-Lou nodded somberly, "Yeah, as long as the Knights of the Golden Circle don't find us first."

Chapter 43

AFTER CHECKING INTO the Blue Ridge Inn, a 10,000 square-foot Southern Georgian mansion, everyone went to work on their assigned tasks. Chet and Corry visited several stores in the small town to buy as much treasure hunting equipment as they could find. They brought back a high-grade metal detector, several shovels, digging trowels, five Swiss army knives and kerosene lamps. Rory scooped up a dozen $500 Fenix RC40 flashlights and hands-free holders that clipped to your belt. The flashlights had a powerful 90-degree aperture to light everything around you. Perfect for exploring a cave - if they found it. He also took the time to pick up some new weapons, ammunition and several cans to carry extra gas. Donna-Lou and Emma were tasked with refilling the cooler with sandwiches and bottled water. After a good night's sleep and a quick, early breakfast, it was 6 AM when the Range Rover drove away from the Inn and the treasure hunters made their way along the scenic Blue Ridge Parkway.

THE SCENERY WAS BREATH-taking, with long-range vistas spread out below them and then close-up views of the rugged mountains that seemed to embrace the Range Rover. But beneath the thrills of excitement the group was feeling, there were the chills that the next vehicle they encountered on the roadway would be filled with Knights of the Golden Circle. Or a horseman would appear on a ridge and the crack of a rifle would be the next sound they heard. Or maybe the last sound one of them would ever hear.

AFTER WHAT SEEMED LIKE an eternity, Chet finally said, "We're there." That was it. Plain and simple.

Rory pulled to the side of the road and stopped. He looked over at Chet, sensing his tension, "This is it?"

Chet had his eye on the Range Rover's GPS system and he took a moment before he nodded, "Yeah. The coordinates we're looking for are just to the north of us." He gestured to the left of the vehicle, "It's that way."

Emma looked across the parkway to a steep hill that rose to the north, fifty yards off the edge of the road, "We have to climb up *that* hill?"

Corry squeezed beside her to look out the window, "Yep. That's where the treasure will be."

"But it's steep and we could tip over," Emma said. She tilted her head to try and see the top of the hill. After a moment of thought, she looked at Corry, a worried look on her face, "You'll have to hold my hand, so I don't fall over and get hurt."

Corry rolled his eyes.

Emma giggled and it broke the tension as Chet and Donn-Lou smiled at each other.

But it didn't last long for Donna-Lou as her smile faded, "So...we're going up there?"

Corry turned to her, "We have to mom if we're going to find the treasure."

Her face glued to the window again, Emma frowned, "I *still* think I'll fall over when we climb up there."

"Why don't we just drive up there?" Corry asked. "We can do that, right, Rory?"

Chet leaned forward to look out up the hill, "I'm not sure that's a good idea. Like Emma says, it looks real steep...."

Donna-Lou shrugged, "I'm with Corry on this one. I don't see why we don't just take this thing up there. That's what it's made for. Right? I'd feel a lot safer and we could get away a lot faster if we see anyone on a horse again."

Shaking his head, Chet glanced back at Donna-Lou, "I'm just not sure that's a good–"

Donna-Lou winked at him, "Who knows what I'll do later if I don't have to walk and use up all my energy on a hike, Chet Calhoun."

"Ewww, mom," Corry complained.

Emma put her hands to her mouth and giggled.

Chet looked across at Rory and quickly offered, "I'll drive if you want?"

Donn-Lou put a hand to her mouth and stifled a giggle of her own.

Rory smiled and shook his head, "No, Chet Calhoun, it's fine." He looked up the hill as he put the Range Rover in reverse gear, "I mean, what could go wrong? Then again, those could be the famous last words of a treasure hunter."

Backing up along the shoulder, he spotted a flat spot between two trees on the other side of the road. He stopped, put the Range Rover in drive, checked for traffic and then drove straight across the Parkway and across the grass to the foot of the hill. A moment later, the big vehicle's 510 horsepower, supercharged engine growled as it began the 45-degree climb.

"Oh, boy!" Corry said eagerly as he leaned against the window.

Emma squeezed herself closer to him.

Corry gave her a small frown and then turned his attention back to the window.

As he drove, Rory switched back and forth several times across the face of the hill to avoid the steepest parts of the climb as best he could. But the Range Rover ate up the ascent easily.

Rory stopped at the top of the hill, put the big vehicle in park and lowered his window.

The others did the same.

Ahead of them was a verdant green forest. The air was warm and filled with the rich scent of Blue Ridge mountain soil and the rich vegetation. Somewhere the caw, caw, caw of a crow broke the silence.

It was Donna-Lou who broke the spell, her voice soft as she asked, "So...what do we look for?"

Corry looked over at his mom, "We look for more signs that leads us to the treasure. Right, Chet?"

Chet stirred in his seat and nodded, "Yeah. Exactly. There should be more signs, like the ones we saw back at Cherokee Ridge. They could be on the trees or on the rocks. Basically, anything that *looks* like a sign, we need to take a look at it. Just call out like we did before and we can stop and check it out. Okay?"

There were mumbles of agreement as everyone shifted in their seats to get ready.

Rory put the Range Rover in drive but sat there for a moment. Then he said, "I hate to break the spell of the treasure hunt but...keep your eyes open for signs of the KGC as well. You see *anyone* on horseback with a rifle...."

There was silence for a moment and then the engine growled as Rory pressed down on the gas.

Chapter 44

THE RANGE ROVER MOVED SLOWLY through the oak-chestnut forest, crisscrossing back and forth so they could get a good look at the trees and rocks from all sides. Nothing stood out for at least an hour of searching as they moved deeper and farther away from the parkway The sun splashed through openings in the canopy of trees and then lit up the larger clearings as everyone watched silently.

As Rory was taking a wide turn in a large open, area to start the next pass in his make-shift search pattern, it was Donna-Lou who started yelling.

"Stop. Stop Go back. We have to go back. I saw something."

Chet stirred in his seat and looked over the seat, "What was it? What did you see?"

Donna-Lou just wind-milled her arm as she looked through the back window, "Just back up. Back up, Rory."

Rory stopped the vehicle immediately, put his arm over the seat and backed up slowly.

Chet knelt on his seat, watching over the back of his seat as Emma and Corry scrambled around to do the same, focused intently on the terrain behind the Range Rover.

The grass hissed softly under the wheels of the Range Rover.

"Stop," Donna-Lou yelled. She jumped out of the vehicle before Rory could even come to a sliding stop on the grass.

The others didn't hesitate either, jumping out and leaving the doors open as they ran after Donna-Lou.

Rory put the vehicle in park and got out. He left his door open as well but he didn't take off after the others. Instead, he took a quick look around first, listening carefully. The only sound was the light wind pushing high through the treetops. Rory reached back into the vehicle, grabbed his handgun and stuck it in the waistband of his jeans. He took slow steps to the back of the vehicle, turning in a circle as he did, watching and half-expecting a horseman to come riding out of the woods. It didn't happen but he still felt uneasy. It *felt* like someone was out there. Finally, he took off at a jog after the others. They were on the far side of the clearing now, standing in front of a large tree, silent. Once he reached them, he saw it.

Carved in the bark was another turtle:

Donna-Lou was running her fingers over the shape in the bark, "So this means we have to go to the left where the tail is pointing. Right?"

Corry shook his head, "No, this one is a bit different, mom."

"Different? How?"

Chet stepped up beside Donna-Lou and pointed to a part of the carving, "Take a look at the tail. What's different about it? What's different from the other one?"

Donna-Lou tilted her head and then ran her fingers over the back end of the carving, "It's bent...the other one was straight...."

Rory nodded his head as he saw it, "So that means we follow in the direction of the bent tail. It's not saying go straight back, but on that specific angle away from the tree."

Chet nodded, "That's right. You got it." He put a hand on Corry's shoulder, "Let's put this one on the map, just in case we have to come back later."

"I'll bring the Range Rover up," Rory said and he jogged back. He took a quick look around again as he closed all the doors. He couldn't see or hear anything but he still felt that unease. Getting back in, Rory backed the Range Rover across the clearing to the others.

Corry quickly dated into the vehicle and brought out the map out, working with Chet to add the sign in the proper spot. Once they were finished, Chet lined himself up with the tail, stretched his arm out and pointed, "Okay, now we go in that direction."

Rory took a look in the direction where Chet was pointing. He picked out a couple trees in a line he could use as a guide to start and then said, "Okay, got it. Everybody back aboard." But as everyone piled back into the Range Rover, Rory held his door open and stayed outside for a moment. He checked their surroundings again. The feeling of unease was still there. Finally, he got in, placing the weapon of the dash in front of him. Then he backed up in a half circle, stopped, and then drove in the direction indicated by the bent tail. Everyone went quiet and back to watching for the next sign. The sun poked through the trees here and there as they drove, splashing highlights on the trees and rocks as they passed.

It was Chet who spoke up after twenty minutes, "I think I see something." He pointed ahead and a bit to the right of the vehicle.

Everyone in back immediately was leaning over the seats, looking through the front windshield.

Rory slowed the Range Rover and leaned forward over the steering wheel, "Where?"

Chet pointed again, "Head for that large rock just up ahead there."

"I think I see it," Corry said in excitement.

Rory drove through the trees and pulled up to a rock nearly a dozen feet high and eight feet across. This side had a large flat surface and it appeared someone had chiseled something into the face. Everyone was out of the Range Rover immediately to see it up close:

Corry and Emma were the first ones out and over to the rock. They ran their fingers over the rough surface.

Chet reached over Corry's shoulder to feel the chiseled sign, "They've carved it right into the rock. It's weathered but it's definitely a treasure sign."

"So what does this one mean?" Emma asked as she ran her fingers over the contours.

"My question exactly," Donna-Lou said as she leaned over the young girl's shoulder and traced the outline of the chiseled sign herself.

Rory only glanced at the sign. He had his weapon in hand and was watching their surroundings again. The others seemed oblivious to any potential threats, not even noticing the gun in his hand, and he felt the need to stay on guard as they did their thing.

Chet put a hand on Corry's shoulder, "What do you think it means?"

Corry ran his fingers across the chiseled sign, "I think...this one refers to a mine or a cave. And I think it's supposed to be below us." He backed up and looked down at his feet. Then he looked at Chet, "Does that mean it's in a cave below our feet?"

Chet shook his head, "No. This is actually one my grand-daddy drew for me when I was a little boy. Me and Bobby Fin *never ever* came across it when we looked for the treasure. But now...I think I know why he drew it for me...."

Donna-Lou looked at Chet, realizing what he meant, "He was probably getting ready to teach you about the treasure. Bringing the next generation into the secret and all that...."

Chet nodded, "Yeah I think so. And then...."

"So what is *does* it mean?" Corry asked.

Chet hitched up his pants, "It means the cave we're looking for will be found in a low spot somewhere around here." He looked up, "Maybe it's even up ahead of us."

Emma's little brow furrowed, "The cave is in a low spot?"

Chet nodded as he looked at her, "Uh, huh. That means it could be in a valley...or maybe just a gully–"

Corry and Emma were off at a run past the rock.

Donna-Lou immediately showed concern and jogged after them, "Careful, you two. Don't go too far without us."

Rory stepped up to Chet, "Do you think we're close?"

Chet shrugged, "I'm not really sure to tell you the truth. But I would imagine–"

Corry yelled back at them, "Hey, guys? Look."

Rory and Chet looked over to see Corry, Emma, and Donna-Lou standing about one hundred yards away. They were side by side, looking at something.

Chet started to run but Rory grabbed his sleeve, "No, no, no. We should take the Range Rover and stay close to the weapons, Chet." He held his handgun up as a reminder, "If we *are* getting close, the Knights of the Golden Circle might not be far behind."

Chet looked at Rory for a moment before a sheepish look crept over his face, "You're right. I guess I'm getting caught up in the treasure hunting stuff and all that. Sorry about that."

"No problem," Rory said. "Let's just keep our wits about us so don't we get caught off guard. Especially us adults. *Always* keep in mind the horsemen that chased us."

Chet nodded, "You're right. Okay."

The two of them climbed back into the Range Rover and drove over to park where the kids were standing with Donna-Lou. When they got out this time, Chet had a Glock stuffed under his belt. He still had to hitch up his pants as he stepped around to the others.

Donna-Lou glanced at Chet, pointing ahead and downward, "*This* must be the low spot you were talking about."

Rory and Chet were surprised to find themselves standing on the edge of a rocky drop-off. Seventy-five feet below them was a grassy field, dotted with trees and boulders, the flat plain stretching out half a mile to a rocky cliff that rose more than two hundred feet high.

"That cliff over there looks like a good place to find a cave," Donna-Lou said.

Rory nodded his head slowly, "I agree. But it can't be easy to find, though. Otherwise, someone would have stumbled across it by now."

"True," conceded Donna-Lou.

Corry pointed ahead, "But there should be signs down there, mom. More signs that will lead us to the treasure."

"Yeah, there'll be signs, Mrs. Haney," Emma said, "and we'll find them. Right, Corry?"

"Yeah, let's get going," Corry said and he ran for the Range Rover.

Everyone followed behind and within ten minutes, Rory found a way down to the lower area. They decided to head straight for the cliff and were soon driving across the open, grassy field. Finally reaching the foot of the rocky cliff, Rory made a decision to turn right and slowly wound his way through boulders and bushes, everyone looking for signs or evidence of a cave.

Chapter 45

EVERYONE HAD THEIR WINDOW DOWN, the warmth of the day and the scent of wildflowers filling the Range Rover as everyone kept their eyes peeled for treasure signs. Corry and Emma passed out cold bottles of water to help everyone cope with the heat. Forty-five minutes into the drive Rory pulled to a stop. "Anybody see any signs?" he asked. "Or anything that *looks* like a sign?"

Chet shook his head, No, "I didn't see anything." He looked at the others in the back seat, Anyone else? Anything?"

Everyone shook their head no.

"Would it be on a tree or a rock?" Emma asked.

"It could be on either one," Chet said.

Corry turned in his seat, "Or it could be up there on the face of that cliff somewhere."

Chet turned in his seat and looked out at the face of the cliff, "He's right." He shook his head slightly, as if he had forgotten that aspect himself, "It could be anywhere. We really have to keep our eyes open."

Rory gave it a moment as thought and then he said, "Why don't we go back and try in the other direction?" Everyone agreed and he put the Range Rover in gear, "Okay. But keep your eyes open on the way back, in case we missed something," He turned in a wide circle to the right and slowly drove back along the foot of the cliff. But this time he took it slower, giving everyone extra time to examine any possible scratches or features that might prove to be a sign.

Everyone was quiet and intense.

Ten minutes later, it was Corry who spoke up, his voice filled with excitement, "Look. Over there." He was pointing ahead and to the left.

Everyone looked at where Corry was pointing.

"Dang," Chet said. "We missed the far back side of that large boulder when we passed. And I should have been the one to catch that. Sorry, everyone."

Rory steered in that direction and slowly approached the boulder. It was nearly eight feet high and some ten feet across. As Rory parked next to the large boulder, Corry was the first to jump out, followed quickly be everyone else.

CORRY SHIELDED HIS eyes from the sun with a hand as he looked up at the sign etched into the boulder, "We either passed the cave or another sign that leads to the cave."

Donna-Lou was a foot behind him, both hands over her eyes and she squinted, "How do you know that? Isn't that one up there telling us to follow the tail and go back across the field?"

"No no, mom. *This one* has those marks on the back," Corry explained. "See? The diamonds beside the arrow head is telling to go in the direction the arrow head points."

Donna-Lou shook her head, "And how was I supposed to know that?"

Shrugging, Corry said, "It's just stuff you have to know about treasure signs, mom."

"Uh huh. It's a good thing we have you here, then," Donna-Lou said. She moved in fast, wrapping her arms around her son and tickling him with both hands.

Corry gave her a big belly laugh as he tried to get away.

Chet took a step to look past the boulder, his excitement evident, "He's right, though. That sign means we passed something important somewhere back there."

"Or we should have gone in the other direction back there to start with," Rory said. "Sorry about that."

"No, no, no," Chet said, "that's treasure hunting. Stops and starts, wrong turns and all that. You make a mistake and you have to spend all day hiking back to a spot to start over again."

"Yep, that's how it works," Corry confirmed. He shrugged, "Otherwise people would find the treasure real easy and it wouldn't be there for us to find."

"He's right," Chet said. "C'mon, let's get going and everyone watch carefully. We're close."

Their enthusiasm was heightened now as everyone piled back into the Range Rover. After waiting for Chet and Corry to mark the sign on their map, Rory then drove slower as they worked their way back along the face of the cliff. They reached their starting point and continued on, a slow steady plod where they made stops to check the back of any boulder or scrub tree they passed.

Thirty-nine more tense minutes passed as they drove slowly, weaving closer and then farther away from the cliff on their right, everyone intent of finding the next treasure sign. And then something popped up.

"Stop," Chet yelled.

Rory hit the brakes.

Chet was out of the Range Rover and running back behind the vehicle, at an angle towards the face of the cliff.

Rory jumped out along with everyone else and ran the fifty yards back to where Chet was standing.

"Up there!" Chet pointed.

Everyone stopped just behind him and looked up at where he was pointing

The treasure sign was chiseled high up on a pillar of rock. It faced *along* the cliff instead of facing outwards.

Chet took a step back, still looking up, "They hid this one really well. I just caught the edge of it as we passed."

Rory nodded, "You're right. You can't see the whole thing unless you're here below the sign like we are now." He looked back across the flat plain, "I'm not even sure you could see it from out there very well."

"That's all fine and good," Donna-Lou said. "But what does it mean?"

Chet hitched up his pants and he looked over the rocks and boulders, "It means the entrance to the cave is right around here. But...."

"But what?" Rory asked.

Taking a deep breath and letting it out slowly, Chet pointed up at the sign, "See that lightning bolt on the right side of the heart?"

"Yeah?"

"That lightning bolt tells us the right side of *something* is booby-trapped."

"Something?"

"Yeah. The thing is, it could be the right side of the entrance to the cave is booby-trapped. Or it could be the right side of–"

"Booby-trapped? What do you mean booby-trapped?" Donna-Lou asked in alarm. She quickly herded her son and Emma away from the face of the rock.

"Aww mom," Corry complained. Emma didn't look too pleased either.

"Don't aww me, young man," Donna-Lou said. "Both of you stay right back here."

Rory asked Chet quietly, "What exactly do you mean by booby-trapped?"

Chet chewed on his lip as he looked at the sign, "Well...the Knights of the Golden Circle used black powder to booby-trap some of their caches. But that was a long time ago–"

Rory shook his head, "Doesn't matter. If any *black-powder* booby-trap is still there, it might be a real problem."

Chet's brow furrowed, "Really? But that was a really long time ago, Rory."

"I've heard some people say black-powder only becomes *more* powerful over time," Rory explained. "I'd rather be safe than sorry. So let's just believe it *is* more powerful and be extra careful."

"Oh great," murmured Chet.

Rory took a step back and looked over the area that rose up the cliff, a hundred yards on either side. It sloped upwards slowly and was strewn with boulders and folds of rock in the face of the cliff. "There are a lot of cracks in the face," he said, "the entrance could be anywhere up there."

Chet nodded, hitching up his pants after a moment, "I'm game to go up there and look if you are."

Giving it some thought, Rory finally nodded, "We didn't come all this way to give up now, I guess." He walked to the back of the Range Rover and opened the back hatch. The others joined him quickly.

"What are you going to do?" Chet asked.

"Like you said, go up and explore, see what we find." Rory pulled out one of the powerful flashlights and a belt holder and passed them to Chet. Then he grabbed a set for himself, slipping it on his belt. Grabbing a Glock 19, he passed it to Chet before grabbing one for himself, stuffing it in the back of his jeans. Finally, he handed a weapon to Donna-Lou, "You can stay here with the kids. Keep your eyes open. Fire a shot if you see or hear anything. *Anything*. Got it?"

Donna-Lou nodded as she held the weapon in both hands.

"C'mon Chet," Rory said. "Let's just go slow and see what we can find up there." They began walking back towards the face of the cliff.

"But mom," Corry said, "we should go up there too. We can't just stop exploring—"

"He said there are black-powder bobby-traps up there. That means a possible explosion and I don't plan on losing you," Donna-Lou said firmly.

"But we *all* have to go, mom. We need *everybody's* eyes, just like we all found different signs to get here," Corry said. He watched the two men begin the climb, "Or the Knights of the Golden Circle get to it first and buys a bomb."

Donna-Lou grimaced, knowing her son was right. But she still worried

Rory and Chet stopped, looking back. Rory realized the kid was right. But it wasn't his place to say anything.

Emma stepped up beside Corry, "He's right. We should go and help. I'll keep an eye on him, Mrs. Haney."

Corry rolled his eyes.

Donna-Lou looked over at Rory, worry over her son and the worry over what might possibly happen with a bomb in the wrong hands warring together on her face.

Rory just shrugged, "It's up to you."

Nodding reluctantly after a moment, Donna-Lou said, "Okay." She held up a warning finger to her son, "*But*...we go slow and no running ahead. You point out something and we all check it out. Deal?"

"Deal," Corry said. He and Emma each grabbed a flashlight and belt clip and then hustled to catch up to Rory and Chet.

Donna-Lou placed the Glock 19 into the back of her jeans, grabbed a flashlight and clip and headed off after the kids, shaking her head, still not convinced this was the right thing to be allowing her son and his friend to do.

The climb was slow and methodical. And difficult. Loose rocks made the way treacherous, constantly sliding out from underfoot. They spread out, maintaining a line so they wouldn't cause boulders or stones to roll down on one another.

One hundred yards up, Rory stopped and looked to the left. He just stared.

Chet called over to him, "Did you find something, Rory?"

He just stood there.

Chet moved carefully across the face of the cliff. The others scrambled behind him.

As they took up spots around him, Rory simply lifted an arm and pointed without a word.

Thirty yards away was a high fold of rock with a dark, vertical crack. It was six-feet wide at the bottom of the crack and rose one hundred feet to a point at the top.

Corry's eyes lit up, "We found it! We found the treasure cave."

Chapter 46

THE SUN BEAT DOWN, hot on his back as Rory stood with his left hand on the rock face, leaning and peering into the darkness of the opening in the cliff. After a moment, he reached down, took the flashlight that was clipped to his belt and turned it on, trying to illuminate the dark space ahead. He shook his head, his voice echoing off the walls and the high ceiling of rock, "I can't see much detail but it appears to go in about one hundred feet and then turns to the right." Looking back at Chet, Rory said, "And I don't see *anything* that could be a booby trap."

Chet stepped up behind him on the right, peering inside, "As you go in, keep an eye out for a red hand on the rock somewhere."

"A red hand?"

"Yeah. They used to paint a red-hand sign near a booby-trap."

"A red-hand *sign*?"

"Yeah."

"Okay."

"Assuming the paint is still there after all these years," Donna Lou said. She stood back behind the two men, a firm hand on Corry and Emma, making sure they didn't dart into the rock cleft. She glanced back over the view below and across the plain, her eyes looking for any sign of horsemen with rifles or vehicles approaching.

Chet looked back at her and nodded, "You're right. It might be faded after all these years. Like Rory said about the black powder, we can't assume anything." He noticed her looking out over the plain and glanced that way himself for a moment, knowing full well what she was thinking, "Anything...?"

Donna-Lou shook her head slightly, still not sure there was something...or someone...she just couldn't see.

Chet glanced out across the plain again and the then swallowed, looking back at Rory, "So...what do you think? You still want to go in?"

Rory chewed on his lower lip and then nodded, "Yeah."

"Be careful, Rory," Donna-Lou whispered.

"Yeah, I will. And since there could be some booby-trap on the right-hand side, I'll follow the left wall." He looked at Chet, "Sound about right?"

Chet swallowed and then gave him a faint nod, "Yeah...I guess."

Rory gave him a smile, "Thanks for the pep-talk."

A sheepish grin settled on Chet's lips, "I could go with you if you want."

"No. There's no need to put anyone else in danger. Everyone wait until I signal you to come in."

Chet put a hand on Rory's shoulder, "Just take your time and don't take any chances. There's always another day in treasure hunting."

Rory nodded and took his first step into the opening. He stayed against the left wall, his flashlight illuminating the way. Loose rocks crunched under his boot as he moved forward carefully. He flashed the light from the left wall to floor of the cave and especially to the right wall of rock, watching for any signs of danger. The coolness of the cave was a respite after the heat of the sun outside. It took ten tense minutes before he reached the corner, where the opening in the rock widened to about fifteen feet. He turned the corner and the light from the flashlight on his belt illuminated the opening ahead. The cave continued to widen out until it was at least sixty feet across at the far end, about two hundred feet away. The shadows at the far gave Rory the impression it split into two branches. The smell was clean and earthy, which meant there was nothing dead in here and no wild animal using it as a lair. At least, he hoped not.

"What do you see?" Chet yelled, his voice bouncing off the rock walls.

"The cave goes down that way at least another two hundred feet," he yelled back. "And it looks to me like there are two entrances down there, one to the left and one to the right." He shifted the beam of the flashlight around, examining the walls and ceiling of the cave. Halfway down the cave ahead, the ceiling disappeared into the shadows, like a massive crack under the Blue Ridge Mountains.

"Can we go in too?"Corry yelled.

Rory could understand his enthusiasm. He turned to light up the right-hand wall again, examining it closely. He couldn't see anything that looked dangerous leading down to the twin caves at the far end. He took a breath and let it out slowly, hoping he was making the right decision, "Okay. C'mon in," he yelled and waved for the others to join him. "Just stay to the left."

Chet led the way, with two excited kids and one nervous Donna-Lou Haney following them. Reaching the corner in the cave, everyone crowded in behind Rory and lifted their flash-lights. Their combined illumination lit up the cave in full detail.

"Wow! A real treasure cave," Corry exclaimed.

"Don't get your hopes up too high," Donna-Lou said. "We haven't found any treasure yet. It could be just a big hole in the wall."

"But we will. I know it," Corry answered as he ignored his mother's pessimism. His voice was filled with excitement and wonder. He pointed ahead, "Can we go farther down there? Can we?"

Emma jumped up and down, "Yeah, let's go find the treasure. Me and Corry have been looking for it for a loooooong time."

Rory looked at Chet, "Considering the warning on that sign back there, I would assume we don't take the cave on the right-hand side either?"

Chet took a deep breath, thinking about it. He finally nod-ded, "Everything I ever learned about signs says that's true. Then again, I don't know of anyone who ever actually found something that was booby-trapped."

"And I never heard of anybody who ever found a real treasure cave like this before," Corry said from behind them.

"Or a booby-trapped treasure cave," Donna-Lou added.

The two men looked around at her.

"I'm just saying," Donna-Lou said as she shrugged his shoul-ders.

Rory looked back down the cave, "There's a first time for everything, I guess."

"Uh huh. Like having your leg blown off for the first time," Donna-Lou said.

Chet raised his eyebrows as he looked at Rory, "You can go first."

"You're such a gentleman, Chet Calhoun."

The sheepish grin settled on Chet's lips again, "Maybe I'm just willing to let you have all the fun."

"Uh, huh. You keep telling yourself that."

Chapter 47

THE CAVE AHEAD BECKONED. So did danger. Taking a deep breath, Rory lifted his flashlight to illuminate his way, stayed close to the left wall and took a tentative step. Once again, small rocks crunched under his boots and echoed lightly off the walls as he made his way ahead.

Chet waited until Rory was about ten feet along his journey into the treasure cave before he stepped close to left wall and began following. After several steps, he glanced back and nodded at the others.

Donna-Lou pressed her hand against the back of her son's shoulder and urged him to follow Chet, whispering, "Remember to stay to the left."

Corry nodded, both delight and fear evident on his face.

Urging Emma to go next, Donna-Lou then pulled the Glock from the back of her jeans and glanced back down the cave towards the entranceway. She blew a light breath between her lips and looked down at her hands. They were shaking. She glanced at the two kids again, feeling the fear for them in the pit of her stomach. Allowing them to get no more than ten feet away, she began following, walking more sideways then straight ahead, to ensure she could keep an eye on both the kids and the cave back behind her.

Rory moved ahead slowly, constantly watching where he was stepping. From time to time, he would splash the light to the right to check the far side of the cave, watching for any indication of a bobby-trap.

Chet splashed his light higher on the right wall of the cave, "Keep your eyes open for that red hand sign as well."

"Right," Rory whispered as he let his own light play higher up on the walls as he moved.

The journey along the two hundred feet of rock floor to the dual cave entrance was tense and seemed to take forever. The sounds of dirt and rocks crunching under their feet echoed eerily off the walls. The lights and shadows played off the rock walls as they moved, every crack looking like a treasure sign. But there wasn't a single thing painted or carved into any piece of rock anywhere.

As Rory finally approached the entrance on the left, he let his light fall on the opening and rock walls to the right, looking for any evidence of a painted red hand sign. He glanced back, his voice a hollow whisper, "I don't see any red hand or any evidence of red paint flecks that might indicate a sign worn away."

Chet didn't say anything as he cast his own light that way. Then he slowed his pace and allowed the others catch up.

Rory splashed his light over the area again, hoping to see something. But there was nothing. Absolutely nothing. There was only the feeling that there was danger somewhere down the cave on the right. Or would that be the right wall down the left cave? Or had the sign been misread? Or was the sign a lie, designed to kill someone who wasn't one of the Knights of the

Golden Circle? A non-member who didn't know the real truth? So many questions ran through his mind. And not one single, satisfying answer. Rory finally turned his full attention to the entrance to the cave entrance on the left, casting his light ahead.

Chet, Corry, and Emma crowded up behind Rory, their combined lights illuminating the path ahead as well. The rock wall curved to the left for a hundred feet or so, then curved back to the right and disappeared into the darkness.

Chet splashed his light up and down the walls on the right, "I still don't see anything about a booby-trap. What do you think, Rory?"

Corry and Emma squeezed their heads between the two men to look ahead.

Donna-Lou was still walking sideways like a crab, the Glock at her shoulder as she watched behind them. She bumped into her son–

Corry jumped. "Mom!" he protested. "You almost made me poop my pants!"

Emma put her hands to her mouth, giggling.

"Yeah, well, I may have to change my underwear when I get home too," Donna-Lou said as she nervously looked behind them.

That sent Emma into more fits of giggling and Donna-Lou winked at her.

Rory splashed his light around with Chet, checking over on the far side to the right several times, "I don't know what to say, Chet." He glanced back, "Anyone see *anything* that looks like a booby-trap? Or a red hand? Corry? Emma? Donna-Lou?"

Everyone shook their head no.

Looking back down the tunnel straight ahead, Rory splashed the light around, whispering, "I don't know...."

"What's that stuff?" Emma asked. She pointed at what looked like dark brown grains of rice. They were piled high in the cracks of some of the jagged rocks over on the right-hand side of the cave.

Rory let the light play high over the piles of rice-like material, "That's just from bats–"

Donna-Lou squeaked, "Would you mean bats? Where?"

Rory pointed up into the shadows with the light, "They're up there." Tiny eyes flashed and black forms took shape as the light passed over them.

Chet looked up and then across to the dark brown material, "Okay. So that stuff over there is guano, then."

Emma screwed her face up, "Gwaw-no? What's that–"

"Bat poop," Corry said and he gave a big belly laugh.

Emma made a face.

Rory smiled then turned back to the task at hand. He took a minute to look at the rock walls under the light, as well as the ceiling of the cave, looking for any hints of danger. "Okay, I guess we might as well move ahead and down this tunnel. Stay on the left side."

Everyone just looked at him, waiting for him to move first.

Rory shook his head. He looked back at the floor of the cave, casting his light back and forth over it. Nothing looked out of place. Nothing looked dangerous. He looked to the right side of the cave. No red hands, no signs, just bare rock. He took a deep breath to steel himself, then moved ahead, watching where he stepped, looking for any possible evidence of buried explosives. When he was ten to twelve feet down the tunnel, he heard the others whisper and begin to shuffle after him. His own ragged breathing mixed with the crunch underfoot and echoed off the rock walls as he moved forward slowly, following the cave as it curved to the left. The going was slow but he wasn't taking any chances. Time passed like he was walking in molasses. One hundred feet down the cave, the high opening curved right and disappeared into the darkness. Rory stopped, flashed his light around again. Still no red hand or any other sign of a booby-trap. He continued on, staying to the left. One hundred and fifty went by slowly. Now two hundred feet...and the cave opened in-to a huge cavern. Rory took three steps and stopped dead in his tracks, his flashlight shining into the darkness ahead.

Chet finally entered the cavern, slowly making his way to stand beside Rory, his flashlight adding to the illumination of the way ahead. Corry, Emma, and Donna-Lou carefully stepped up to the right of Chet and stopped. Their lights dancing into the enormous cavern dead ahead.

Corry's voice was the only sound, a loud whisper that echoed off the rock walls underneath the Blue Ridge Mountains, "Wow!"

Chapter 48

THE CAVERN WAS ENORMOUS. The roof disappeared hundreds of feet overhead, disappearing into the darkness. Far off to the side, in the shadows, huge stalagmites and stalactites met together in a strange mineral forest, long pyramids from the floor meeting long pyramids dropping from the ceiling. But it was the man-made items that were the most interesting to the treasure hunters. Fifty feet ahead were dozens of old wooden crates, stacked haphazardly one on top of another, forming a wooden pyramid that stood ten feet high and was twenty to thirty feet across. Faded labels designated the various contents as ammunition, high explosives or oranges.

Donna-Lou put a hand on Corry and Emma, holding them back, her voice shaky, "Are those really old ammunition and explosives crates?"

"Maybe we just found moldy oranges, mom," Corry whispered. He looked around and splashed his light over the rocks off to the side, "And look at all the bat poop." He was right. There *was* a considerable amount of bat droppings around the cavern, including considerable traces of it on the boxes.

Chet took a step, his voice an awed whisper, "No, this *must* be the treasure. When they shipped everything on the train, they used old crates and barrels to put the money and other stuff in. This is amazing."

Donna-Lou shook her head, "No. It can't be, Chet. That's not a lot for the nine trains we were all told they used."

Chet shrugged, "True. But maybe this is all our grandaddys could dig up and move before they was...."

Corry looked at everyone just standing there and then he looked up at his mother, "Let's make sure. Can we go look at it? Please?"

Donna-Lou looked at Chet and Rory.

Chet looked at Rory and then shrugged, "I guess this is what we all came here for. Let's take a look." He looked over at Corry, "*But* be careful until we know it's not dangerous–"

"All right!" Corry shouted and he was off running with Emma right behind. His voice and running steps echoed off into the darkness

Chet looked apologetically at Donna-Lou for about a heartbeat and then took off after the kids.

Donna-Lou shook her head and placed the Glock in the back of her waistband, "You're all just a bunch of kids."

"I'm still here," Rory said with a smile.

"Yeah...and you got ants in your pants to join them."

Rory nodded, winked at her and headed off after the other three.

Donna-Lou shook her head and walked over to join them in their exploration, "Just be careful around those ones marked ammunition and high explosives until we're sure." Her voice echoed through the chamber and no one paid the least attention to her.

"What do you think is inside?" Emma asked Corry as she joined him at the wall of crates.

"It's probably gold and silver, right?" he asked as he looked at Chet.

Chet nodded as he ran his hand across the wooden crates, his eyes lit with anticipation, "That's what they say. Whatever they are, these are really old crates."

"Yeah, look at this one," Corry said as he reached up to a crate in the second row. He pushed his fingers into a slight crack in one of the boards and pulled on it, "It's kind of rot–" There was a 'crack' and Corry jumped back.

Silver coins spilled out of the box like a slot machine paying out a winning jackpot, the metallic jingling echoing around them.

Donna-Lou pulled Corry back as she looked up at the stack of old crates, "Be careful! You don't want to bring it all down on us–"

"But it's treasure, mom," Corry said excitedly as he jumped forward and bent down, along with the others, to pick up a few of the coins.

Chet held one against the light from the flashlight at his waist, "This one says Republica Mexicana." He flipped it over, "And the date is 1865."

"This one is 1827," Rory said as he examined one in the light of his own flashlight.

"The value on this one is one is 8 R.G. How much is that?" Corry asked as he looked at his.

"I have no idea," Chet said, "but part of the Confederate treasury that was moved was supposed to contain Mexican money. I would say this is it. I wonder how much–"

"Hey y'all," Emma called. She was standing off to the side of the wall of wooden crates and pointing behind it.

Everybody walked over to see what she was pointing at.

Donna-Lou's her hands went to her mouth in surprise at what she saw, "Oh my!"

Chapter 49

THE CAVERN EXTENDED a long way back into the darkness behind the wall of wooden crates. As the group stood there, their combined flashlights highlighted hundreds and hundreds of wooden barrels and kegs, stacked in high piles and pyramids that extended back into the shadows. The barrels and kegs had faded labels that indicated they once held items like sugar, coffee, flour or gunpowder. They also saw hundreds more of the stacked wooden crates with faded labels of ammunition, high explosives, oranges, whiskey, soap or apples.

Rory walked thirty yards past the wall of crates to one of the barrels.

The others joined him, silent as they tried to take in the immense find in the cavern.

Rory brushed bat droppings off the top of the old barrel with the back of his hand. Then he pried the barrel top off with his fingers, dropping it as he looked inside, "Wow."

Chet quickly looked inside the barrel, dipped his hand in and pulled out a handful of gold coins. He slipped them under his light, looking closely, "Wow is right. These are 1866 Liberty Head Double Eagles,"

"Double Eagles? That's $20, right?" Donna-Lou asked.

Chet nodded, "At face value, yes. But...."

Emma walked to a wooden crate, lifted the lid up a crack and peered inside, "What's this?"

Corry ran over and peeked inside with her. His mouth dropped, "I think...I think it's gold bars."

"Really? Take one out," Emma said and she held the lid up while Corry reached inside. He grunted, "I can even move one of them."

Chet trotted over and looked inside the crate. He groaned as he lifted a bar, "Wow. This thing has to weigh 30 pounds."

Rory walked over and looked inside as well, "That would probably mean these are 400-ounce gold bars."

Chet let the bar drop with a dull, metallic clink and he looked at Rory in surprise, "Do you know how much gold is worth *per ounce* today?"

Donna-Lou stepped up between Rory and Chet as they were examining the contents of the crate, "How much do you think is in here?" she asked in a hushed voice.

"Enough to buy you a new house," Chet said as he looked at her with a big grin on his face.

Donna-Lou smiled back at him, delighted at the thought.

"Look up there," Corry said, pointing high off to the side. "Neat."

Everyone looked up to see bats roosting high in the rocks.

"They look cute," Emma said.

"Yeah, until they start getting in your hair," Donna-Lou said and she shuddered.

Corry laughed and then he and Emma were off running, exploring around the array of wooden barrels, boxes, and crates.

"Careful you two," Donna-Lou called after them. Then she shrugged, "Although, I can't blame them for being excited. *This* is amazing."

Chet nodded and stepped over to another barrel, pulling off the top. He put his hand inside and scooped out the contents. "These are 1878 Morgan silver dollars!" he said in excitement. He extended his hand to Donna-Lou, "Look."

She stepped over and took a handful out herself, gasping in astonishment. "How much is silver worth these days?" she whispered.

"I'm not sure. But think about it. They're not only valuable for the silver, they could be a lot more valuable as collector's items," Chet said.

"You're right. I never thought of that," Donna-Lou said.

"Isn't this incredible?" Chet said as he and Donna-Lou shared a big smile.

Rory walked over to a number of crates sitting off to the side. He couldn't get the top off so he kicked at the side to break one of the wooden slats. Nothing spilled out. He knelt down to allow his light to shine through the broken slat and then felt inside with his hand. "This one looks like silver bricks," he yelled.

But no one was really listening. Everyone was off looking into any container they could pry open.

Rory got up and wandered through the treasure trove himself. Eventually, he met up with Donna-Lou and Chet who were looking inside another barrel. "I think you guys can buy more than one new house," he said with a big grin.

"You too, Rory," Donna-Lou said. "You helped us find this."

"Yeah, she's right," Chet said.

"Thanks, but I got my reward when we got the two kids back."

Donna-Lou dropped a handful of old coins and threw her arms around Rory's neck, wrapping him in a big hug. "Thank you so much. If it wasn't for you, Rory, I don't know if we would have ever gotten Corry and Emma back. *Or* found any of this."

"Yeah. Thanks, Rory," Chet said as he held out a hand. "You're a great treasure hunting buddy."

Rory shook his hand as Donna-Lou continued hugging him.

Corry and Emma came running back between the crates and barrels, their loud, excited voices bouncing off the rock walls

"There's a lot of water way in the back," Emma said. "A big pool of it."

"Yeah. And there's a stream of water tumbling down from way up high in the ceiling back there," Corry said. His hand tumbled like water going over cascades.

"And more bats," Emma said in disgust.

Corry looked delighted, though, "Yeah, lots and lots of bats way up high like you said. This is a really amazing treasure cave."

"Yeah, I bet there's even pirates in here somewhere," Emma said.

"This isn't pirate treasure," Corry complained. "This is Confederate gold treasure—"

"I can have pirates if I want," Emma protested as she crossed her arms in defiance

Rory smiled at their antics and then spoke up, "Okay everybody. Now that we know what's back here, let's go back on the other side of the boxes and talk about what we do next."

"Sounds like a plan," Chet said as they headed back. He stuffed some gold coins in his pocket as he passed an open barrel and handed some to Donna-Lou.

Corry and Emma picked a couple of the coins up themselves and skipped back around the first wall of crates where everybody gathered in a circle.

Rory stood in front of the others, "Okay. We have to figure out a plan to get all of this out of here and hidden somewhere else."

Chet looked back for a moment and then raised his eyebrows, "How in the world do we move all of this? That would require a whole fleet of trucks."

"We can afford them now," Donna-Lou said with a large grin and a twinkle in her eye.

Chet nodded and smiled at her, "That's true, I guess. But—"

A line of powerful flashlights lit up behind Rory, bathing them all in a harsh light. A moment later, the sound of someone clapping their hands slowly echoed off the walls of the cavern. Everyone's blood ran cold as they slowly turned to see the harsh outline of Tucker Watley Calhoun - Old Tuck - grinning like a fiend and slowly clapping his hands. Behind him stood a dozen, hard-looking men, each one with a light on their belt - but more importantly - each carried a powerful Winchester rifle with a hunting scope.

Chapter 50

EVERYONE STOOD FROZEN IN POSITION, shocked to see the old, white-haired man standing there, backed up by a dozen gunmen. These men now spread out slowly behind Old Tuck, their rifles aimed and ready to fire at a moment's notice.

Chet's jaw was working in surprise but no sound came out. Then he sputtered a "How–?"

Old Tuck laughed as he clapped several more times, fully enjoying the situation. Then his raspy voice echoed off the walls as he talked and pointed a finger at Rory, "We found Steele's Jaguar. People at a dealership in a small town up by Greenville were wondering why a vehicle they didn't own or they didn't know about, was parked in with their other vehicles. So they reported it to the state troopers, in case it was stolen." He jerked a thumb over his shoulder and grinned fiendishly, "*These* men are those troopers. They're also loyal members of the Knights of the Golden Circle. When they saw the report, they went to investigate 'cause I had alerted everyone to keep an eye out. They was told about a man who had arrived in a Jaguar and rented a big Range Rover. Well...we put two and two together...especially since we already had your license plate from when you were stopped before. All these men had to do was work as State Troopers with the dealership to access the GPS system on board the Range Rover, which was set up to track the vehicle in case it was stolen. Funny how a thing like that it can lead you right to where you need to go. Thank you, Mr. Steele." The tall, thin, white-haired man grinned fiendishly at Rory.

Rory cursed himself silently inside for not thinking about that. It was stupid, short-sighted thinking on his part. Thinking that might just have killed them all.

"Now, I know you have weapons," Old Tuck said, "so why don't we make everything nice and safe and you toss them over here?"

As Rory, Chet, and Donna-Lou tossed their weapons over to the line of men, Old Tuck's eyes looked with delight on the wall of old crates behind the group, "Thank you for cooperating. And *thank you* for finding the treasure for us. Couldn't have done it without all your help, folks. Never would have found this place in a month of Sundays."

After tossing her weapon, Donna-Lou pulled Corry protectively behind her, "You old son of a–"

Old Tuck grinned fiendishly, "Oh don't worry. I don't need the boy anymore. In fact, I don't need *any* of you from this point on." He looked around at the enormous cavern, "This place will make a nice mausoleum for all of you–"

Chet took a threatening step toward Old Tuck.

Two of the men took a step forward, their Winchesters trained on Chet.

Chet stopped in his tracks, clenching his fists as he glared at Old Tuck.

Old Tuck sneered, "Just like your daddy and grand-daddy. All wind and no guts–"

Corry quickly moved around his mother before she could stop him and he tugged on Chet's sleeve, his voice low and urgent, "Don't let them take all the boxes in the other cave too, Chet. Don't let them. That belongs to us...." His voice trailed off quickly and he stopped tugging on Chet's sleeve.

Old Tuck's eyes went hard as he looked at Corry, "What's that, boy?"

Corry lowered his eyes and took a step back.

Donna-Lou putting her hands protectively on his shoulders.

Old Tuck stepped forward menacingly, "Speak up boy. What are you talking about? Other cave−?"

One of the gunmen spoke up, a cocky grin on his face, "The boy must mean that other tunnel on the right side when we came in,"

Old Tuck's face broke into an evil grin, "Ahhh, right. The other tunnel back there. We heard the faint echo of you folks talking when we first came in. Led us right down the tunnel to here."

Rory and Chet exchanged glances.

Old Tuck nodded his head gleefully as he backed up a couple of steps, pointing a gnarly finger at Corry. "Thank you, treasure boy. You helped us after all. Once we get all these crates of out of here, I'll make sure you're the last one to go...as a reward."

Donna-Lou stepped forward and put herself between Corry and Old Tuck.

Old Tuck gave her a dismissive grin. Then he turned to the men behind him and jerked his head to the junction of the two caves back behind them, "Let's go see what's on the other side." He looked back at the front wall of crates, "I knew there had to be more. We're gonna need a lot more to pay the bill." Old Tuck pointed to one of the men, "You stay here and guard our *friends*."

The gunman nodded.

Old Tuck turned his head to look at Rory and the others, "Anybody in here so much as twitches, put a bullet between their eyes. You hear me? Man, woman...or child."

The gunman nodded and grinned as he clutched the rifle to his chest.

Old Tuck's laugh was low and dry as he gave them all a last dismissive look. Then he turned and led the men away to secure the rest of the treasure.

Everybody stayed quiet as they watched Old Tuck and the eleven gunmen march away. They could still hear their feet shuffling and echoing as they disappeared around the curved rock wall.

Rory waited, trying to mentally count down to the time when they would be entering the right-hand cave. As he did, he gave some thought to getting further away from the entrance and the force of an explosion that could come through at any moment. He looked at the gunman, "Do you mind if we move away from these crates behind us? I'm afraid they might fall on the children." He gestured carefully off to the right, "If we can just move over there—"

The man pointed his rifle directly at Rory's head, "Don't even think of taking a step."

"Please," Donna-Lou pleaded.

The man grinned wickedly, "You're all going to die, lady, one way or another."

Emma began to sob.

Rory gestured off to the right again, "All we want to do is move over that way."

"Please," Donna-Lou asked again as she put her arm around the girl.

The man took a deep breath and let it out in a huff. But he backed up and waved the rifle for them to move away from the crates, "Do it slow."

They all complied, moved slowly away from the crates.

After they had only moved about twelve feet, the gunmen yelled, "Stop! No further."

Rory looked back at the pile of crates. Then he looked at the gunmen and pleaded, "Please. We need to get away farther. If you can back up closer to the entrance, that'll give us room enough to—"

"Fine! But no further," the gunmen said harshly. He carefully backed up ten feet, letting them move as well as he kept his rifle trained on the group. Then held a hand up, "That's it. No—"

BOOM!

A tremendous explosion ripped apart the rock wall at the entrance, the concussive force violently knocking everyone off their feet. Any screams were drowned out by the savage thunder-clap that shot through the cavern. A massive cloud of black smoke and gritty material shot through the air. Jagged splinters of rock ripped through clothing and embedded themselves into the pyramid of old wooden crates.

Chapter 51

RORY MACK STEELE OPENED HIS EYES. He was lying on his back and there was a ringing in his ears. Where was he? The light at his waist was pointed straight up and all he could see was dust. It hung like a smoky mist in the air and he could taste it on his tongue. His hand went to his waist and he looked down. Why was he wearing a flashlight at all? He saw bloody cuts on his hands. And there were bloody rips through his shirt sleeves. He sat up quickly and grabbed his head as the world went for a spin. What had happened? He struggled to remember. Then he heard a low cough that echoed behind him. Turning his head, he saw a woman struggling to sit up.

Donna-Lou's voice was low and husky as she called out, "Corry? Emma?" Her voice echoed but there was no reply.

It all came flooding back to Rory. The explosion and the others. He looked around and his heart beat harder when he didn't see anyone else. Then he turned to look the other way and saw the kids. Corry and Emma had been flung back to the wall of crates by the explosion. But they weren't moving. He rolled over and began crawling on his hands and knees towards them. He emitted a low cry of pain as sharp shards of rock bit into the flesh of his hands and knees. Struggling to his feet, he shuffled to the kids, "They're here, Donna-Lou," he said. His own voice was raspy from the dense air in the cavern. Reaching the two forms, he knelt down and pulled on Corry's sleeve to get him sitting up, "Corry, you okay?"

The youngster opened his eyes slowly and nodded his head. "Where's my mom...and Emma...?"

Rory shuffled around to the little girl as Donna-Lou reached her son and hugged him.

Emma was limp as Rory sat her up and cradled her in his right arm, pushing her hair away from her face, "Emma? Emma? Are you okay?"

The young girl opened her eyes and swallowed. It took a few moments for her eyes to focus.

"She seems to be okay," Rory said.

"Chet? Where's Chet?" Donna-Lou asked in a panic. "Chet," she called out.

Chet Calhoun suddenly sat up just a few feet away, pieces of rubble falling away from his body, "What? What happened?" He looked around for a few moments in bewilderment. "Oh...right." He squeezed his eyes shut tightly and shook his head gently. Then he opened his eyes and looked around again, "Everyone okay?"

"Yeah. We all look good," Rory said as he looked around at the others.

"Except for that gunman that Old Tuck left to guard us," Chet said as he got his feet. He pointed towards the area where the entrance had been only moments before. A boot was all that was visible of the gunmen, now buried under a ton of exploded rock. Chet walked slowly over to Donna-Lou and the kids and helped them to their feet.

Rory left them and walked to the former entrance area, surveying the damage. He climbed the pile of rubble, looking for a way out over the top, searching for any slight opening, but there was nothing. He stopped his search and carefully moved back down to the cave floor, "It looks like the way we came in is totally blocked. It would take a mining scoop or a bulldozer to move all this rubble."

"I'm sorry," Corry said in a subdued voice. "If I hadn't said anything...."

"No, you did great," Chet said. "In fact, I'm proud of you," he said as he gave Corry a hug.

"He's right," Rory said. "That was some fast thinking. They would have...well...you did great like Chet said."

"But how do we get out?" Donna-Lou asked.

"I said it was great, not perfect," Rory said as he looked at Donna-Lou.

Donna-Lou nodded. "Still better than the alternative," she said and then she bent over, coughing.

Chet walked over and placed his hand on her back, patting it a few times, "You okay?"

Donna-Lou nodded and straightened up, holding her hand to her throat, "It's all this stupid dust." She coughed again and waved her hand in front of her face, trying to clear some of the dust away.

Chet waved his hand at the dust as well as he looked to Rory, "So, what do we do now?"

Rory looked at the pile of rubble, "I'm not sure. It's going to take a lot of digging before we can get out of here."

"Maybe somebody will come looking for the Range Rover," Donna-Lou offered in optimism.

Rory shook his head, "No. Remember what Old Tuck said. The dealership where I rented the vehicle is expecting the state troopers to look for us."

"And those troopers were members of the KGC," Chet added. "The dealership will probably just write the vehicle off through their insurance, figuring the state troopers just couldn't find us."

"And anyone else who does come looking will probably be Knights of the Golden Circle," Rory concluded.

"Oh great," muttered Donna-Lou.

Chet looked at the pile of rubble, "I guess we just have to try to dig our way out."

"Too bad we left the shovels out in the Range Rover," Donna-Lou said. "*And* all the food and water. I have an idea it's going to take a while."

Chet looked at the kids and then said in a low voice to Rory and Donna-Lou, "How long do you think we can hold out?"

Rory took a deep breath and did some thinking. Then he grimaced, "As Donna-Lou said, we have no food and water. The good news is we can go three weeks without food, so we have three weeks to dig ourselves out. *But*...we still have a big problem according to the Rule of Threes."

Donna-Lou's brow furrowed, "What's that?"

"As a rule of thumb," Rory said, "you can live 3 minutes without air, you can live 3 hours in a harsh environment without shelter and you can make it 3 weeks without food like I said. So yes, we *might* make it out. Except...we'll only last *3 days* without water." He glanced at the pile of rubble, shaking his head, "Three days."

Donna-Lou and Chet looked very somber.

"But we have water," Emma interjected.

"Yeah," Corry said as he jerked a thumb over his shoulder, "we have a whole bunch of water back there, remember?"

Emma looked at Corry and made a face, "And maybe we'll have to eat bugs."

Donna-Lou held a finger up, "*Nobody's* eating bugs!"

"Maybe we'll find some squishy caterpillars," Corry said.

Donna-Lou made a face and her son let out a belly laugh. Then he suddenly began coughing violently.

Donna-Lou placed her hands on his shoulders as he bent over. "Do you need some water?" she asked her son.

Emma started to say something and then she coughed.

Rory watched the kids, feeling helpless. And then his blood ran cold. He whirled around, looking at the dust that hung heavily in the air throughout the large cavern. He found himself clearing his own throat. It felt like sandpaper. He took a few steps, looking at the cavern floor. He took his flashlight and looked off to the sides of the cavern. He turned in circles, shining the light around, searching.

Chet coughed as he stepped up beside Rory, "What's wrong? What do you see?"

"It's what I *don't* see," Rory said.

"What do you mean?"

The guano," Rory said as he took a few steps in another direction.

"The bat poop? What about it?"

"Where is it?" Rory asked. He pointed off to the side, "Remember how it was all piled up...?"

Chet looked at where Rory was pointing. He took his flashlight and shone it at another spot. "Yeah. Where is it?"

"It's in the air," Rory said. "The explosion and the subsequent shock wave pulverized all those tiny grains–"

Donna-Lou's eyes shot open in alarm, "We're breathing in bat poop?"

"That can't be good," Chet remarked.

Rory shook his head, "No it's not. It's not good at all. Fungus and mold spores grow in the bat droppings. At the very least, it could mean histoplasmosis...."

"Hist...? What is that?" Chet asked.

"It's a fungal infection that affects the lungs," Rory explained. "Also known as cave disease or cave fever–"

"It's treatable, right?" Donna-Lou asked. She looked like she was about to panic.

Rory looked at her, "If treated in time...."

"If...treated in time? And we're stuck in here?" Donna-Lou whispered. Her face turned white as her son continued coughing.

Chapter 52

THE SERIOUSNESS OF THE SITUATION struck Rory, Chet, and Donna-Lou hard, as Corry and Emma bent over, coughing. The sound echoed off the walls of the dark cavern, basically their tomb for all intents and purposes.

Chet's voice filled with anguish as he went over to Emma to comfort her, "We definitely have to get out."

Donna-Lou gently rubbed Corry's back as he bent over, her face showing she was close to breaking down with the worry.

Rory took a few steps, turning slowly as he looked at the darkness around and above them, looking for a solution. Then a thought struck him. He shone his flashlight around, looking intently. There was something he couldn't see. After a few minutes more of looking, Rory stepped over to Corry, who was still bent over, the boy's breathing ragged.

Corry looked up when he heard Rory's footsteps, "Am...am I going to die?

"No," Rory said. "The coughing is just because of the dust–"

Emma cleared her throat and complained, "And the bat poop. Yuck."

"True," Rory said. "But it will take some time before you get infected. Corry, you said you and Emma found some water and a high, cascading waterfall somewhere?"

Corry cleared his throat as well, nodded and pointed past the pyramid of wooden crates, "It was way back there, behind all those other crates and barrels and stuff."

Rory moved past Donna-Lou and walked around the wall of wooden crates, where he stopped and shone his flashlight towards the back.

A moment later Donna-Lou, Chet, Corry, and Emma joined him. "What are you thinking?" Chet asked.

"I'm not sure," Rory said. "Just a thought." He began walking past the other wooden crates, barrels, and kegs.

Donna-Lou looked at Chet, "We should stay together and go with him. Right?"

Chet nodded. He looked at Emma and Corry, "Are you okay to walk?"

Corry and Emma nodded, each clearing their throats again, Emma coughing lightly again.

Rory flashed his flashlight back and forth, keeping an eye on his footing as well as looking for the water the kids had talked about. The air was thick with the dust and guano mixture here as well; cutting the distance their flashlights could shine. It also made breathing difficult and Rory coughed. He waved his hand through the air, trying to create some cleaner air to breathe as he walked. "Am I going in the right direction?" he called back.

"Yeah," Corry said and he broke into a fit of coughing, stopping for a moment and then nodding to his mother that he could keep going.

Rory kept walking further back. The ceiling of rock dropped to a little over twenty feet overhead and then the cavern widening out into an immense, canopy of rock again, totally disappearing into the darkness overhead. The sound of falling water echoed from up ahead. Finally, Rory's light shone through the hazy air and reflected off a thin, clear surface of water one hundred yards away. "I see it," he called back. Then he waited for them to catch up and they continued forward as a tight group. The sound of falling water got louder. They reached the edge of the pool and stopped. Rory's voice was low as he flashed his flashlight off the surface of the water, "That is a *lot* larger than I expected."

"It's like a mini-lake," Donna-Lou said

"It really is," Chet said in astonishment. "It's a mini-lake in a cave."

Corry started coughing again.

Donna-Lou pulled her son close and wrapped her arms around him, "We have to do something, Chet."

"I know, I know," Chet said. "Any ideas, Rory?"

Rory wasn't really listening. He was turning in circles as he shone his light up into the high nooks and crannies in the dome of the immense cavern.

"What are you looking for?" Chet asked him.

"Bats," Rory said.

"Bats? But why...?"

"Because there weren't any on the other side. Corry...Emma...you both said you saw bats back here as well?"

Corry nodded as he pointed and looked up. "They were way up there. You could see their eyes. But I don't see them now...."

Emma started to talk and then coughed.

Chet put his arm around her, pulling her close.

Rory was looking towards the sounds of falling water and he spotted the source of the lake now, off to the left. Just as Corry and Emma had said, there were a series of cascading falls that started in the deep shadows hundreds of feet above them. The water tumbled and splashed its way down through craggy tiers of rock. Rory hustled around the edge of the mini-lake to get a closer look.

Donna-Lou called to him, "Why are you so interested in bats?" Shouldn't we be figuring out how to get out of here?"

"That's *exactly* what I'm doing," Rory yelled back.

Chet and called Donna-Lou exchanged glances and they quickly moved with the two kids over the jagged rocks to join him. As they caught up with him, Rory was wading ankle deep into the mini-lake, carefully watching for any unexpected drop-off.

"Are you going swimming?" Emma asked.

Rory didn't answer. He just kept moving towards the lowest cascade of water where it splashed into the clear mini-lake.

"What are you doing?" Chet called. "You need me to help?"

Rory still didn't answer as he concentrated on his destination. The water was at his knees now as he slowly moved across the wide expanse of water. One hundred and fifty feet across, the water was at his waist and he shivered from the cold, spring water as he reached the lowest cascade and climbed out. He stood on the first level of rock, flashing his light upward, examining a series of wet rock steps climbing up towards the roof.

"What are you doing, Rory?" Chet called again.

"Think about it," he yelled as he looked back at the group. "Where did the bats go?"

Chet shrugged and looked at Donna-Lou. "I have no idea," he yelled back.

"They had to go somewhere," Rory yelled again as he pointed up, "I'm going exploring. The rock looks slippery from all the moisture in here but...I should be okay."

Corry started coughing again and he bent over, hands on his knees.

"Do you really think there's a possible way out up there?" Donna-Lou called out frantically as she went to her son.

Rory looked around from his perch on the first level of rock, "I don't really see any other way out of here," he yelled back. He looked up at the cascading water, "If the water can come in...and the bats can get out somewhere...then maybe...?"

"We're going up with you," Donna-Lou yelled.

"It could be dangerous. And it might *not* be a way out. If someone falls–" Rory yelled back to her.

"And it's dangerous if we stay down here," she interjected loudly. "If these kids get infected, how long can we last, even if we do have this water?" Donna-Lou's voice trailed off as she knelt beside her son. She looked up at Chet, "We have to go up there. Right?"

Chet blinked as he looked at Donn-Lou. Then he looked over at Rory and his eyes followed the cascading water up into the deep shadows far above them. He opened his mouth...closed it...and swallowed.

Chapter 53

CHET CALHOUN LOOKED into Donna-Lou's eyes, feeling the weight of a decision on his shoulders. Then he looked at the two kids, coughing, hands at their throats and he decided. Looking across the pool of water, he called out, "Rory–" His voice caught and he put a hand to his dry throat and then tried again, "We're...we're going with you. We're going up, too." He looked back at Donna-Lou.

She gave him a nod and whispered, "Good, good."

Across the pool, Rory said, "Okay." It was quiet and more to himself but he slipped back down into the cold water and began wading back.

Chet and Donna-Lou helped the kids to get closer to the water, talking with them, reassuring them everything would be okay before long.

As he neared the edge of the pool, Rory called out, "C'mon, Corry. I'll give you a piggyback across to the rocks."

"I could swim it," Corry told. "I'm a good swimmer–" He began coughing again.

"You'll drown if you try to swim across with that cough, young man," his mother said sternly. "Now climb on and Rory will take you across."

"This water is very cold, Corry," Rory said. "If you get the shivers, you'll have a hard time breathing, and that will only add to the problem."

Corry nodded, "Okay."

Rory sloshed out of the water and crouched down so Corry could get on his back.

"Come on, Emma," Chet said, "I'll be your horse."

Emma grinned and climbed on board with Donna-Lou's help.

Chet stood up and waded into the water.

"Giddyup horse," Emma said with a giggle. Then she put her face against Chet's back and coughed.

A few feet into the water, Chet looked back to Donna-Lou, "Will you be okay? Or do you want me to come back and...?"

Donna-Lou placed her hands on her hips as she stood at the edge of the water, "Why Mr. Calhoun, are you suggesting we horse around while we're in this danger? Can't you wait till later?"

Chet gave her a stupid grin and shook his head.

Emma giggled, "She's funny."

"She is," Chet said as he headed across to the rocks.

Donna-Lou waded slowly into the water, shivering from just the touch of the cold water.

"Be careful," Rory yelled back to them, "there's a drop-off just to the right and the footing under the water is slippery from algae buildup."

Chet nodded but kept his head down as he followed Rory through the water, carefully watching each step as he waded towards the wall of rock where the water was cascading down.

Donna-Lou followed closely behind, pushing her way through the water.

Chet's right foot slid to the side suddenly and he nearly fell in before he righted himself. "Emma," he said with a hoarse voice, "you're choking me...."

"Well," the little girl complained, "I don't want to fall in."

Rory turned as he reached the rocks and allowed Corry to get off.

Corry knelt down on the first tier of rock and started coughing again from just that exertion

Rory waited for Chet and Emma to reach him and then helped the young girl to climb the rock.

Corry's cough lessened enough to allow him to grab Emma's arm, pulling her up beside him.

Donna-Lou was about ten feet away when she yelped and slid sideways, falling under the water and disappearing from view.

Chet turned immediately in concern, "Donna-Lou!" Not seeing her come back up, he pushed through the water and dove in after her.

Corry was on his feet in a heartbeat, desperately looking for his mother, "Mom. Mom."

"He'll find her," Rory said as he took a step toward the area where they had gone under. He looked for any sign of movement under the water, getting ready to dive in himself. The only sound was the echo of the water spilling into the mini-lake.

A few long seconds later, Chet shot up from the water, his arm around Donna-Lou. She coughed and water shot from her mouth. Chet waded his way back towards the shallow area, pulling her with him. She coughed and spit out more water, pushing the hair from her face as she allowed herself to be dragged. Just before the first tier of rock, Chet stumbled and he went backward with Donna-Lou. And she yelped.

Rory jumped into the shallow water and grabbed Chet's shirt, pulling both of them back

"Thanks," sputtered Chet as he turned Donna-Lou around to the rocks.

Donna-Lou grabbed onto the rough, jagged rock, pulling herself out of the water and up to her son.

Rory and Chet then pulled themselves out of the water and up onto the first level of rock where they both flopped face down.

Donna-Lou was coughing, still on her hands and knees with her son tapping her on the back with his hand.

Chet got to his knees and moved to her side quickly, "Are you all right?"

Donna-Lou nodded as she coughed, waving her hand that she was okay.

Rory rolled over and lay on his back to rest, his arms stretched out across the wet rock. "That was fun," he said, "and that's only the first level."

No one said anything for a minute. And then Donna-Lou started a small laugh but a cough cut it off.

After a few moments of rest, Rory rolled over again, this time getting to his knees, "Okay. Guess we might as well start our way up."

Donna-Lou and Chet looked at each other. She gave him a small smile and nod before she got up onto her feet, "I'm ready when you guys are." She checked on the two kids.

"Okay," Rory said as he rose to his feet, "I'll go first and try to find the best route up there." He walked carefully across the slippery rock and began to look for handholds and footholds to get started

Donna-Lou urged Corry and Emma to get up as she said, "Keep the kids in mind as you climb, Rory."

"Right."

Chet and Donn-Lou worked together with the kids to move across the wet rock. Falling and getting hurt before they even started to climb would be disastrous. As they stood just below Rory as he made his way up, Donna-Lou looked up at the rise of stone and shook her head, "I don't know about you guys but...*that* is a lot higher than I thought it was. It's like...mountain climbing...."

Corry put his hand in hers, "I'll help you, mom. We can make it." But when he looked way up himself, his face didn't show the confidence he expressed.

Donna-Lou put an arm around his shoulder and pulled him close, "I know you will. We'll help each other."

Rory called down from ten feet above them, "Okay. Stay just on this side of the falling water but watch for wet spots. Make sure your hands and feet are firm so you don't slip. Just take it slow and you'll be fine."

Chet and Donna-Lou exchanged serious, worried looks. Chet gave her a nod, "You go first with Corry and then I'll send Emma up after you. If someone slips, I can catch them."

Donna-Lou gave him a nod in return and then urged Corry to start his climb. She followed closely.

"Okay, Emma, your turn," Chet said.

Emma looked scared but she did as he asked.

Chet took in a deep breath and let it out slowly, flexing his hands before he started the dangerous climb himself.

Chapter 54

THE CLIMB WAS LONG, slow and difficult. Moisture beaded on the stone and made the climb beside the cascading waterfall treacherous for everyone. Reaching the first ledge of rock where the water cascaded forty feet to the pool below, Rory had them all stop and rest. It was more important for the kids to keep their energy up but there was no doubt Chet and Donna-Lou were finding it difficult. As a private investigator who could meet danger at any moment, Rory had a daily routine of exercises to keep him fit, even on the road. That didn't appear to be the case for the others. He told himself to keep an eye on them.

The next part of the climb went easier but the kids would break into fits of coughing every so often. That was worrisome. Not just because it could be energy draining, but a sudden, involuntary fit of coughing could cause one of them to lose their grip on the rock.

After another short rest, Chet and Donna-Lou stayed as close as they could to the kids, just in case they did lose their hold on the rocks. But the kids still had to do the physical climb on their own. There was no way to hold their hand or do it for them. And that added to the stress, making the climb more psychologically difficult and energy draining for the adults. Donna-Lou and Chet exchanged glances, trying to keep each other encouraged.

Rory couldn't do much to help. He just had to keep climbing above them. It was his job to find and point out the handholds and footholds and to keep looking for the easiest route upward. The problem was, there really wasn't one. The upper levels where the water cascaded past the group on their way to the pool far below were steeper and more treacherous and it took nearly twice as long before they found another suitable area to rest. Everyone was breathing heavy.

Another long slow climb took them up into the shadow areas of the cavern where they took another brief rest. Rory had hoped the higher areas would be dust free but that wasn't the case. The air actually seemed heavier with the dust from the explosion and breathing was difficult at times for all of them. Rory became convinced they had to get out as soon as possible and he had them on the move again, despite some grumbling.

But getting to the next level seemed to take forever. He wasn't sure if it was slower going because they were tired or because of the difficulty in breathing, due to the thick dust in the air. It didn't matter. They were slowing down and that worried him. He looked down several times, watching each individual struggle as they moved upward. Their flashlights danced through the shadows off to the sides. They were close now. Finally reaching the top of the cascading waterfall, Rory saw something hopeful and he crawled upward over the angled wet stone.

Emma reached the upper ledge and scrambled forward on her knees.

Corry got onto the ledge but flopped onto his face, exhausted.

Chet flopped onto the rock as well, just off to the left.

Donna-Lou moved past her son on her hands and knees, her breathing heavy, "C'mon, Corry. Get away from the edge–"

Breaking into a bout of coughing, Emma's body went into a spasm and her foot slipped on the wet rocks. She slipped backward towards the edge of the rock level and let out a scream.

Donna-Lou frantically grabbed for her but missed, screaming, "Emma!"

Emma frantically grabbed for a handhold, but her fingers slipped over the wet rocks and her body plummeted over the edge.

Chapter 55

CORRY SCRAMBLED AROUND and dove across the slippery rock surface, reaching out to grab Emma's left wrist with both his hands, just as she disappeared from view.

Donna-Lou screamed in panic as she saw her son's upper body sliding over the edge. In another second, he would be falling to the pool below.

Chet spun around and threw himself across the wet rock surface, grabbing Corry's right ankle and stopping his forward momentum.

Rory scrambled back down quickly and grabbed Chet's shirt to keep him anchored, "Have you got him?"

Chet nodded his head slightly and grunted, "Yeah...."

Emma was nowhere in sight and Rory feared the worst, "Corry? Do you have hold of Emma?"

Corry was near tears, "Y-yeah...but...I... I can't...hold on...please help me."

Rory looked at Donna-Lou, "I want you to hold onto Chet."

But Donna-Lou was in a panic and she looked from Rory to Corry.

"Donna-Lou? You need to hold Chet."

Corry whimpered under the strain.

Rory spoke calmly, "Just a few more seconds, Corry. Hold on to her." He looked back at his mother, whispering, "Just trust me."

Donna-Lou nodded faintly. She was shaking but she slid across the rock and sat down on Chet's legs. She reached forward and grabbed onto the waistband of his pants to hold him in place as well.

Rory carefully slid past Chet and then past Corry's body. Sliding between two shards of rock, he spotted Emma's jeans. He looked for a way to move lower to try and get underneath her. The rock was very treacherous here. Rory clutched at the rock surface, looking for a solid hold on the wet, slippery rocks as he moved downward.

Corry saw him from the corner of his eye and he whispered frantically."Please hurry."

Rory had no time to move any lower. He held onto a slippery rock with his right hand and shuffled left, extending his left arm towards the young girl.

"I can't–" Corry said in a strained voice.

Emma screamed as Corry's hands slipped from her wrist.

Rory leaned down urgently and grabbed

Emma fell - and stopped suddenly!

Rory's fingers had gone into the waistband of her jeans at the back.

Emma screamed as she looked at the long drop below her.

Rory strained to pull the young girl closer to him, "I've got her. Pull Corry up."

Corry's body slipped upward.

Rory slowly pulled himself back, bringing her closer to safety. "Grab hold of something, Emma," he yelled in a strained voice.

The young girl frantically grasped for the rocks, desperately looking for something she could wrap her hands around. After a few attempts, she grabbed onto a pointed rock for a brief moment. Then her hand slipped off and her body swung away from the edge

Rory nearly lost her.

Emma screamed.

Rory pulled hard, pulling her body back towards him.

Emma frantically grabbed at the rocks

Corry was peered over the edge, "C'mon Emma. Grab something."

Donna-Lou was yelling frantically, "Corry! Corry, get back."

Emma finally grabbed a pointed rock with her right hand and pulled hard.

Rory groaned as he pulled the young girl's dead weight upward.

Emma swung across the face of the rock and landed hard across Rory's knees. She immediately scrambled around and threw her arms around his neck, sobbing heavily.

"It's okay," Rory whispered. "You're safe now." He kept his left arm around her as he climbed back up to where Donna-Lou, Chet, and Corry were sitting in a group hug. Rory sat down heavily beside them, still holding onto the young girl. He was breathing heavy from the exertion.

Corry looked across at his friend, "You okay, Emma?"

Emma looked at him and nodded, wiping the tears from her eyes with the back of her left hand. But she wasn't letting go of Rory's neck with her right.

"We're right at the top," Rory said to Emma. "Are you okay to climb a bit more again?"

Emma nodded but didn't look too happy about it.

"It'll be okay, I saw something up there," Rory said encouragingly.

"What did you see?" Donna-Lou asked.

"Let's all go take a look," Rory said. "You stay in front of me and I won't let you fall," he said to Emma as he turned and set her down on the rocks.

Emma nodded and began moving upwards on the angled rock surface on her hands and knees. Rory stayed close behind her as they climbed while Corry followed closely behind him. Chet and Donna-Lou stayed close behind Corry, watching his every move.

"Hey!" Emma said with excitement. She scrambled up through the falling water and over the top edge of the rocks. She splashed her way into a five-foot-wide, ten-foot-high tunnel carved into the limestone over centuries by the water.

Rory moved up beside her, stepping into the water rushing along the bottom of the tunnel. "Move ahead a bit and wait," he said to Emma. Then he turned and helped the others up over the edge and into the tunnel.

"Do you think this goes above ground somewhere?" Donna-Lou asked as she crouched in the cold water, her hands on Corry's shoulders.

Corry was shivering.

"I bet this is how the bats got out," Chet said as he splashed into the tunnel. "And it's a good thing you thought about it, Rory. Thanks."

Rory nodded and he turned back to Emma. Her teeth were chattering. "The water's cold, isn't it?"

Emma nodded, too cold to answer.

Rory rubbed the outside of her arms, "Just hang in there. You're doing great."

Emma nodded as she hunched her shoulders up against the cold.

"Let's go see if we can find the warm sun," Rory said as he took her by the hand and made his way forward through the cold water.

Corry, Donna-Lou, and Chet splashed through the cold water behind him as they all made their way forward.

Rory saw a sliver of light in the ceiling of the tunnel about one hundred feet ahead. "I see light up ahead," he yelled back to the others. He began pushing his way as fast as he could through the cold water with Emma. Corry, Donna-Lou, and Chet all moved faster now, splashing through the cold water behind Rory and Emma as well, eager to get to safety.

Within minutes, Rory reached the light and found an angled exit to the surface above. The opening was filled with thick tree roots crisscrossing over each other. "Let me go up first just in case," he said to Emma.

She nodded and wrapped her arms around her shivering body.

The others caught up, their bodies shivering as they waited in the cold stream flowing along the bottom of the tunnel.

The fit was tight but Rory used the roots as pull bars to lift himself upwards. He slowly worked his way up a small incline to the side of the stream of cold water that now tumbled past on his left. He saw the surface! Slowly pushing his way up he found himself at the bottom of a gully that was surrounded by trees. The small stream stretched out ahead of him, disappearing into the trees.

Everything was quiet. There was no evidence of anyone around.

Rory moved back down, using the roots as stairs until he reached the opening in the tunnel ceiling, "Okay, give me your hand, Emma." She reached up and Rory pulled her upwards. "Use the roots to help you climb," he told her and Emma began climbing.

Corry came up next, followed closely by Donna-Lou and then Chet, all of them passing Rory and headed for the light above.

Rory followed Chet back to the surface where he soon joined everyone on the dry bank of the stream, under a long canopy of trees. He sat down heavily, breathing in the clean air of the Blue Ridge Mountains. After giving them a few moments to rest, Rory saw how cold everyone was, "How about we get right into the sunshine and warm up?"

Donna Lou nodded as she got to her feet, her teeth chattering, "That's a good idea. Do you think any of the Knights of the Golden Circle are around here though?"

"I have no idea. Maybe back at the Range Rover."

Chet shook his head, "And we don't have our guns anymore."

"We can't worry about that, now," Rory told him. "We can go that way and see if anyone is there. I doubt Old Tuck left any men outside to guard the Range Rover and I doubt they'd still be there after the explosion no doubt buried that entrance. But if we have to, we'll just head over to the highway and hitch-hike. Let's go." He led the way up the side of the gully and through the trees. It wasn't long before they found a clearing and stepped into the warmth of the sun. Smiles lit up everyone's face.

It was Corry who spoke up after several minutes, "What do we do about the treasure?"

Donna-Lou looked at her son, shaking her head, "We almost died and you're still worried about the treasure?"

Chet looked at Corry, "Don't worry. We know where it is and I can come back with climbing gear and masks–"

"But what if other people come and find it before we get back?" Corry protested. "We're going to need a new house, mom."

Rory had his face up to the sun and he said, "If people haven't found this upper entrance to the treasure cave after all these years, Corry, I doubt they'd find it now."

"And the Knights of the Golden Circle didn't know anything about it until they tracked us here," Chet added. "Now those members are dead and buried below us so the secret should be safe."

"Okay," Corry said, finally convinced. "But *we* need to be able to find it." He began searching the area around them.

"What are you looking for?" Donna-Lou asked him.

"This," Corry said triumphantly. He had a sharp-edged rock. Walking back over to a tree at the edge of the clearing, he began carving into the bark, "I'll make treasure signs so we can find our way back."

"Good idea," Chet said as he looked for a rock of his own.

"Boys and their treasures," Donna-Lou said as she shook her head again. But this time she smiled.

Chapter 56

HILTON HEAD, SOUTH Carolina
6 Months Later
RORY MACK STEELE stepped into the beachside restaurant and took off his sunglasses. He slipped them into the top pocket of his shirt and squinted, trying to adjust his eyes in the darkness. The tantalizing aroma of sizzling steak and baked seafood started his taste buds anticipating the meal to come.

"Ohhh! There he is," Jesse Flint squealed as she advanced rapidly on Rory and wrapped her arms around him.

Rory groaned, a smile on his face as she squeezed the breath out of him.

Jesse unwrapped her arms and grabbed his hand, pulling him through the crowded restaurant, "Everybody is in the private side room, waiting for you."

Rory laughed, nearly tumbling because she was pulling him so fast around the tables loaded with diners. He was pulled into a large side room overlooking the ocean. Everyone inside the room exploded with delight. Chet Calhoun, Corry Haney and his mother Donna-Lou, as well as Emma-Mae Lynn Houston, took turns giving him a hug.

As Emma stepped away from Rory, Donna-Lou spoke, "Rory, this is Emma's mother, Charlene Houston."

Charlene Houston, a tall, thin woman, rushed to Rory and threw her arms around him, tears spilling from her eyes, "Thank you for saving my Emma. I can't thank you enough."

"You're welcome. But there were a lot of others involved."

Charlene nodded as she stepped back from Rory, wiping tears from her eyes, "I know. But if you hadn't persevered...."

"This is for you," Corry said. He held out the gun case holding the gold LeMat revolver.

"Are you sure...?" Rory asked in surprise

"Your sister told us you like to collect things," Donna-Lou said.

"We even put a bunch of different old coins in there as well," Emma added in delight.

Rory took the gun case, "I don't know how to thank you...."

"We're the ones who need to do the thanking," Chet said. "If you hadn't stepped into our lives, maybe most of us might not be here." He held his hand out to Rory.

Rory shook his hand firmly and then he changed the subject, "How was the honeymoon?"

Donna-Lou slipped her arm around Chet Calhoun's waist, "Perfect," she said with a big smile.

"Except they wouldn't let me go and search for treasure in Hawaii," Corry complained.

Donna-Lou messed his hair up with her left hand, "Boys and their treasure."

Corry let out a big belly laugh while moving away from his mother.

"Speaking of the treasure, how did you folks make out?" Rory asked.

"Thanks to your sister Skye, and all that equipment she supplied, we were able to get back down there," Chet said. "But we're playing it smart, though, staying under the radar. Items like all those 1866 Liberty Head Double Eagles down there can be moved easily to coin collectors. The 1866-S with no motto on them are are in mint condition and going for ten grand each."

Rory whistled.

Chet grinned, "So far, we have far more money than we could ever spend."

"I wanted to buy a helicopter to fly in and get it, but they don't want to," Corry said as he stuck his hands in his pockets, a little miffed.

Chet laughed, "That he did. But as we explained, we don't want to attract any attention. We split up the money and really don't need much more right now," he said as he looked at the others, "the rest will stay put in the cavern, waiting for a rainy day."

Everyone nodded.

"We bought a condominium overlooking the ocean and all of us are living there," Donna-Lou added.

"Us too," Emma said. "Me and momma can go swim in the ocean anytime now."

Jesse Flint beamed, "And I also bought this restaurant."

Rory was surprised, "You did? I thought you'd retire to a life on the beach?"

"Oh, I do a lot of that. But I *always* wanted my own place like this near the ocean and now I got it, thanks to all of you."

Rory, happy for all of them, changed the subject to something more serious, "Any signs of our friends?"

Everyone went a little somber.

Chet shook his head, "No. Nothing so far. Like we surmised, the fact there no troopers guarding the Range Rover would seem to indicate all the ones who followed us up there was killed. I would imagine the other members are back to guarding the old spots."

Donna-Lou squeezed Chet's waist, "Chet, Jesse, and Charlene gave their houses back in Golden to friends. I did the same with my property and someone can rebuild there. We don't intend on going back. Right?"

Chet nodded and pulled her closer, "Right."

AFTER A GREAT LUNCH, Rory stepped out of the restaurant, the Civil War gun case held securely under his arm, and he gazed out over the sparkling ocean. The scent of the salt water was pleasant and soothing. Hearing the light laughter of everyone back inside, he felt relief wash over him. Hopefully, they had all seen the last of the Knights of the Golden Circle.